NIGHT SOIL

Other Books by Michael Cochrane

NONFICTION

Surviving Your Divorce: A Guide to Canadian Family Law

Surviving Your Parents' Divorce

Do We Need a Marriage Contract? How a Legal
Contract Can Strengthen Your Marriage

Do We Need a Cohabitation Agreement? How an
Agreement Can Strengthen Your Relationship

Class Actions: A Guide to the Class Proceedings Act

Strictly Legal: A Guide to Canadian Law

Family Law in Ontario for Lawyers and Law Clerks

FICTION

Olympic Lyon: The Untold Story
of the Last Gold Medal for Golf

NIGHT SOIL

A Novel

Michael Cochrane

Legal Intel

ISBN 978-1-988344-37-9 (paperback)
ISBN 978-1-988344-38-6 (e-book)

Production Credits
Copy editor: Allister Thompson
Proofreader and project manager: Karen Milner
Interior design and typesetting: Adrian So, Adrian So Design
Cover design: Adrian So, Adrian So Design
Cover illustration: Huzaifa Mohamedbhai

Published by Milner & Associates Inc.
www.milnerassociates.ca

This work is dedicated to my sweet wife. Rita, I'm always grateful for your patience and understanding when I slip away in the wee hours to write. I know, this one took a while.

And to Bonnie Lenzo (June 1, 1947 - August 6, 2015), faithful assistant in preparing the original manuscript. She made me promise to publish this story because it made her laugh and then cry. As promised.

Contents

Was I unwise to shut my eyes and play along?
—Natalie Merchant, from "Carnival"

1

The Grim Reaper

AS A GENERAL RULE, divorce lawyers are not welcome at weddings. I think the other wedding guests imagine us gazing around the reception hall like grim reapers, paying special note to the contemptuous eyeball rolling and bickering that signals the end is nigh for a once loving couple. Their marital contempt carries a subtle, somewhat pungent smell that only we can detect.

And yet I was invited to a huge Italian wedding, just a few summers ago when life was much simpler and such gatherings were not considered life-threatening. Unwelcome at this wedding? Yes. But there I stood, budget scotch in hand, waiting for the moment I could slip away unnoticed, a ghost. If not welcome, then why come in the first place, you ask? Not to bathe in the reflected love of two young people, I assure you. It was much more mercenary than that.

The bride's father, Carlo Bruni, had been a long-standing client. He asked me to make sure his precious daughter, Conchetta, would be "safe" marrying her boyfriend of just eight months. Wedding a little rushed? Yes. Some things don't change. Let's just say that her name suited her situation. Oh, and by "safe," Carlo meant he wanted me to protect his considerable wealth with a prenup for his daughter. He'd made a fortune in the food business and was damned if he was going to risk leaving any of it to Conchetta just to end up having her share it with her husband-to-be, the very average Marco D'Angelo. He'd been frank with me: "Bierce, make it tight." He squeezed his hands into fists the size of cantaloupes. "Make it bulletproof; it won't last a year."

In fact, the marriage contract negotiations were an unholy war as I bloodied my knuckles on his future son-in-law and his lawyer. No one likes to put all their financial disclosure—assets and liabilities—on the table, but Carlo was worried Conchetta was marrying a debt rather than acquiring an asset. So there was hardball. And I mean expensive hardball.

At one point not two weeks before the wedding, I told Carlo to threaten to cancel the whole thing if the contract I'd drafted was not signed as presented, word for word. No changes. If the marriage ended, Marco would get nothing. Even though the reception hall was booked and four hundred expensive invitations had been sent (custom laser-cut invites, which, when opened, played "The Prayer" duet between Céline Dion and Andrea Bocelli), Carlo took my advice. The D'Angelos didn't like it, but Marco signed. And as the song said, "Guide us with your grace to a place where we'll be safe . . . "

I understand that when the wedding guest list was being finalized, there was some heated discussion about my presence at the blessed event, but Carlo put his foot down, so I pretty much had to come. Truth be told, I actually skipped the wedding itself and arrived at the reception in time to learn that the wedding planner had parked me at the back of the hall. I assumed I would be stuck at a table with some of the more remote family connections, the ones who drink too much and insist on carrying the bride around on a chair.

But after wandering around with my drink for a bit, I discovered that I was in fact seated at the ubiquitous table of wedding losers: five divorced but still single women. Three of them had retrained as real estate agents after their divorces. That was in vogue for divorce settlements a few years ago. Then it became yoga trainer, then early childhood educator, then home staging, and the absolute last resort was life coach. Divorce lawyers encourage husbands who don't want to pay spousal support in perpetuity to their now discarded wives to at least pay them to find careers. "Invest in them," we would say. A real estate licence, a yoga certificate, whatever, was fast, relatively cheap and doable for these fifty-somethings who had absolutely no marketable skills after twenty-plus years of marriage. Once they had launched their children, most of these women only had a "Shop therefore I am" world view, could drive to Pilates, meet at Starbucks, or help to use up their husband's monthly at his golf club. Too harsh? The fact that it's a cliché is what's harsh.

Now, did these divorced women actually have a shot at making it as a real estate agent? Yoga instructor? Life coach? Honestly? Not my problem. Maybe they would meet someone and remarry. Seriously? No, they would soon learn just how rough it is out there in this new world of repartnering. Tinder's not tender. Meeting someone new is not exactly as advertised on eharmony or in those treacle-soaked Hallmark movies where the career girl returns to her small-town roots to win the pumpkin pie contest and find her long-lost love.

I gazed around the table at these women, each stuffed into an impossibly tight dress and wearing high-heeled shoes like stilts. Except one.

Shit.

Just my luck that one of these women was the ex-wife of one of my most infamous clients, Drago Markovic. As she sat across the table from me, I could see that she was still brimming with the bile that poisoned their marriage and brutal divorce.

"Monica." I acknowledged her presence.

She said nothing, glaring at me from her wheelchair.

She hadn't always been in a wheelchair, but I get ahead of myself.

Let's rewind for a glimpse through a Judas hole. I had wrapped up Drago's divorce from Monica after what had been several years of spectacularly ugly litigation. Finally, when there seemed to be no end in sight and after each of them had spent well north of $400,000 on lawyers (not to mention even more on forensic accountants, tax lawyers, child custody assessors, and a couple of very expensive but frankly useless PIs Monica had hired), everyone decided to take a breather. We decided to go to our respective corners and think about somehow settling this cow pie of a divorce.

Monica's lawyer, Sharon Burda, suggested we take one last crack at a mediation, so we agreed to assemble at 9:00 a.m. on a Friday at the offices of one of Toronto's top mediators, Cormac McKenzie. He has a sign over his office door, a quote from Robert Frost, "The afternoon knows what the morning never suspected." He was an eternal optimist who could get a deal where others could not.

Shortly after we arrived, Cormac started doing his Kissinger thing, shuttling back and forth between two rooms, trying to find some middle ground that would make Drago and Monica each miserably equal, or at least equally miserable. He had his work cut out for him. I made sure of that.

My law clerk, Bonnie, told me that she had actually gone to church the night before the mediation and lit a candle, praying the case would settle. She loathed our client and the file. Not without reason.

Drago was not what anyone would describe as a good-looking man. Serbian, not a handsome people. He was too angry to be handsome. I sometimes wondered what he might have looked like twenty-five years ago. And how did Monica, a good-looking woman—not great, mind you, but decent-looking—end up with this swarthy human spider?

Regardless of the time of year, Drago would arrive at my office for meetings in sweat-soaked short-sleeved polyester shirts, pungent like a can of vegetable soup decades past its best-before date. Let's leave it at that, because that's generous. His forearms were huge and covered in thick black hair. His chest hair burst out of his shirt collar where a necktie or even a simple button could have kept that tangled mess out of sight. His eyes? Two black holes and, in a word, ferocious. A bushy black unibrow cut across his forehead like a charred fireplace mantle, eyes burning below.

When Drago was angry, which was often, I found him genuinely frightening. It felt like something awful was about to happen. My skin would crawl listening to him. And yet from time to time over the years, during tough moments in the negotiations, there was something about him, a strange musky male warmth, a feeling that he was on my side. No, it felt like we were on the *same* side. Subtle difference, I know, but it was as if the two of us, brothers in arms, were in something together, something dangerous. A battle was coming to our village, and it would be fierce. We would not only survive, but at the end of the fighting we would be standing together, up to our knees in blood, victorious like the Crusaders who had stormed Jerusalem and killed every living thing. Being with him at that moment felt weirdly good—for just a fraction of a second—but then my skin would begin to crawl again.

Monica and Drago's divorce had been a bitter one about many things, but initially it was about custody of their three children. The lawyers and mental health professionals agreed that all three of these kids were utterly screwed up, and personally I could not understand why either parent would want one of these cretins, never mind all three. It became clearer.

Let's start with the youngest, Drago Jr., age fifteen when we finished. I think he was seven when we started. In the middle of the divorce, when Drago was back in Serbia on "business" (actually at a Bulgarian sex hotel) and Monica was abroad "resting at a spa" (yet the Visa bills revealed anything but rest with a $50,000 non-stop shop), their youngest had a totally forbidden house party. Three hundred-plus kids showed up at their beautiful multi-million-dollar Rosedale home and proceeded to pretty much tear it down to the frame—and broadcast it on social media while they did it. The YouTube videos are still out there with over 100,000 views. Oh, and a neighbourhood kid was shot and killed on the street in front of their house. No arrests were ever made, and there were no consequences for Drago Jr., of course. His excuse? With a literate sneer, "I'm a child of divorce."

Incidentally, a little footnote. Drago Jr. inherited his father's name because within about ten seconds of his head popping out of Monica, his paternity was in serious doubt. Drago Sr. can trace his hairy family back hundreds of years, but there was not one red-headed man or woman until Junior arrived. Monica insisted he be named Drago Jr. to reassure "Dad." I often wondered when ginger would figure out that his real father was actually a young Newfie landscaper who laid more than sod at the family home during its construction years ago.

Now, the middle child was all of seventeen when we wrapped up. Her real name was Madison but, a Bowie fan, she renamed herself Ziggy. In the middle of the divorce, she disappeared for over a year, couch-surfing around Toronto as a street pharmacist using, buying, and selling a cornucopia of drugs. She wouldn't be too hard to recognize if you saw her lying with her mangy kerchiefed dog in an empty storefront on Queen Street

West in Parkdale. She was there often, along with three or four other *enfants des rues*. Some of her hair was purple, some was green, and some was blue. She was tattooed from head to toe in brilliant colours, animals, flowers, and kooky Asian sayings and symbols. I can't say either parent was looking very hard for her during that time. As I explained to a Superior Court Judge one day, "Your Honour, Madison has withdrawn from parental control in accordance with s. 65 of the *Children's Law Reform Act*." (Translation: she ran away from home.) She was pretty much considered a writeoff by the family. No more evidence was needed to establish that fact than a look at her Facebook page or Instagram account, which were basically ads for a horror movie. Poor Ziggy. No ground control.

Their oldest child, Mitch, was the pride of the herd though. Nineteen going on thirty-five. Extreme Goth. He frightened even the mental health professionals. Bipolar? Probably. Unpredictably violent; none of the social workers would meet with him alone. To make matters particularly nerve-racking, no one was ever sure where he might be lurking at any given time. His track record of mindless violence had everyone worried, even Monica and Drago. A home security system and deadbolts only go so far to allow sleep when your firstborn has vowed to "come for you" because "your divorce ruined my life."

His high school yearbook had an interesting comment though: *Mitch is most likely to be a Columbine copycat.* And that was a teacher.

It turned out that Drago and Monica were each claiming custody of these misfits, not because they actually wanted them, but because they were damn well determined not to have to pay child support to the other. It was all about leveraging the money. Model parents.

What I have just shared is a very thin shaving from this family's meat grinder divorce. We—lawyers and clients—fought about everything from property division to support, from furniture to pets. Mitch had abandoned three pit bulls at their home, and no one could take care of them without taking their life in their hands. Odd parallel, I thought. We agreed to put them down. The dogs, that is.

You can understand why my clerk Bonnie hated the file. At the halfway point of the divorce, she had already been with me for several years, and she had seen just about every possible marriage depravity, but Drago was different. She blamed him and the file for going back to cigarettes and a significant weight gain. I thought people smoked to stay thin. What do I know.

Things were looking good for a settlement in the mediation. We had resolved the property issues around Drago's business. The home had been staged and sold with a quick closing date that was just a few weeks away. But we were stuck on spousal support for Monica. She had agreed to do—you guessed it—real estate agent training but was insisting she needed $20,000 a month support until she passed the course, got up and running as an agent, and actually sold a house. I know that seems like a lot of financial support, but given this family's considerable wealth, it was actually a reasonable request to everyone, that is, except Drago.

The law was pretty clear. She was entitled to the support. However, a divorce lawyer's job is not simply to follow the law. If we did, there would be a lot less work. There are, I like to think, *nuances* in the law that deserve exploration, extrapolation, and exploitation. Drago had heard the horror stories about husbands paying alimony to their wives forever. Granted, I was the one telling him those stories. Alimony, spousal support, the money IV, plug it in and she is on life support, or, in the less elegant words of Drago, "She's sucking my tits."

Put yourself in Drago's shiny, pointy-toed Payless shoes. He was a self-made millionaire businessman, achieved in large part because he had a special gift for being an awful human being. It didn't matter that he made his millions liquidating everything from mattresses to expired pharmaceuticals and garbage inventory from someone else's failed business. I think he would have been a millionaire, even if he had been a hotdog vendor. To him, commerce was about the survival of the fittest. He was a warrior who had climbed over more sorry bastards than anyone could count, least of all him. His favourite business maxim? "Fuck them." Not exactly Warren Buffett.

During our meetings, he would often launch into furious, long-winded, expletive-laden speeches about self-made men, capitalism, and success. He respected one thing: power—regardless of how it was exercised, wisely or unwisely. Bonnie refused to meet with him alone, and frankly I hated spending time with him too, but at $1,000 an hour, I would just paste a tight smile on my face and listen to his lessons in commercial terrorism all day. He, on the other hand, loved me for the simple reason I was making Monica's life—and Burda's life—miserable. I was making her divorce expensive, very expensive.

Drago was confident in my total war strategy: "Make it nasty. Sometimes you spend money to make money. She will fold like a cheap mattress." Really? I didn't have the energy to correct him, because we both got the point.

I had played that kind of hardball with Burda and Monica for years, drowning them in requests for disclosure, updates on disclosure, medical reports, updates on medical reports. Monica says she is depressed? I need an independent medical and a list of her prescriptions. Her Visa bill shows a $482 purchase at a naturopathic health food store? I need a breakdown. On and on, hoping she would fold. In terms of the cost to Drago, I still recall our first meeting, when he said the magic words every divorce lawyer longs to hear: "I would rather pay you than her." Cha-ching.

Bottom line, though, in this mediation was clear: Drago did not want to pay what Monica was reasonably entitled to receive. He wanted a full-support release. Permanent. After a very long marriage? Not likely. We offered her a lump sum, tax-free, but nothing serious. I expected Monica's lawyer either to tell us to get lost or come back with a counteroffer. So we sat and waited in our breakout room.

Sharon Burda was an experienced family law lawyer. I mean, she was competent, but for some reason she always felt it necessary to carry on like she was smarter than everyone else in the room. She was not. Always with a remark about the "big case" she had just settled or the "judge who complimented her on her Factum." I knew that grinding teeth make a noise, but eye-rolling did too when she got going. Always something to prove, even when things were going her way. The big woman-lawyer chip on her shoulder was balanced delicately by an expensive designer purse on the other. Biggest obstacle on every case she ever had? Herself.

At about fifty, she was tall and worn-looking, thin as a rail, not a hundred pounds, no ass to speak of, and always wearing too much makeup, a real cake face kabuki. Well dressed, though. To the mediation, she wore a very sharp pink linen suit. Looking at her as she teetered around in ridiculously high-heeled shoes, she reminded me of something. I couldn't put my finger on it. It was like watching a tightrope walker weaving along, trying to hold a valuable piece of crystal between her tiny ass cheeks. To add to her unique look she had trademarked her own oddball hairdo, a wispy straw-coloured bird's nest piled high and tucked into place with some twigs and a feather comb device. It added another six inches to her height, which meant she towered over everyone, especially McKenzie, who at 5'4" was practically a little person.

Background. Burda had worked for several years with Stan Corbett. Now there was a great divorce lawyer. He knew his stuff. Firm. Great advocate. Healthy dose of common sense. For three years, Burda soaked Stan for mentoring, training—and as it turned out, clients. She bolted from his firm in the middle of the night with a bunch of his best clients and set up her own law firm. Not a classy move, and it did not go unnoticed among the local Bar. I think what made it even harder was her ongoing attempts to trade on his reputation, as if she had taken some of his DNA along with the files. I don't think anyone bought it. I know I didn't. Stan was the man. Burda? Not even close.

Stan died a few years back in a car accident that happened shortly after insuring himself for a few million bucks. Single car. Cottage country. Late at night, railway crossing. No alcohol. When the police came to Stan's home, they explained the situation to his wife as—and I quote—"a horrible accident." When his wife, who was at that time in her late seventies, heard the news, she lost it and sobbed to the officer that Stan had been depressed, that they had financial problems since his junior associate (that's right, Burda) scooped a bunch of his clients. She said she was worried he might do something crazy. Well, that cop cut her off, took her gently by the arm, and steered her into the kitchen.

He said softly, "Look at me, Mrs. Corbett. We did a full investigation, and in my report I said it was a 'horrible accident.' When the insurance people come to ask you questions, that is what you tell them: 'The police said it was a horrible accident.' Understood?" It took a few seconds for the insurance penny to drop, but she understood. Accident equals payout on insurance. Suicide equals, well, problems.

The cop sat her down with a cup of tea and explained that Stan had looked after his messy divorce, got him custody of his two kids a few years back, and he owed Stan. I heard later that the insurance paid out in full. The best parts of human nature can emerge at the strangest times.

Oh, and how do I know all that? I did that cop's next two divorces.

As I sat waiting for a counteroffer in the lounge at McKenzie's office, Monica teetered in and fell dramatically into a big coffee-coloured club chair. It was just the two of us. She, in her pink suit, stretched out her long, skinny legs, kicked off her shoes, and laid her bare feet out for me to admire. Her bony feet were bruised, bloody, and covered in Band-Aids. How strange. But in that moment, seeing her stretched out like that, I suddenly knew what she reminded me of. It was something I had captured and tormented as a boy: *Sipyloidea sipylus*, the pink-winged stick bug. No sooner was I enjoying the flashback to my youth when she suddenly slipped her shoes back on, rose, and said with misplaced authority, "We'll have a counteroffer for you in a few minutes." Her skinny rear disappeared around the corner.

As I went down the hall to warn Drago that a counteroffer would be coming and to brace himself for more back and forth, I could see Monica and Burda through the glass panels of their meeting room. They were hugging like two sisters in arms who had successfully launched an assault against the evil king Drago and his equerry lawyer. Pathetic.

I popped into our meeting room, told him of my experience in the lounge, and to expect a counteroffer. He detested Burda and began calling her every filthy name he could think of—and he had a much better command of that aspect of the Queen's English than any other. I had to ask him to cool it a couple of times. "Drago, take it easy. The last thing we need is her taking this personally. It's business. She's a divorce lawyer. You're not supposed to like her." Instead, my advice triggered a spewing of Serbian cussing (something to do with the steam off his piss), the frightening sound of which made me wish he would switch back to swearing in English.

The counteroffer arrived. I read it aloud with a smile. "She will take $200,000 lump sum, tax-free for a full release." If we agreed to pay it, then the case was over. Everything done. Burda even offered to look after the divorce paperwork. As I looked at Drago, my smile widened. A multimillionaire was about to get rid of a spousal support obligation to his wife for $200,000? It was a joke. It would be negligent if we didn't take it. So we did that deal. I made Drago do an e-transfer of the funds on the spot and had them sign a triple bulletproof release. I was not going to risk buyer's remorse in the morning. This deal was done.

Drago's reaction after he made the payment? "My strategy worked. I told you. It was easy." Suddenly I was just a tool of this evil negotiation genius.

I said dryly, "You should teach negotiation tactics at Harvard Law School." He thought I was serious.

As we got ready to head our separate ways from McKenzie's office, Drago insisted we grab a drink across the street at the Sheraton to celebrate his victory. Mercifully, he said he could only stay for thirty minutes, which meant three fast double vodkas for him while I nursed a twenty-five-year-old Macallan. He was buying. As we toasted his strategy, he told me that he was anxious to get home and clear out his stuff. He didn't like living in the home alone, having to keep it spotless as endless agents and their clients poked around. They had done well on the sale, expecting $5 million but getting a typical Toronto bully offer of $5.3. It was a pretty home on one of the nicer streets in Rosedale. I heard the neighbours threw a street party after this hideous family broke up and moved away.

As Drago and I chatted, I could see Monica across the bar with a woman who looked like her sister. Burda was nowhere to be seen. I assumed she'd had enough of this shit storm and had gone home to soak her battered hooves and her other ninety-nine pounds in a hot tub.

Monica and her sister apparently stayed on at the Sheraton for a while and had a few more gin and tonics. A little drunk and assuming Drago would carry on drinking for the evening, Monica decided to Uber over to take one last look at their family home. The security cameras showed her walking around outside and then letting herself in to use the washroom and telephone. She had left her cellphone in the Uber. She had the home security codes because she had been doing the staging during the listing and prepping for showings. She wandered upstairs and into the master bedroom to find Drago in bed with none other than

Sharon Burda. That's right. Monica's bony stickbug lawyer was buck naked and furiously fucking the furry human spider. And with quite noisy stridulations, I was told.

At that moment, Burda's betrayal of Monica in what had been her own bedroom was so jaw-droppingly complete that Monica simply walked across the room to a set of French doors that opened out to one of those little Juliet balconies and jumped. It was only two storeys to the flagstone patio that surrounded their beautifully lit infinity pool, but it was enough to drive Monica's shin bones up into her pelvis. That's an image I will never get out of my head.

This *liaison sexuelle*, we all learned later, had been going on for several months under our collective noses. I still don't get it. You could put a hundred men and women in a room, and you would never match those two. The insect world, go figure.

The fall paralyzed Monica from the waist down, hence the wheelchair. For life. Not really conducive to being a real estate agent. Unable to work, Monica turned around and sued Drago to throw out the settlement and pay her spousal support. We defended her claim and of course won. After all, Monica had signed a bulletproof release with independent legal advice from Burda—and she had received her money. It wasn't Drago's fault that Monica jumped out a window or that she couldn't trust her lawyer. Don't believe me? Look it up. The trial and the Court of Appeal rulings are both reported decisions. I billed Drago for my handiwork and collected a cool $600,000 for the two cases. Nice work if you can get it.

That next phase of Monica's life was pretty ugly. Burda was suspended by the Law Society. Monica then hired the biggest dick lawyer in Toronto to sue her and McKenzie, even though he had no idea we were all being played. It took a couple of years to clear up the fallout from the settlement and the insect affair. Probably more of interest to entomologists than lawyers now.

Anyway, that was all history by the time I ended up at the Bruni–D'Angelo wedding with a scowling Monica sitting across from me in her wheelchair and my only thought being, *It's going to get very awkward if I don't get out of here before the dancing begins*. I was about to get up, grab another drink, circulate and make sure Carlo saw me when another "divorced and still looking" woman flopped down beside me, splashing her large glass of Pinot Grigio on my very expensive burgundy monk-strap shoes.

She began to slur cheerfully through her bleached teeth, "Hello there, isn't this great? . . . I love weddings . . . Are you at our table? . . . What do you do for a living?" A seamless stream of banal thoughts and questions.

Out of the corner of my eye I could see Monica flinch, spin one wheel, and turn to leave. Without taking a breath, Ms. Bleached Teeth stretched out her hand and said, "I'm (insert name I didn't care to know)."

I extended my hand. "I'm Andrew Bierce. I'm a divorce lawyer."

It took a second as she paused and pursed her lips, perhaps trying to recall the name of a former client. But then she glanced at Monica wheeling away and withdrew her hand. "I've heard of you."

She said it as if sickened by the thought.

2

Grains of Rice and the Rule of Law

MY LAW OFFICE IS IN DOWNTOWN TORONTO, high up in one of the towers at Bay and King. I park underground. It's expensive, and there have been unfortunate complications, but the convenience of a reserved spot close to the elevators is unbeatable, especially with the huge black briefcase on wheels now needed to haul even the most mundane divorce to and from court. While they can be a pain in the ass on the subways, these big briefcases are now standard operating equipment for anyone doing court work. A few years ago Bonnie dubbed mine "Black Beauty," and it has taken a lot of punishment, bouncing off curbs, streetcar tracks, subway turnstiles, and a few toes.

Sometimes, if I don't have to boot it up to the office, I will head straight from my car to the University Club for a workout. Being in my sixties has meant trying to do a better job of taking care of myself. I'm not going to lie; there were a few issues—before and during my own ugly divorce — of the pharmaceutical variety in the past, but I worked through them, on my own, I might add. I got my teeth fixed up, run now, work out, stay a trim 6 feet, 185 pounds and, alas, if I could just grow a little more hair, I would be a much happier man.

Entering the reception area of my firm, Andrew Bierce, Q.C., and Associates, I always feel a genuine measure of satisfaction. (Note: I don't actually have any associates. Never have, never will. Not after Corbett's experience with Ms. Burda.) My clients arrive by appointment only and enter through a set of high-polish stainless steel doors using a personal code. They are scheduled one at a time, with no overlap and well spaced for privacy reasons. The waiting lounge has a very contemporary modern feel, with two immaculate and authentic (and I mean genuine original) black Barcelona lounge chairs, Nagucci coffee table, high-def flatscreen displaying continuous calm spa-like scenes. The art, hand-picked personally (I've been told I have an eye), is on loan from the Art Gallery of Ontario (I'm in the Curators' Circle), and I try to change it up every six months or so, keep it fresh. The lounge area determines a client's first impressions, so I have taken it seriously. On the one hand, it cannot be too much, or they think their fees are paying for artwork rather than legal work. On the other hand, they want the reassurance that they have chosen a successful, sought-after, and, dare I say, feared advocate. It's a delicate balance.

I must be doing something right, because I have never had any shortage of clients. Many of them are referrals from senior commercial lawyers and in-house counsel around Toronto who need to keep their business clients satisfied but would never dare sully their hands with a divorce. You see, divorce clients are never happy—no matter how things turn out. The referring lawyer makes sure that someone else wears the blame for the divorce nightmare. Divorce work has also become very specialized, both in terms of the number of areas of law that are involved and "the dark tactical arts" of pulling marriages apart. I don't really care about the referring lawyer's motives. At $1,000 an hour, why would I? *Pro bono?* Haven't you heard? Latin is a dead language.

My favourite type of divorce—assuming the client can pay—is the proverbial shit storm. Example: A beauty of a case was referred to me by in-house counsel at a large cable company. It was a nasty custody dispute involving a lesbian couple. They got married and decided to have a child. Mom #1, a former athlete and at forty-four a little past prime conceiving years, underwent very extensive procedures to conceive. And when I say extensive, I mean full-blown gamete intrafallopian transfer (GIFT). However, the "gifts" she received included not only a lovely little boy but also a punctured bladder. With very unpleasant complications, she was in pretty bad shape for several months, and Mom #2, a prof at one of our better law schools, decided she hadn't signed up for that kind of life. She called it quits just a few months after the little fellow arrived and moved out to live with one of her students. The night she dropped that bombshell there was a brawl in their kitchen that sent Mom #1 back to the hospital and the baby to Mom #2 on an interim basis. Well, to me, that's a terrific case. Shit storm + ability to pay + results = model case. All parts of that equation are equal—but results are absolutely necessary. Clients who come to me demand results, no excuses, hence total war.*

When a new client contacts me, Bonnie does the preliminary intake and fills in the client background with an overview of the history of the relationship, the client's financial wherewithal, and their expectations. (Do they want the moon? More? Solar system? Usually.) She has become something of an expert at sizing up clients, weeding out the nutbars, and deflecting the routine cases. She does the conflict checks, gets their ID, and a credit card authorization for $10,000. No money, no meeting.

Setting a fee for an entire divorce can be tricky, and there is little business sense in scaring off a good client by telling them that the whole divorce could cost over $500,000. No one would ever undertake their first battle if they thought the war might consume all their RRSPs, drain the equity in their home, or even bankrupt them. No, quoting a fee has to be a bit more subtle. I like to tell a client, "Here is my hourly rate, and I recommend that we take things a step at a time."

Sometimes I feel like the Chief Counsellor who asked the Sultan if he could be paid for his advice in grains of rice. The Sultan, intrigued, asked him to explain. The Counsellor pointed at the Sultan's chessboard and said, "All I ask is a grain of rice on the first square, two grains on the second, four on the third, eight on the fourth," and so on. The Sultan smiled and accepted the proposal. It looked like a great deal—a chessboard covered in rice. Of course, by the last square on the chessboard the amount of rice required to pay the Counsellor would bankrupt the Sultan, since the number of grains of rice—9,223,372,036,854,775,808—would exceed the worldwide production of rice.

------

* Remind me to tell you how that case turned out the next time we meet.

So a step at a time, a square at a time, a little rice at a time. I like that compensation model.

Part of Bonnie's work is making sure we don't have a client who is going to run out of rice halfway through the war. I have to be honest, though, money is not the soul (that's not a spelling mistake) determining factor. Even if a client has bags of rice, I may not take the case. It has to be at least interesting in some way. I have turned down many a rich but boring file. The client must also be prepared to surrender to my advice, my recommended strategy. I'm not one of those lawyers who sits patiently with the client setting out options, going through pros and cons and cost-effectiveness strategies. Life's too short. My advice amounts to, "Here is what we are going to do. Sign these documents." No arguments. If the client gives me a hard time, I tell them I'm not interested, and if that isn't enough, I may need to turn to the infamous "fuck-off fee."

The fuck-off fee is a request for a retainer so large, the client can't swallow it. They flinch at the dollar figure requested and then politely say they'll "think about it." Nine out of ten times they don't return. Word in the profession is that Eddie Greenspan, Q.C., (may he rest in peace), at one time one of Canada's top criminal lawyers, coined the phrase on one of his cases.

Helmuth Buxbaum, millionaire owner of a chain of nursing homes (but also full-time cocaine addict and part-time consumer of prostitutes) wanted to hire Eddie to defend him at his murder trial. Who did he murder? His poor wife Hanna. Presumably having met with some young lawyer who did a cost-benefit analysis on a divorce (I'm still bound by solicitor-client privilege, even though he's dead), Helmuth thanked him for his advice and decided murder was faster and cheaper.

He then hired a contract killer for $10,000 and, figuring he might as well go for gold, took out a million-dollar life insurance policy on Hanna. The killer then met Helmuth at an off-ramp on Highway 401 near London, pulled the unsuspecting Hanna from the car, and shot her in the head three times. Once caught, the gunman fessed up and, of course, it was game over for Helmuth. I guess Eddie didn't want the loser of a case on his record, so he asked Buxbaum for a cool million dollars as a retainer. Helmuth pulled out his chequebook, wrote the cheque on the spot, and promised Eddie a $250,000 bonus if he got him off. What could he say? He pretty much had to take the case, but it turned out as Eddie predicted—conviction—and Helmuth died in Kingston Pen at the age of sixty-seven.

Buxbaum's daughter found my number on his desk and reached out to me for advice about her father's estate, but I wasn't interested. I heard that she ended up homeless, living on the streets of Toronto. I wondered sometimes if Helmuth ever sat in his cell and thought, *You know, maybe a divorce would have been better . . . Oh well.* Now that could all be a bullshit urban legend, but it's still a great story, and the fuck-off fee survives, if only on a smaller scale in divorces.

But I digress. Back to the unfortunate complications that arose around parking. I'm not even sure how much of this problem I should share. The day started like any other. Bonnie had a new client scheduled for a consultation with me. This client's case stands out in my mind for two reasons. First, it was the same day I had trouble coming into the office—well, the parking garage to be more precise. I was driving a rental, a big cherry-red Cadillac Escalade. I had been visiting a client over the weekend at her home in Muskoka. I generally don't go to a client's home, but for this particular client I had been making exceptions—overnight exceptions. That's not really recommended under our Rules of Professional Conduct, but she is pretty open-minded and she has a great case, which means it is an expensive absolute horror show. Let's leave it at that for now.

There had been a forecast of shitty weather up in cottage country, so I rented the Escalade. The cost will show up on my client's bill as a "travel disbursement," a bill which, incidentally, she never reads because she runs every one of them through her well-known clothing business. She is basically deducting her divorce on the corporate tax return as a business expense. Rev Can has no idea. Since the client's paying, I always get the maximum car insurance in case of trouble—which brings me to this particular morning in the parking garage.

This Caddy barely fit under the garage roof guide bars. I started to wheel down to my reserved spot on P2. It's a perfect spot, near the elevator, between two concrete pillars so no one can park on either side of me. The spot has a sign, *Reserved 24 hours 7 days a week*, and a warning about towing. I used to have a nameplate, but the disgruntled (to put it mildly) husband of a former client trashed my car one night, so now I keep the spot anonymous. Anyway, as I was wheeling down to this spot enjoying the slight squeal of the tires, I came upon a large car parked in a spot near the corner. That particular spot has a sign posted very clearly—*SMALL CARS ONLY.* I recalled that every time I go by that spot, I have to pay extra attention because invariably someone has parked an obviously Not Small Car there. This particular day I stopped and saw that, once again, it was this big grey Lexus GX 470 V8 with vanity plates that said INV EST. Obviously a Bay Street financial dickwad.

I considered the problem for a moment and then looked around to make sure the coast was clear. The building has two pretty useless guys dressed like members of a paramilitary SWAT team wandering around as security guards. And yet they cannot even ensure that this entitled person understands that large cars are not supposed to park in the *SMALL CARS ONLY* spot. That sign is there for a reason. I backed the Caddy up and took the corner again, but a little tighter. I gave the Lexus's rear taillights a kiss with the front end of the Caddy. It was just enough to push it right up against the concrete pillar. There was barely a sound except for a crunch and a delicious pop as the taillight caved in. I finished my turn and parked one level farther down, nose first, to hide any damage to the Caddy. In a couple of days I would get the rental company to come and pick it up and blame bad weather up north. I have had to change rental companies a couple of times because, sadly, this problem with large cars in small spots has occurred more than once.

As I walked back up through the garage to the elevator that morning, I saw that the impact with the Lexus had actually made quite a mess. The owner was standing looking at it with one of the security guards (who was wearing everything except night-vision goggles), and he was just fucking furious. Chewing out the guard. Hilarious.

I stopped and looked at the damage with him. "Jesus, what a mess . . . but INV EST . . . wow, clever plate."

He stopped his rant, smiled, and said proudly, "Thanks."

This whole thing has been very annoying. People should follow the rules. After all, it is the Rule of Law that separates us from barbarians.

Oh, and the second reason I remember that day? The client Bonnie had waiting for me in the office, well, just when you think you've heard it all . . .

3

Septic Shock

BONNIE HAS BEEN WORKING WITH ME for over a dozen years. She was thirty when she started, and we celebrated her fortieth birthday a while back. I think I know no more about her now than the day she started. Would you believe she took a pay cut to come and work for me? She had been working at a bank, making a decent buck, but was bored. So bored that after seeing the movie *Erin Brockovich*, she started looking for a new legal secretarial job. Seriously. Her girlfriend, whom I had dated briefly, told her I was looking for help but that she would need to hold her nose and tolerate some pretty ugly scenes. That was all Bonnie needed to hear. We met, it clicked, she minds her business and I mind mine. Occasionally she will let it slip that she was on a date or saw a movie or was away for a weekend, but that's it. I don't ask questions because frankly I'm not interested. She's not married, no kids, lives to work. I think she comes in from Pickering or Ajax everyday.

Her workstation sits outside my office, within shouting distance across a hall. We can see each other, which sometimes means a lot of chatter back and forth. I can see her hunched over her keyboard all day, unlit cigarette hanging from her lips, until she can't stand it anymore and jumps on the elevator to head down for a smoke with all the other post-modern gargoyles that hang around our building—all of them well within the nine-metre restriction. I'm working on dealing with that breach of the rules.

Bonnie's hair is jet-black, so black I assume it's dyed. The cut is blunt and has been unchanged in all the time I have known her. It hangs straight down along her pale cheeks. Makeup? If so, not enough. Her fashion sense is pretty straightforward—if it's black, she'll wear it. To spice things up, she might switch to gray or charcoal. She has a lavender sweater, which I only know because every time she wears it, I make a point of saying how great it looks, "What a beautiful colour," hoping that it might trigger even a hint of other colours in her wardrobe. But no, the next hundred days will be a steady cortège of black sweaters, black pants, black shoes followed by a joyful stretch of grey, then back to black. I imagine her closet to be like a dark star collapsing in on itself. After a few years of these fashion hints, I gave up. Maybe she's in mourning and just hasn't had the heart to tell me, and now it's too late for me to ask who died.

She is also a bit of a softy, a total wuss. Every stupid cause that comes along, she is in for a pound. Speaking of pounds, the folks who run those sappy TV ads for abandoned pets have her on speed dial. For some reason she is also a sucker for immigrants in trouble and works a couple of weekends a month at some shelter in the east end. She said the name, but it didn't register, something Asian, I think. Maybe South American. Honestly I don't know why or how she does it.

But she works hard. She is in early, stays late. Many days I have to tell her to go home. I pay her well, bonuses, gifts, lunches at Christmas and birthdays, benefits, extra vacation (she never takes all of it anyway), the whole nine yards. I treat her well and I keep my hands off her. That is something of an accomplishment because I've had a few office marriages blow up in my face after a little too much wine over lunch led to lost afternoons at a little boutique hotel nearby. Lose a day of billings and a secretary in one fell swoop? Dumb move. Three times in a row? There must be a name for that. Never again. Without Bonnie I am lost, and I cannot say that about anybody else in my life.

But as much as I like her and respect her, on this particular morning, as I arrived at the office after the parking problem, I wanted to absolutely smash her in the face.

I discovered that the new client, a Ms. Wood, had been scheduled for an early consultation, but I could find no intake form. Nothing but her name. No conflict search either. I searched the trust ledger and couldn't see a $10,000 deposit for the consult. Bonnie would not be in for another hour, and I couldn't leave this woman just sitting in the reception lounge. All I could find was a yellow Post-it note on my computer screen: *Your brother called—again.* Great.

I have been at this for a very long time, and I was concerned about seeing this client without a conflict search. I don't want to risk getting conflicted out without money in trust. This conflicting out move was a very smart game I played with well-heeled clients many years ago, so I guess in some ways I got what I deserved when it finally happened to me a few times.

It works like this: the wealthy client comes in to retain me, and I get him or her to set aside a budget of $5,000–$10,000. I then send him for four or five brief interviews with the top family lawyers in Toronto. The client gets in their offices and spills enough information to justify a bill for the consult. The client shells out but never has any intention of hiring these top-tier lawyers. But now none of those lawyers can act for his or her spouse because they have a conflict. It's worth every penny to force his/her spouse to go to the B list of divorce lawyers. Or worse. After I got stung a few times myself, I started to charge $10,000 just for a consult. If some lawyer in one of the towers across the street wants to conflict me out, I'm flattered, but it will cost their client.

Angry and against my better judgment, I brought the new client into the boardroom. Ms. Wood was mid-forties, I would estimate. Plain. Good taste. Nice business suit. I figured Annie Aime, maybe something from Nordstrom or Holt Renfrew. Her hair could have used a bit of colour, but I don't always see clients when they're at their best. I recalled as she got comfortable that I was seeing her early because she had to catch a flight.

I made up an excuse about not having her intake form and vowed to deal with Bonnie later.

"It's not a problem, Mr. Bierce. I transferred the $10,000 for this consult last night when I flew in from London. Your assistant said she would look after it this morning."

"I understand you have a flight this morning as well?"

"Yes, I am off to Vancouver for a few days and wanted to meet with you before I left."

She seemed together, but a huge red flag popped up when she opened her briefcase. She started to spread out a sheaf of documents on the boardroom table in front of me. Each one was in a plastic sleeve. There were tabs, lots of tabs, and dozens of sticky notes. I could see on one document that passages had been highlighted in yellow, some in blue, others in green. The initial red flag was now being overtaken by alarm bells because there is a fine line between being well organized and crazy. All of these things are the hallmarks of a problem client. Mind you, it's not as bad as the client who shows up with everything in a blue IKEA bag. IKEA stands for *I Know Every Angle*.

She got right into it. "My husband and I separated two weeks ago. He is a firefighter."

Uh-oh. I knew where this was headed. Firefighters start more fires than they put out.

"I insisted that he move out." She kept spreading documents on the table.

"What do you do?"

"I'm a VP at TD, Asia Division."

Nice, that meant rice. "Children?"

"No. I travel a lot."

Uh-oh. No kids + firefighter + a wife on the road = perfect storm.

"What caused you to separate?" I was practically writing down her answer before she could even speak (e.g., client found firefighter husband's other cellphone and guessed his password was FIRE1234, only to discover unseemly texts and intimate pictures of someone he met at the photoshoot for the charity calendar), but then she spun a thick binder around and pushed it in front of me. It was open at Tab J, and there was yellow highlighting of an invoice from Bryson's Septic Systems, $638. Pumping septic.

She flipped to the next page, Tab K—BC and Son Excavating—$2,000 cash. Green highlighting. Lots of highlighting, so much so, the page looked like it had been caught in a green downpour.

Hmmm. Okay. I looked at my watch. Proceed with caution. "There was a problem with your septic?"

Stone-faced, she flipped to Tabs N through S, a series of photographs. They were all tucked neatly into sleeves in what looked like a family photo album, except they were pictures of the excavation of her septic system. First shot was from the edge of the property, with each photo getting closer and closer into the open trench. In a few of the photos I could see that two mud-covered contractors had climbed down to hand-shovel the exposed pipe, which I assumed led to her home.

My mouth got a little dry. *If there is a body in there . . .*

"We had been having a problem for a few months, with the smell. My husband refused to deal with it, and one day while I was home early after a trip, I decided to handle it. I called the septic guys in—"

"I'm sorry Ms. Wood, I don't see the issue."

She turned the page to the final series of photos, Tabs S to V. One of the contractors was laughing, and the other was sheepishly lifting a shovel of something that had come out of the joint where the pipe entered the septic tank chamber. I couldn't quite make out the problem until I saw the last photo, a close-up.

Condoms. All different colours. Dozens of condoms had been flushed down the toilet. Their packages too. They had jammed the septic.

I looked up at her. There were no tears; instead there was that special form of slow-burning rage reserved for betrayal of marital trust.

"Mr. Bierce, we don't use condoms."

"I see."

"I need clarification on a couple of things." Ice water was now being poured on that rage.

"What's that?"

"I earn considerably more than my husband—with bonus and my investments, over $2 million a year. He earns about $110,000 with overtime. He has a landscaping business, referees some local hockey, and does some snowploughing in the winter for cash, really just to keep busy." I could see where this was going.

She carried on in a very business-like manner. "I have done a little research on support . . ."

I bet you have. "We can discuss that . . . I can run some calculations for you."

"Am I at risk of paying him support?"

I had to be honest with her. "Yes, there is a very serious risk. Technically, his behaviour has nothing to do with his potential entitlement to support."

"Mr. Bierce, we've been married twelve years. I have been faithful throughout. I make more than ten times what he makes. He's been fuc . . ." she couldn't say the word, " . . . everything in sight, and I just got my test results for STDs . . . " She named three, one I had not heard of before. So much for all those condoms. "Is there anything that can be done?"

"Well, as I say, he has a very strong entitlement to spousal support, but we can make it difficult for him to pursue it."

"Difficult?"

"It's one thing to be entitled, but it's another to actually 'survive' making a claim. It can be, you know, made difficult."

"Made difficult? How difficult?"

I tried not to smile. "It can be expensive for you, but for him I can make it like he wished he had never been born, difficult."

With those words I noticed her attitude shift to just plain marital meanness. "I'd rather pay you than pay him."

Now, I have heard those words before from angry clients, but the way she said it sent a chill down even my frozen spine.

Bonnie knocked on the door and stuck her head in to the boardroom. "Mr. Bierce (she calls me that in front of clients), there is an urgent call from you—"

"Not now, Bonnie. We are in the middle—"

"It's your client—"

"Bonnie—"

"He's calling from jail."

"Ms. Wood, can you excuse me for a moment?"

"Of course. I have to be leaving to catch my flight in any event." She gathered a few binders and papers together and muttered softly, as if relieved, "I guess I can just leave this stuff with you now . . . " Her tone shifted again as her meanness subsided into that weary sadness that follows having exposed one's most embarrassing experiences to a complete stranger.

I stepped out of the boardroom into the hall. "What is it?"

Bonnie looked worried. "It's Paul Campbell."

I had been trying to reach him for the last few days, without luck.

"He's been arrested—again."

Oh God, what fresh hell is this?

4

Roll Up the Rim to Win

PAUL CAMPBELL. WHERE DO I BEGIN? Never have I become so entangled in a client's life. That day, when I was meeting with Ms. Septic Smell, Paul was calling from the Don Jail, a different septic hellhole that later closed about hundred years after its best-before date. It never ceases to amaze me that our wise citizens' interest in so-called Law and Order usually only extends to catching, convicting, and incarcerating criminals. TV shows are dedicated to real life takedowns, but God forbid you should see the inside of a real, live Canadian courtroom through a camera lens. And nobody cares about that rare innocent person who must sit in these warehouses until their trial. They get to experience a penal Lord of the Flies for days, even weeks, until they get to see a judge. So, yes, the Don Jail is now closed, but not soon enough for Mr. Campbell.

When I got on the phone, it took a minute to get Paul calmed down. He was talking so fast, I could hardly make out what he was saying. He was in a panic, which was unusual for such a young, savvy guy. At that point he was making a very good buck on his way up in an insurance company, specialized stuff, reinsurance, global. Whatever. I had actually begun to represent him about eighteen months before and the divorce had certainly had ups and downs. He and his wife had separated a couple of years previous after a very short marriage, and I use the term "marriage" loosely because what he described to me during his original consultation back then was nothing like what you or I would describe as marriage.

His wife Chloe, admittedly a beautiful young woman of twenty-nine, was sadly also quite crazy. They got married in a fever, so to speak. Neither of them knew diddly about the other before they got married impulsively on a beach at a Bahamas resort with a couple of drunken hotel guests as witnesses. That was their first big mistake. Their original sin.

Second big mistake? Chloe got pregnant, and by their second anniversary they were living at every baby boutique in Toronto from Advice From a Caterpillar to Moschino Kids to Luxury Kids. Looking through their credit card statements, I was appalled to see among other purchases a child's Versace Medusa Black Tracksuit—$519. And Robert Cavalli Sandals for $377. I had to meet this child. Now, I realize that all of what I have just described—young couple, marriage, baby—could easily have been the beginning of a happy story. It was not.

Their marriage took a turn when Paul came home one day around the time their baby, named Angelina Jolie (I'm serious), was about four months old. Let's get that name out of the way. Chloe, an avid reader of *People* magazine, thought it was a "sign" that the actress was on the cover of the magazine the very week the baby was born. It should have been a sign, all right—an exit sign. Anyway, when Paul opened the door to their home (a two-million-dollar townhouse in the Beach that he owned before he met Chloe), he gagged on a wave of bleach fumes. He rushed in assuming something was wrong, only to find out that, well, something was terribly wrong. Chloe was cleaning the house from top to bottom with bleach—for the second time that day. Angelina sat, watery-eyed, in her Cybex Sirona baby seat on the kitchen table, green garbage bag spread beneath her so she would not contaminate the kitchen. Chloe, on her hands and knees scrubbing, began screaming at Paul to take off his shoes.

Within a few months, he was not allowed to wear shoes into the house. They were "filthy." Then no mail, newspapers, flyers or magazines could come in because they had germs. Then no people could come in because they were filthy *and* had germs. When Paul demanded that he be allowed to have guests over to celebrate his thirty-fifth birthday, he had to agree to Chloe's condition that guests would not use their home's bathrooms. They would have to use the toilet at the Tim Hortons on the corner. I shit you not.

Chloe, it turns out, had full-blown OCD and apparently had always had it. Her kookiness just never emerged into the full light of day until she stopped taking her meds during the pregnancy.

When Paul came to see me eighteen months ago for his $10,000 consult, he was cowed and ashamed. He and Chloe were now living in the basement laundry room, sitting on plastic lawn chairs, eating their meals off TV trays because the house could not get dirty without triggering a full-blown bleach breakdown from her. If Paul was caught upstairs, out came the bleach. He told me that things changed one night when they were in the laundry room, with the dryer going, listening to the radio. He looked at Angie and then at Chloe reading the latest *People* magazine and realized he could not keep living in eighteen square feet. Clearly he could not leave without the baby. So he came to see me to discuss options. Chloe was refusing help, so he ran through some scenarios: Stay put and try to work it out? Not possible. Move out with Angie? Chloe might harm herself. Split but stay in the house, she gets the basement? She might harm him. Children's Aid Society? No. That was bottom of the barrel. Nothing looked realistic, and every option had a serious downside. I recommended a course of action that could be summarized in two words: total war. He balked. After three hours, he couldn't make a decision, so he went home to think about it for a few days.

The next time I heard from Paul, it was a few weeks later on his first call from Toronto Police, 55 Division. He had been arrested. Chloe's personal trainer in a way had made decisions for both of them.

Chloe could keep it together for the most part outside the home. She could make it to and from her fitness club in the Audi Quattro that Paul had leased for her. She would drop Angie in the club's daycare program, spend the morning working out with her personal trainer, Jason, and then head home for some heavy bleaching. At first.

Unfortunately for Paul, after whipping Chloe into very buff post-pregnancy form, Jason had started polishing the floor with her. It had been going on for several weeks when Paul found a series of filthy (which seemed ironic in retrospect) text exchanges between Chloe and Jason (complete with startling photos as she demonstrated her amazing new-found flexibility).

Paul flipped. Who wouldn't? The only reason he had been hanging in was to pay the bills and make sure Angie was safe, but he discovered Chloe was getting down and dirty with Jason, who despite his high-level training in kinesiology was clueless about her compulsive problems. (I thought the rosy red dermatitis on her hands would have been a giveaway but what do I know.)

When Paul angrily confronted Chloe about the pictures, she called the police and said that he had threatened her. This, she later said, was based upon advice she heard on CBC Radio during a lunchtime call-in show. Cops arrived, took one look at the very beautiful buff but traumatized young mom, asked a few questions, and put the cuffs on Paul. Off to 55 Division.

That night I met him at the police station and persuaded the cops to cut him some slack and release him—which they never do. But this particular evening was different because the police were up to their eyeballs in the dozens of protesters they had been arresting all day. Actually, it looked like they had simply arrested everyone on the Queen streetcar along with anyone who happened to get caught in their kettle at the intersection of Queen and Spadina. Half the people who had been arrested didn't even know Toronto was hosting the G7 and that there was some kind of protest going on. It was so chaotic at the station, they released Paul, but with a stiff warning and on condition that he not go back to his home in the Beach. It was take it or leave it, so we took it.

The day after that catch and release, Paul was at my office with even bigger problems than when we had met a month earlier for his initial consult. Jason had now decided to move in to protect Chloe. He was still a long way from cluing in to her mental health challenges, as the doctors would later describe them. I assume he was prepared to have any intercourse in the basement laundry room, because there was no way Chloe would allow that upstairs. Maybe he was turned on by the smell of bleach. Trust me I have heard stranger things. Bottom line though, Chloe was in the house with the baby and Jason, and Paul was on the hook to cover all the bills.

And he had no access to Angie.

Suddenly my earlier recommendation for total war looked more attractive. Paul was all-in now. Blank cheque. Where do I sign?

Chloe retained the biggest asshole lawyer in the Greater Toronto Area. This was not even a lawyer whom I would think to try and conflict out: Albert Fernstein, a real nut job who had been in and out of practice with his own problems. A few years back, he had to take a leave of absence from his firm when his partners learned he had spent over $50,000 of lawyer time and $2,000 in disbursements chasing a $3,500 account receivable. Zero common sense. The firm docked his draw and sent him home. A few months later he was back at work on new meds. When Chloe met with him, he—as would be expected of him—promptly had her collapse $50,000 in RRSPs for his retainer. That is a ridiculous move from a tax perspective, but he wasn't paying her taxes, was he? Never mind that the only reason the money was in her RRSPs was because Paul had made the spousal contributions for her in the first place. Fernstein put her cash to use drafting and filing an emergency application to Superior Court, carefully pointing out that Paul, having been charged with uttering a threat and barred from being near them or the home, was a danger to Chloe and Angie.

As busy as I was on the lesbian mother battle at the time, I dropped everything and we—Paul, Bonnie, and I—spent a day preparing our response. We were due in court in just two days, on a Thursday morning at 393 University Avenue, 9th floor, 10:00 a.m.

That Thursday morning, the march of the lawyer penguins had begun much earlier, the same way it does five days a week, every week, Monday to Friday. We start in our offices, doors shut, slipping into our grey double pinstriped court pants, black linen skirts for women, white tuxedo-style shirts, some fresh from the dry cleaners, others not so fresh with armpits the colour of old lemons from repeated sweat soakings, black waistcoats, long black gowns thrown around our shoulders, fastened in the back by two long black strands and, last but not least, the famous starched white tabs fastened around our necks. We are robed and ready for appearances in Ontario Superior Court. With our big black briefcases on wheels loaded with files, textbooks, the Rules of

Practice, iPads, laptops, and other tools of our trade, we all head off to the courtrooms spread throughout buildings on University Avenue. For the more involved matters, there might also be luggage carriers loaded with banker's boxes pulled by articling students in ill-fitting suits. All are summoned to the courthouse. Away we go, striding to the office tower elevators, descending to the streets, flowing out onto Bay Street, King Street, Queen Street, Adelaide, Richmond, and Wellington. Dozens of us in our black robes and white shirts beginning our march north to the courtrooms. Legal penguins marching off in search of justice. It's all quite comical.

But not this particular day.

At 9:45 a.m. we were milling around in the hallway on the ninth floor of 393 University waiting for the court clerk to open Courtroom 903 for the hearing of Campbell (Chloe) v. Campbell (Paul), emergency custody motion. I had parked Paul in a corner with Black Beauty. Fernstein and Chloe kept a safe distance at the far end of the hall near the photocopier.

I walked over and scanned the court docket on the bulletin board outside the courtroom. *Shiiiit.* Bad news. The matter had been assigned to Justice Newsome, otherwise known as "No Nuts" Newsome. He is widely considered to be a bit of a non-judge. Why make a decision when it can simply be adjourned for some arcane reason? Let some other judge make the tough choices. He has rarely read the materials filed by the parties and cannot get out of the courtroom fast enough at the end of his list. As I stood there, I thought this is totally the wrong judge for Paul's matter. I even considered trying to get it moved to another judge's list. Not easy. The good news was that at least Newsome had only two matters on his docket. The bad news was that his list was short and therefore unlikely to be split. We were number two on it, so I checked to see who was the lawyer on the first matter. It's always a good idea to track them down and see how long they're going to be. If it's going to be hours, then we can head off for a coffee downstairs, otherwise we hang in hall limbo. The docket list I was reading couldn't be right, though. It said that the lawyer ahead of us was Lester Donald. I was pretty sure old Lester had died a few years ago. It had to be a mistake.

No sooner had I read his name than Lester came toddling around the corner in a rumpled set of gowns, which he surely had purchased during the reign of Queen Victoria. His briefcase, screwed up under his arm, was an old green leatherette zippered sleeve that could not be holding more than a dozen sheets of paper.

"Good morning, Mr. Donald. I see you're number one on Newsome's list. How long do you think you'll be?" I wondered if he could detect my shock that he was still alive.

"Hey, Bierce." I was surprised he remembered my name. I had not had a file with him in years, if ever. He was in a very different league of lawyers. If this was hockey, he would be the guy on the bench gasping for air in the old timer's league while his teammates searched for the defibrillator. "I'm just reporting a consent settlement with a self-rep on the other side." He nodded toward a man sitting near the men's washroom. Based on the way he was dressed, he looked like he might be homeless. "We won't be long. What have you got?"

I cringed at the sound of Lester's voice, which was something you had to hear to believe, so raspy and worn he sounded like he should be on a ventilator. "Emergency motion. Fernstein's on the other side."

At this statement, Lester's tangle of poorly trimmed peppery eyebrows shot up as if to say, "Yech."

Once we were all assembled in Newsome's court, I could see that Fernstein was clearly thrilled to have him deal with this matter—or not deal with it—by finding a reason simply to order the matter be adjourned. I could practically hear his thoughts: "Status quo. Status quo. Status quo to be maintained." That type of order would put Chloe in the driver's seat for months.

But first we had to endure Newsome dealing with Lester Donald's matter. Lester read slowly from a handful of yellow legal sheets. He introduced the homeless man, who was there without a lawyer and was presumably consenting to some godawful order that would surely make his life even worse. Lester's congested voice coughed out the terms of the agreement. When done, he sat down and Newsome asked the self-rep if he had anything to say. Unfortunately, he did. Twenty minutes later, after a rambling speech in which he mentioned the US Constitution, free speech, Nuremberg and the United Nations, he agreed with everything Donald had just read out to the judge. He sat down satisfied that he could have argued his case successfully in the Supreme Court of Canada.

Newsome then decided that this was a good time to give his standard speech about what a good job they had done, how it was good for everyone to settle matters and not fight, and how overburdened the courts are these days. He reminisced with Lester about days gone by when matters were less acrimonious and everyone got along. He then turned his comments to the lack of civility among lawyers and how this needed to change. I looked at my watch. Fifteen more minutes of his sermon followed. I looked at Fernstein, who struggled to catch Newsome's eye and nod in firm agreement with everything the learned judge had to say about the sorry state of the justice system, notwithstanding the fact that he himself engaged in that very same uncivil behaviour on virtually every file he touched.

I knew what was really going on. Newsome was simply stalling, hoping that another judge would finish his or her list, and our matter would be shifted to another courtroom. His list would be done, and he would disappear from the courtroom like a wisp of smoke. At a minimum he was probably going to suggest we should all take a midmorning break, and the lawyers could talk about settlement before carrying on with the second matter on his list.

All this while a genuine emergency matter sat waiting to be heard.

At long last, Lester and the self-rep packed up and bowed their way out of the courtroom. The clerk slid the Campbell file in front of Newsome. It was already thick with the affidavits and financial statements we had filed. It also looked like it had never been cracked. Newsome likely knew nothing about the case other than its name.

The clerk called the case. "Number two on Your Honour's list, Campbell v. Campbell."

Fernstein was on his feet in a split second, suggesting that, given the pending criminal proceedings, the matter should be adjourned to allow for further disclosure and questioning—and that the STATUS QUO be maintained in the meantime. He proposed that Chloe would stay in the home with the child, Paul would pay the bills, and we would await the outcome of the criminal charges. He said "CRIMINAL" as if Paul had already been convicted of murder. He closed with a classic line, "Your Honour, it is in the child's best interests to leave the status quo in place until further order of the court or agreement of the parties."

Those are magic words to a lawyer whose client has physical custody of the kids. Get a status quo, then adjourn, then delay, delay some more, demand disclosure, adjourn until it is provided, when it is provided adjourn because you need time to review it—possibly with a financial expert who can help you read a VISA statement—then, after reviewing it, ask for more disclosure: "What's this item here on page three? Victoria's Secret? What was purchased at Victoria's Secret?" After a few months of this nonsense, the next judge to deal with the matter is asking, "Why would I disturb the status quo? These children need stability. It's in their best interests." It works. I know it works because I have done it hundreds of times, screwing some parent out of time with their kids to create leverage. You would be surprised what someone will agree to just to be able to see their kids after suffering through six months of FaceTime calls. I recall one case, the Glidden family, a couple of the decisions were reported, so you can look it up if you are so moved. I had that case so tangled up in adjournments that the father, broke in every sense of the word, just gave up and walked away. It cost a fortune, but my client got what she had demanded, sole custody of the two boys. It is a real skill to generate that kind of result for a client.

But this day, with Paul's situation, the shoe was on the other foot in front of Newsome. I thought Fernstein's pitch must be music to his ears. Adjourn, punt the file, go for an early lunch. But I was not going to let that happen, not on my watch. Newsome finally turned to me and said, "Mr. Bierce, is there anything you would like to add?" He said it as if surely maintaining the status quo was a foregone conclusion.

I knew I had to engage Newsome. Get him interested. I would need to push hard. So I started with the gory stuff. The bleach. The baby with watery eyes. The pissing at Tim Hortons. Living in the basement. I was firm and patient. Even when Fernstein jumped up to interrupt me—three times, no less—fairly shouting the words "Status quo!" I stopped my submissions and said, with just a touch of self-righteousness, "Your Honour, in your remarks to Mr. Donald just moments ago in this very courtroom, you reminded us that civility is needed among the profession. I sat here patiently while Mr. Fernstein made submissions for his client, and I would ask that I be shown the same courtesy by him." How could he disagree? He nodded disapprovingly at Fernstein.

And then it happened. *Click.* Newsome actually started asking questions. *Where is this particular evidence? Direct me to the affidavit and the paragraph. Show me the exhibit.* He began to read the material carefully. He was actually interested. Very interested. Fernstein, jumping half out of his seat objecting to my submissions, looked like he was trying to sit on a hot stove. It didn't help his cause that as I made my submissions Chloe sat beside him, hissing loudly into his ear after every statement.

Two hours later, I had an order from Newsome that Angie was to be alternated between the parents on a regular schedule. The Office of the Children's Lawyer would be appointed to investigate her needs. Chloe was to attend meetings with Dr. Petrowski, a very good psychiatrist. She could stay in the home but she had to pay occupation rent, which would be knocked off her spousal support. Here was the best part: she had to pay Paul's legal costs of the day. (I had made a very good Offer to Settle before we went to court, knowing full well that Fernstein would never accept it. Idiot.) And the amount was to be sorted out by the lawyers; if not, then Newsome would make a costs order. Total war brought total vindication.

It was a good order, and Paul was walking on air. I packed up my briefcase, rolled it out into the hall, and waited for the clerk to bring out a copy of Newsome's order. Paul was pulling around my briefcase like he was my goddamn articling student. I could see Fernstein and Chloe having words at the end of the corridor. He grabbed her arm to move her out of earshot, but it was clear that she was mightily pissed. He had not delivered as promised. Even Jason, who was there for the proverbial moral support, looked a little unnerved by her foul-mouthed ranting. I thought to myself, Jason will be gone within the month now that he was seeing—and hearing—what a nut job she was. He would be back to the gym, grazing for another insecure young mom.

In a few minutes, Fernstein was at my side with his usual kooky look on his face. "Off the record?"

"Sure."

"I cannot believe Newsome grew a pair and made that fucking order."

"Sorry, I thought you wanted to talk about my client's costs? I will be looking for about twenty-five grand plus disbursements, and let's not forget HST." I smiled, of course.

"Fuck off. I can barely get her to agree to honour Newsome's order. Costs will have to wait. Let us get out of here ahead of you, or there will be a brawl at the elevators. "

"You better keep your client under control, or I might have to call the police." I couldn't resist a little sarcasm.

No sooner had he disappeared around the corner to deal with her than Lester Donald limped over toward me, half dragging a foot. I had never really noticed his weird but pronounced gait. He had his leatherette briefcase tucked under his arm as he applied his stained teeth in a vigorous chew on the rim of a large Tim Hortons cup. He was struggling to roll up the rim in search of a prize. He stopped and turned to me. "Hey, Bierce, I heard that Newsome made quite the order in your matter."

"Wow. Word spreads fast. I know, it's unbelievable. Wife has OCD, total loon." I turned to keep an eye on Chloe.

Without missing a beat, Lester said, "Newsome's wife had that." He chewed the rim of the cup a little bit more, tearing at the cup. "She went off the deep end a few years ago. He tried to get her help, but she was pretty screwed up. She died or something. Yes! Free coffee and donut!" And with that joyous pronouncement, Lester walked away, slightly dragging one foot and still chewing off the winning scrap. He was so thrilled, you'd think he'd won the LottoMax.

I called after him with a laugh, "Roll up the rim to win, Lester." He raised his arm to acknowledge me and promptly dumped his sleeve of papers all over the floor. I watched as he struggled down onto his knees to gather them up, cup still firmly held in his teeth.

"Who's that guy?" Paul asked.

I shook my head and laughed. "Nobody."

At that moment, Fernstein and Chloe passed Paul and me on the way to the elevators. I commented to Fernstein that I would wait a day to hear from him about costs and made sure to give Chloe a good look so she wouldn't forget who she was dealing with. I mouthed "Bye" with a smile.

Suddenly, she wheeled around and snarled at me, "Say hello to your sexy brother, Father Sean."

I was stunned. I didn't know what to say. How on earth did she know my brother, Toronto's worst priest?

That glorious Thursday in court with Paul just months ago felt like an eternity had passed as I showed Ms. Septic Smell out of the office. Now Paul had been arrested again and was in the Don Jail, and I would need help to get him out.

5

Canada's Funniest Home Videos

BY THE FOLLOWING MORNING, I had still not found a lawyer who could help me get Paul out of jail. Normally I refer all criminal defence work to Peter Deacon, a former Crown attorney who switched to the defence side after he got a couple of thousand prosecutions under his belt. That's how it works, take a low-paying job as a Crown for a few years, learn the ropes, the judges, and the tricks of the trade, then switch to a more lucrative career as a defence lawyer doing high-profile murder trials for millionaires. That's the plan anyway, but few pull it off. Most end up just grinding it out in the trenches on legal aid certificates.

Deacon's an exception. He has a steady flow of quality work. But this particular morning I found out that he was off to California to see grandkids. A lot of that seems to be happening lately. That's not something I will ever need to worry about; no kids means no grandkids. Without my go-to guy, I had to turn to my B list of criminal defence lawyers. Then my C list, but no one is available on short notice. Paul is a good client, pays his bills, so the unthinkable was becoming thinkable: going to the Don myself.

I had one last thought. "Bonnie, did you call Singh?" He's a smart guy who has been trying to build a defence practice for years but doesn't seem to have that private practice touch. He's a bit of a softy and too academic to actually help people in trouble. They don't really care how inefficient the justice system is and how it should be reformed. They need you to deal with reality. Get me out. Get me off. Pretty straightforward.

"Didn't you hear? He was appointed a judge last week."

I had not heard that. I'm not sure that was such a good decision, but these days appointments to the bench are, shall we say, complicated.

Bonnie pointed at a thick package on the counter of her work station. "In the meantime . . . " She used her pen to push it toward me. It had several large orange Personal and Confidential stickers on it and a half dozen Fragile notes. I mean, even two stickers is enough, but seven?

"No return address. Bomb?"

"You tell me. Why don't you open it in your office, though. And your brother called again. Call him."

Notwithstanding his name practically being spat at me by Chloe Campbell, I was in no hurry to return the calls of my brother the priest today, if at all.

I carried the package into my office, set it down on my desk, and zipped it open so I could gently slide out a handwritten letter. I called out to Bonnie. "Coast is clear. It's from that idiot Laurier." He was a new client facing a boatload of trouble, and at the rate he was going, a container ship of legal bills. As I read his weirdly scrawled note, it occurred to me that no normal person writes like this, and perhaps I should send it for some kind of psychiatric handwriting analysis. The note said something to the effect of, "Here are some DVDs. Let's book some time ASAP to go through this material together." The word "together" was underlined twice in red and highlighted. It was also followed by three exclamation marks. Whatever. I opened the package and held the DVDs up to Bonnie with a smile. There were five of them, and as I closed the door to my office, Bonnie winced and said, "I don't even want to know." We had been here before.

I slid a disc into a computer we kept around for precisely such occasions and started clicking through files. There was no obvious order, random photos, scanned tax returns, Notices of Assessment, and some oddly titled short videos. Oh God, I prayed this was not homemade porn. I opened a file and knew immediately that it was not going to be pretty.

Professional porn is made for a reason; the quality production removes reality, along with all the ugly warts of participants. Seriously, no one wants to see real people having intercourse. I have never understood why people film themselves in all manner of sexual activity. Nor can I understand why they take pictures of their private parts and send them to each other, to people they supposedly like. Those pics usually look more like autopsy photos or something from an old medical encyclopedia. Brutal.

There is never anything erotically stimulating about these pictures, and to make matters worse, along with the pictures, people include cringe-inducing messages to their lovers and other strangers. Their cache of lusty images is of course later discovered by their horrified spouse, who has no problem identifying their life partner's pudgy tattooed ass. Those shocked husbands and wives show up in lawyers' offices with Canada's funniest home movies, emails, text messages, cards, notes, and love letters. Occasionally, just occasionally, in the middle of this garbage, there is a quality sex video. This can be enough reward for having to wade through all the other muck, plus it makes for a bit of fun when we actually get to meet the star of the film in the flesh, so to speak. But most of the time we are sifting through the garbage, wincing, laughing, gagging, and ultimately trying to figure how and why any of this stuff is remotely relevant. I guess some pictures will help establish adultery, but so what? No one uses adultery as grounds for divorce anymore, even after that scary leak at Ashley Madison. Unless of course you are the wife of a certain hockey player whose wife made sure his affair with an uptown girl ended up on the front page of the *Toronto Sun*. That was pure fucking revenge, I assure you. I know. I was there.

As for that Ashley Madison scare, it was totally overblown, and there were few if any divorces actually triggered by it. I think I know why. I met a young woman who got into trouble in her own divorce when she had to disclose sources of income. She had been working part-time pretending to be an eligible woman on one of these sites, enticing men to stay engaged but never hooking up with them. Let's just say there was more fantasy than fornication.

One time, a client showed up with a recently discovered banker's box of her husband's sex tapes (Seasons 1 through 6). Some of it was on VHS, for Christsakes. Bonnie had to go find a VCR to screen this technologically ancient archive of lust. He had secretly set up a camera in an old TV in order to record his encounters with hookers (uh, sorry, sex workers) in the basement guest room of the family home.

It was a nicely decorated room, with a frilly yellow comforter on the bed and matching pillowcases with a nautical theme. Pretty if you were decorating based on a *Harrowsmith* magazine from 1978. But for him I guess it made for an innocent setting for his guilty liaisons. Any genuine guests of the family would have been physically ill if they knew what was going on in that room, on that bed.

There was a lot of standard stuff on the videos, lots of grunting, groaning, flipping and flopping around, and him making furtive glances at the hidden camera. I guess by acknowledging himself, it made watching it later a little more real. I found it unnerving, even creepy, each time he stared into the camera and smiled knowingly.

There was, however, one epic VHS moment when his guest for the afternoon arrived, a full-bodied, flaming red-headed, middle-aged woman. Aside from the hair on her head, there was no other evidence by which one could determine her hair's natural colour, if you know what I mean. There she was buck naked and bouncing around on the bed, with his legs dangling off the end right in front of the TV, his little lighthouse of a pecker pointed to the heavens. Big Red was attending to it like her life depended on it, occasionally throwing out an, "Oh yeah ... oh God ... oh yeah." The host could be heard moaning more like a man left to die on the battlefield than anyone in the throes of ecstasy. But then, in a classic turn of events, she stopped bobbing for apples, looked at her watch, and rolled her eyes before getting back to work. Hilarious. I played it for Bonnie in the boardroom and nearly pissed my pants laughing. Bonnie, of course with no sense of humour, was furious and stormed out. Not impressed. But seriously, it should be on YouTube.

The "Law of Pornography and Divorce" is pretty straightforward. That's probably why there were no classes dealing with it in law school. Did the porn video evidence have the slightest impact on their divorce? No. On support? No. On custody of the children? No. Child support? No. Spousal support? No. Property division? No (except that the wife didn't want any of the furniture from that guest room). Was the evidence relevant in any way? No. And yet the scorned and betrayed spouses arrive with the grim stuff and insist that here, surely, is evidence that will not just alter the outcome of the whole case but send the guilty spouse straight to hell in the eyes of the world. Sorry, it does not work like that. Still, I'll pop in a disc or video, turn the sound down, and work on something else and double-bill for my time on two files at once. If something interesting pops up, so to speak, I can always rewind.

Bonnie knocked, cracked the door a bit, and with a tinge of mild disgust said, "If you are finished with that . . . I still have no good news on a criminal lawyer for Paul. What next?"

I pushed the pile of Laurier's DVDs aside. "I'm going to the Don." Even I couldn't believe that I had said it. "I'll go up to Old City Hall and do it myself if I have to."

What was I thinking?

"You're going to Old City Hall? That's criminal court . . . "

"I know it is criminal court, Bonnie."

"Do you know what to do in criminal court? Have you ever appeared there? I don't think I ever—"

"I'll figure something out."

"Can I come and watch? You're always telling me I can come and watch."

This was true. Bonnie had been bugging me for years to come to court and see what was actually going on. It's also true that I have promised that she could come—sometime—but the time has never been right. "Some other time, Bonnie. Look after any appointments that will need to be cancelled."

I cannot stomach the idea of an innocent guy in jail, but even more than that, I could not bear the thought of Bonnie seeing me absolutely clueless in a courtroom.

6

The Don

NO SOONER DID I GET INSIDE the shithole Don Jail than I found out no one would be seeing any prisoners because some scissors had gone missing from the infirmary. I looked around at the ragtag collection of people being held in a waiting area and couldn't tell if they were visitors, family, or lawyers. God, from the look of their shabby clothes, I hoped they weren't lawyers. I decided to wait. Thirty minutes later, good news, they found the scissors. Then, fifteen minutes after that, bad news, they only found "half" the scissors. Now someone had a weapon, so the jail went into full lockdown. Then it got worse. The union rep for the guards threatened to call for a walkout because the missing scissor piece was suddenly a safety issue. Seriously? Wasn't every day at the Don a safety issue? After being there a full two smelly hours, a woman whose name was surely Brunhilda stepped out and told all of us to go home and come back tomorrow.

Decision time. It was 1:00 p.m. Thursday. If I didn't do something to get Paul out, he faced not only another night in jail, but possibly the whole weekend, a long weekend. I decided to boot it directly to Old City Hall and hire a lawyer on the spot to spring him or take an even bigger gamble and try to do something myself. Gulp.

I parked at my office and made my way up Bay Street to that once proud Romanesque building at the corner of Queen and Bay. The gargoyles on the facade are a pretty accurate reflection of the losers who pass through its revolving courtroom doors. I took the front steps two at a time past the cenotaph, thinking that if the men and women who died in those wars knew what goes on inside this building today, they would have wondered what they had fought for.

I would hazard a guess that at any given moment, 99.9 percent of the accused people in this building are guilty of something. Maybe not what they are charged with, but something. I calculated that all their actual acquittals, convictions, and unknown illegal activities must average out over the course of a lifetime. Which is why so many of them look blasé when convicted. They think, *Oh well, I guess I had to get busted for something eventually*. It's pretty rare to see a case of outright injustice in here, you know a real, "But Your Honour, they got the wrong guy. I'm innocent. I wasn't even there. You gotta believe me!" That bullshit is for TV.

By the way, if family law lawyers are on the bottom rung of the legal ladder, then most of the criminal lawyers eking out a living at Old City Hall don't even know there's a ladder. Sorry, but a life devoted to non-stop legal aid, dump-trucking guilty pleas for a living with the same clients over and over again, dealing with petty criminal shit? You might as well be that guy who got sick shovelling elephant shit at the circus. When he was told by his doctor that he had to quit, he said, "What?! And give up show biz?!" But what do I know if I'm only one rung up.

Now, I haven't told you what circumstances led to Paul's second arrest and brought him to the jailhouse, have I? Remember that great order that Judge No-Nuts Newsome made at the emergency motion brought by Fernstein? Well, it didn't last long.

A few months after the order was made, Paul and his buddy had gone to see a movie, a safe little flight from reality surrounded by other escapees. He was sitting in the Cineplex lobby area, enveloped in the usual teen mayhem and long lineups for popcorn, waiting for his friend to come out of the men's room. Unbeknownst to him, Chloe and Jason happened to be in theatre #21, watching some rom-com. When they came out and saw Paul sitting there, they did the only reasonable thing people do in the middle of a divorce: they phoned the police to report a breach of his bail conditions. Six cops in three cruisers arrived at the theatre. Overkill? A bit. They threw the cuffs on Paul and frog-marched him out in front of the gawking—and video recording—teenagers who thought they were watching a real life episode of *COPS*. All of the "takedown" video was posted online before Paul even arrived at the Don Jail.

Breach of restraining order. That's the call that interrupted my meeting with Ms. Septic Smell. That's why Paul was in jail and this was what dragged me to Old City Hall. There was a line up of losers twenty deep waiting to get through the metal detectors at the front door of the courthouse. I jumped the line by flashing my lawyer's ID card and could hear the guilty people in line grumbling about "effing lawyers." It was a relief to leave them behind sorting through baskets for their expensive phones, fake bling, and knock-off watches.

I stood in the middle of the main hall and gazed around. I was a little out of my league here and felt uneasy. This was not my turf, and my gut tightened. At the family courts I know the clerks, the court reporters, the lawyers, the judges, and I even know most of the security guards. They may not like me, but they know me and respect me because I know what I'm doing. Here at Old City Hall, the lawyers don't even wear black gowns. For all anyone knew, I could be a criminal standing there, albeit a very well-dressed one, but a possible criminal nonetheless.

I decided to head toward a throng outside a courtroom and try to figure out if one of them was a lawyer. Surely one of these lowlites could use a quick cash-paying case. Maybe I would know someone. I scanned the crowd, no luck. The mob outside the courtroom was a veritable whirlpool of guilty people, their families, girls huddled in clutches of two and three, cellphones in hand, drama queens, talking too loud about things of no consequence, girlfriends of wannabe gangsters.

I watched as these twenty-somethings sized one another up as if to say "stay away from my man." They were there to support loser boyfriends instead of working or going to school. As I watched, it occurred to me that poor people always seem to have money for cigarettes, the best cellphones, multiple tattoos, and mean dogs. These young ladies pushed cheap overloaded strollers with diaper bags, knockoff purses, and yoga mats stuffed underneath, and pulled a toddler by the hand. I don't know why it is, but these girls always seem to be so angry with their children, shouting at them with their celebrity-inspired names, "Kobe, you stand still. Paris, you get yourself over here." Pulling them, tugging them, making them sit still like unwanted pets, constantly scolding them, especially the boys, as if to say, "See I'm a good parent. I'm on this kid's ass 24/7." Yeah, right, you'll be on the cover of *Parents* magazine next month. I wonder what they'll say when their little one takes his or her place in line at this whirlpool in a few years?

I stood at the edge of this scene, trying to figure out what to do next but couldn't help thinking that I had seen some of these kids and their parents before. I recalled my many cases in which these drama queens sat with some twenty-four-year-old social worker from the CAS, a newbie MSW who had just graduated from York and hadn't even framed her degree yet. That was because she still lived at home with her mom and dad in Richmond Hill. But that wouldn't stop her from giving sage advice to her clients on how to raise two children on social assistance while their father was gone or in jail. She would explain the secret formula for getting blood and child support out of a stone. She might even shake her finger and warn, "You better clean up your act or CAS will come in and supervise your troubled life." (Meaning you will need to be home when she pops in to ask about the kids and your yoga classes.) It is a cruel joke—on both of them.

It is cruel because you know what happens next? Breaking news, they don't get their act together in this family apocalypse. Instead, I arrive with an order for custody and apprehension—along with the police—to scoop up those little ones and get them over to the safety of Grandma and Grandpa, who finally had enough of their daughter or son's neglect of their precious jewels—as the little heart-shaped sign on their fridge says.

Where did Nonna and Nonno get the rice to hire me? They used a chunk of their savings or home equity to pay my hourly rate because there was no margin of error. They would take no chances when it comes to their grandchildren. They need results, not excuses. Total war. Maybe one or both of them will need to head back to work part-time to pay for "Operation Grandchild" extraction. Most of the time they'll be too late to change the trajectory of this kid's life, but I'll still come for them with the sweet, albeit expensive, sword of justice. I love those cases.

But I couldn't get distracted by these thoughts. I needed to do something for Paul, so I headed into the courtroom, only to be greeted with a slap in the face of BO. The ripe room was packed, so I took a seat at the back on a well-worn bench and surveyed the scene. Who was in charge here? Anyone? The judge looked vaguely familiar. He barely lifted his head as the assembly line passed in front of him. I could only see the back of what appeared to be the Crown attorney. She looked young, black hair in a ponytail, in an ill-fitting suit. I watched her. She seemed to run a tight ship, though. Respect. She was moving the packages along the conveyor belt of justice while a steady stream of shabbily dressed lawyers in cheap sports jackets and Dockers shuffled in a line toward her. They would bend at the waist, whisper in her ear, "Here's the deal, here's my client's plea. Here's an adjourn date." She never even looked up, except occasionally, when she would give a lawyer a look of absolute disgust. What could he have suggested to her? Her face said, "You must be kidding? Your package is not doing that. Your package is going somewhere else." I watched as the chastened lawyer stepped back, whispered something to his client, and then returned to her ear. "Okay, here's what I can do." She nodded. "That's better." And she moved the package along.

As she worked, the charges were read in open court by the clerk, and the guilty would march up before the judge for disposition and a new shipping address. What I heard that day was a litany of behaviour you and I pray does not occur in our neighbourhoods. Guilty pleas were recorded and sentences imposed. Next.

A cellphone rang, and I recognized a popular kooky ringtone, Baby Shark. The clerk warned everyone to turn their cellphones off. I edged down and got in line to move toward the ringmaster, watching her, trying to listen to how she handled this list. Up close, her suit showed its wear with the ass shiny from standing and sitting repeatedly all day. Finally, I was close enough even to smell her perfume and musky sweat. It was a relief from the pungent pot of stew surrounding me. I could see her face, porcelain white, apparently never exposed to the sun, thick black-rimmed glasses, bright ruby-red lipstick. Interesting.

I leaned over her shoulder and said, "Hi, my name is Andrew Bierce, and I'm not a criminal lawyer . . . I'm a family law lawyer. But I was hoping you could help me out. I need a minute of this judge's time for a client of mine, an innocent man . . . " I could not believe I actually said that. It sounded so stupid. "He's in the Don and . . . "

She didn't even look up. "What number is it on the list?" Her voice was deep, husky, tired.

"What? Sorry?" I stammered.

"I said. Are. You. On. My. List?" Each word was punctuated as if to say, Are. You. Deaf?

"I leaned in a little more. "No, I am not—"

She cut me off again. "If you're not on my list, then get the fuck out of my face and my courtroom. I'm busy."

Her words hit me as if someone had opened a furnace door. I was stunned. Whatever happened to civility in the profession? Thank God Bonnie didn't witness this. Another lawyer squeezed by me and slipped to her side, burbling, "Okay, I spoke to my client and we can . . . " Reeling, I stepped back to the seating area.

I heard a very calm voice behind me. "That didn't look pretty."

I turned to the voice, which was coming out of a mouth that sat about eight inches below a very bald middle-aged head. My first instinct was to size up whether this man was a lawyer or perhaps a criminal who had more experience here than me. I couldn't tell based on his clothing, a worn caramel corduroy sports jacket and a pair of black jeans. He wore Blundstone boots that looked like he had just finished hiking the Bruce Trail.

He smiled. "She's a real ball-buster of a Crown, but at least you have a story to tell your friends."

"Tell my friends?"

"Yeah, you know that TV show on CBC . . . "

"No." Where is this going? Do people still watch TV?

He looked toward her and said, "There was a show a few years ago, and it had a character on it, a Crown attorney, who was a real witch. The writers based the character on her, Lorelei Novak. The Witch." Another weird ringtone pulsed in the court, Bieber's "It's Too Late to Say Sorry," and the clerk reminded everyone to turn off their cellphones. The bald man continued, "She runs a tight ship. She's good but a little bit of a control freak. Just out of curiosity, what did you say to her?"

I explained the situation, including my lack of experience in criminal court and even the fact that I said Paul was innocent. When he stopped laughing, he made a face as if he was Robert De Niro weighing an important decision about whether he would do another sequel to *Meet The Parents* simply to help pay for his own ugly divorce. He rubbed his chin and ran his hand over his bald head. "Well, look, I would say Judge Harold is bored out of his gourd right now."

"That is Harold?" I was shocked. I knew him in law school. We played hockey together. Law practice took us in different directions. He was, as we say in private practice, a grinder, not a minder, who never aspired to be a finder. Harold's hair was bone-white, and he looked exhausted. I bet he regretted applying to be a judge. He probably never imagined presiding over this stinking factory day in, day out. A ringtone sounded out the opening bars of Michael Jackson's "Beat It," and the clerk reminded everyone to turn off their cellphones.

"If I were you . . . ," Baldy now ran both hands over his head, face, and chin as if to make sure they were still there, "I would just walk up there in front of the clerk and ask Harold for a minute of his time. Explain the situation and ask that your guy be brought to bail court tomorrow morning. They bring a van of them over every day. Throw in a reference to *habeas corpus* and you're golden." He smiled as if to say, "Why not?" And smiled a goofy De Niro smile, pleased with his advice.

I nodded to the Crown. "She will not be happy."

"True. But so what? Are you coming back here soon? No. The only reason we're scared shitless of her is because we have to deal with her every day. You don't." A cellphone chimed the theme from *The Godfather*, and the clerk reminded everyone to turn off their cellphones.

The fact that it was Harold gave me a little more incentive. I started to think, how bad can it be? And besides, to put it very mildly (and by mildly I mean I had a fucking rage building in me), I didn't like the way she had treated me, senior counsel. I'm a Q.C. for Christsakes. I marched down directly to counsel table and stood in front of the clerk. She looked up at me as if to say, *What do you think you're doing?* She glanced at Novak, who was busy listening to a lawyer's proposal.

I made my move. "Your Honour? Good Morning. My name is Bierce. Initial A."

Harold did not even look up. "What number are you on my list?"

"It's a matter that is not on Your Honour's list." Now he looked up, and I could see that his eyes were dead pools.

Suddenly the Witch was on her feet, practically knocking over the lawyer whispering in her ear, "Your Honour, I spoke to this gentleman, and the matter is not on my list and is therefore not properly before this court." She was not happy, but in her anger she had made a little slip. She referred to the list as *her* list, when it was actually Harold's list. Small point, but Harold's eyes flickered like a computer rebooting after a power failure. His interest had been piqued simply because the mind-numbing routine had been broken. This package is different.

Harold spoke. "*Your* list, Ms. Novak?"

"I'm sorry, Your Honour, *your* list. Regardless, this matter is not on it." She didn't sound very sorry to me.

Harold turned his gaze to me. "A little far from divorce court, aren't we, Mr. Bierce?" Ahh, he recognized me.

"It feels like a million miles right now, Your Honour. And I would not put myself here disrupting *your* list, unless it was important."

The Witch was on her feet again. "Your Honour, do we have time for this today? There are ways to deal with his matter, and this isn't one of them. There are ten more matters on Your Honour's list. I mean, really? Is this the best way to handle this?"

But it was too late. Harold was interested now. The monotony of this tidal wave of stupid people had been broken. His day would be different now. Thursday would be different from Monday, Tuesday, Wednesday. He would have something to tell his wife at dinner tonight. "You won't believe what happened in court today. Pass the peas."

"What do you want me to do, Mr. Bierce?" He said it not in a puzzled way but in a rather generous way, as if to say, *How can I help?*

Novak was beside herself and fell dramatically into her chair. Harold did not like it. "Ms. Novak, do you have a problem? Because if you do, I can fix it." He seemed to enjoy seizing control of his courtroom again. He was sitting up straight, looking down at the flotsam washing up against the bench. The courtroom was suddenly dead quiet. A cellphone chimed out the theme from *Rocky*. The clerk sat stunned, looking at me and then the Crown. Novak stood, apologized, and sat down, clearly shaken.

I explained Paul's situation to Harold as Novak sat at counsel table, resigned to the fact that this was not going to be her day. It took all of ten minutes. Harold made an order to bring Paul over in the morning and even told the clerk to make a point of getting his order to the Don ASAP because it was getting late in the day. "With the lockdown over there, things may be slow." She smiled at me, a little shocked but enjoying the change of pace.

I thanked Harold for his order and apologized for the interruption.

"I assume I will not be seeing you anytime soon, Mr. Bierce, so have a nice afternoon. The court will take a fifteen-minute break."

He stood as the clerk called out, "All rise. This court stands adjourned for fifteen minutes." Someone at the back of the court actually applauded.

Harold wasn't out of the room three seconds before the Witch was on me. Defence lawyers and clients all stepped back as if making room for a schoolyard brawl. "You fucking bastard. Who the fuck do you think you are? If you so much as set foot in my courtroom again I'll make you and your client wish they were . . . " Her words were lost in the buzz of people around us.

The group turned to me for my response. I waited a beat and then said coldly, "Then you'd better pray that you are never in my house." I turned and walked away. As I did I heard a wannabe gangster say, "Oh man, what tha fuck zat mean? Come on, hit the bitch." His lawyer grabbed him and pushed him aside before Novak could see who said it.

Baldy was waiting for me in the hall and raised a hand for a high-five. "I didn't see that coming. Well done."

I thanked him for the help and asked for his card. He handed me a budget business card like the ones that come a hundred for free if you buy an ink cartridge. I looked at it. "Alvin Shank. LLB. Criminal Law."

I passed him one of my cards. He fingered it and said, "Nice." It was nice. Gold-embossed, bone white, linen, watermark, Expensive. "Man this is going down in history over here. She is going to be a handful after this. I wouldn't want to be the next lawyer in line."

"Listen, I really appreciated the help. If you're ever over my way, I expect a call."

"Divorce court? Ha, not likely." He laughed and for good measure massaged his face and head from top to bottom with both hands.

With a wave, I was off and called back to him, "Well, you never know. Ya never know."

7

The Keg

SATISFIED WITH A GOOD DAY'S WORK, I went back to the office to catch Bonnie before she headed home for the day. I needed a drink, and after that experience, it would have to be something strong. When she looked at me as if to say *Well?* I poured a large bourbon and told her a slightly modified version of what had actually happened, with the bottom line being that I got Paul out but still needed to meet him at bail court in the morning. "You seem surprised that I could handle myself so well in criminal court."

"I am surprised . . . maybe if you let me come and watch some-day . . . But it looks like today's appearance was a handful." She glanced at my beautiful blue Canali suit, and I suddenly realized that the armpits were soaked through with perspiration.

I wasn't going to take the bait about her coming to court and slipped into my office for three more fingers of bourbon. As I sat there retracing the whole unnerving experience at Old City Hall, I vowed to never do it again. Criminal courts? Never again.

My review of the day was interrupted when Bonnie called out from her desk. "Guess who died?" Before I could blurt out my top-ten list of celebrities who deserved to die, she pronounced solemnly, "The Keg."

The Keg was dead? It was the end of an era.

Keg. Kegger. Both were short for Powderkeg, his nickname for the last forty-five years or more of law practice. Tom Warden, Q.C., dead. It was like learning an old hockey enforcer, maybe Eddie Shack, had died. Warden had been at it as a litigator in Toronto for decades, and for every single minute of it he was furious. He was a short man but powerfully built. Apparently a former rugby player, he walked like he was about to either draw pistols from both hips or tackle someone. Or both. His intimidating athletic stance and stride were unmistakable around the courthouse as he practiced law into his late seventies. But it was his constant slow-boiling rage that made him infamous among lawyers and judges. He could explode on a moment's notice about anything that tipped over his internal jar of nitroglycerin. Boom.

I once witnessed him demolish a vending machine in the hallway of a small courthouse in Cobourg. Why? Because his articling student, a young man who should have known better than to accept a job with him, delivered a document brief that had, brace yourself, several pages out of order. It was a simple copy and binding mistake. Happens all the time. But it pulled Keg's hair trigger. He might as well have been told he missed a limitation period (every lawyer's nightmare) or been denied an appeal to the Supreme Court of Canada on a technicality. Five minutes later, after an unprecedented level of swearing and the destruction of one vending machine, he carried on as if nothing had happened. The student quit law the next day.

Everyone had a Kegger story. In the old days you could get away with those antics, but these days the Law Society wants lawyers to be civil with each other. Civil to Keg meant no hitting, well, no hitting hard. One time, years ago, I watched as he stood up at a Bar Association meeting held in the august dining room of Osgoode Hall. The panel discussion was entitled, *Bringing Civility to the Legal Profession*. There, surrounded by the rich wood-panelled walls, shelves laden with dusty law books, and with the light pouring down through stained glass windows, a red-faced Keg called the chairwoman (and I quote) a "pussy" and told the room that she was trying to turn all lawyers into pussies like her. And then he said, "No offence." And sat down with his standard grimace. The room exploded into laughter as a group of old male lawyers chanted "Keg, Keg, Keg." She burst into tears and adjourned the meeting.

And now Bonnie said he was gone. I tried to imagine what might happen to his face once his fiery pulse had stopped. Would it finally relax, go smooth? Or would it stay etched with deep wrinkles and still carry those huge, red, inflamed bags under each eye, his expression a constant cartoon caricature of fury.

Bonnie called out again, "Keg's memorial is tomorrow night at 6:30 p.m."

"I can't go. I have prep for Fabio's matter in OCJ."

"You have to go. It'll be a who's-who. Fabio's matter is ready to go. There's no more prep."

She was right. It *would* be a who's-who and Fabio's matter was ready. "Where is it?"

"Burdettes Funeral Home. Queen Street. Out Parkdale way. And don't forget that tonight you are doing MIP."

Fuck, not Burdettes, that hideous chocolate-coloured brick dungeon of a funeral home. I had passed it a thousand times. I used to stop and look at the 8 x 10 glossy pictures of the recently deceased posted in the window. They creeped me out. Did the departed ever imagine that this would be the picture in the window of a funeral home? *Smile, say cheeeeese. Oh, that's beautiful. I'll get this right over to Burdettes.*

I heard a terrible story about a part-time guy who was fired from Burdettes and charged with what lawyers call "offering any indignity to a dead human body or human remains." That is a nicer way of saying he was caught humping a dead customer. So whenever I go by there I get a sick, sour feeling and my mouth goes a little dry.

When I die, I don't want to be laid out at Burdettes. I have even thought about adding a special section to my will directing my estate trustee that under no circumstances are they to use Burdettes. But then I remember that I don't have a will. Most lawyers don't, because secretly we know that making a will can actually lead to death. And perhaps Burdettes.

8

MIP

MIP. MANDATORY INFORMATION PROGRAM. Anyone applying for a contested divorce must attend this educational seminar, which is designed to provide people with an overview of the divorce process in the hopes they will gain some understanding and consider settlement options. It stresses how couples should play nice and cooperate in their divorce, even though they now hate each other with a passion once reserved for their sex life. They must attend and get their attendance form stamped by the lawyer who presents the seminar. I was scheduled to deliver one of these educational sessions, not because I care about either of those goals, but because I was forced to do it by the Law Society as a part of a reprimand. Why was I reprimanded? Long story, but bottom line, I was "rude and unprofessional to a client." I "agreed" to apologize to the former client, Darla "Hi May," and do evening MIP seminars to resolve the matter. This was the last of three scheduled sessions at the courthouse on University Avenue.

Hi May was not her real name. That was the nickname Bonnie came up with. It was short for high-maintenance. When she retained me, I had no idea just how high. Darla always needed more. During her case, which went on for a couple of years as I squeezed her husband for support and a generous property settlement, we would get close to a settlement, but then Hi May would back off. She needed—wanted—more, and the potential settlement would drift away. Some clients actually enjoy the divorce drama. Their new strong, ugly emotions become a substitute for the strong, loving feelings they once enjoyed. The struggle gives their life meaning. They want to separate but cannot let go of the only person they have had in their life for ten, twenty, even thirty years. They're pathetic.

All things considered, when I finally wrapped up her divorce after a couple of years of screwing around, it was a remarkable settlement. It was tidy, because there were no kids, and we only had to worry about spousal support and property. She left a fifteen-year marriage with a cool $7 million, comprising a beautiful mortgage-free home, a pile of cash in good investments, and some spousal support locked in for five years until it terminated forever, with no possible review. She would never have to work again. Her ex schmuck, though, he got to keep working to rebuild his business and his savings. But he was still delighted to be rid of her. When he signed the agreement, he turned to his lawyer and said, "The support payments are less than her credit card bills every month—and they're tax-deductible." We had a good laugh over that one.

So what was wrong with this sweet settlement? Not even a month later, Hi May was calling my office, unhappy. A girlfriend of hers got a much better settlement, she said. She learned that fact over lunch at the Toronto Lawn and Tennis Club, where she had apparently become a full-time resident and soon-to-be alcoholic. She was eating breakfast, lunch, and dinner there. In between meals she was taking tennis and pickle ball lessons, yoga, and Pilates classes, and every other class or lesson they could offer a fifty-two-year-old divorced woman with too much money. Every day, she would follow all of her activities with too much white wine in the lounge. I heard through the grapevine (I am a member but rarely go anymore) that some of the gentlemen at the club have taken her home for a romp after a few drinks. But it only happens once, and then word would spread about Hi May.

She was calling my office, leaving long-winded wine-fuelled complaints about how she couldn't afford anything, she needed to save her money, maybe she would need to get a part-time job, she couldn't afford to travel and on and on. This with a net worth over $7 million. I ended up just deleting her messages. One day I picked up the phone by mistake. It was her so I said, "Look Darla, the case is finished. The file is closed. I am not a counsellor. I'm not here to listen to these complaints, especially not for free." But the calls continued. So I billed her three grand for "telephone calls, emails, and text messages." She called the office, screaming at Bonnie—which I will not tolerate—so I took the phone and "spoke frankly" to her. I admit I should not have used some of those words. I generally shun vulgarities, but she caught me on a bad morning. Truth be told, I was already annoyed because I had to deal with another NOT SMALL CAR in the parking garage. Do people never learn?

You can guess what she did next. A couple of weeks later, I got a letter from the Law Society. Personal and Confidential. Hence, MIP.

I'm glad Bonnie reminded me of my last session. I had been thinking about making it a sort of swan song. I wanted to bill for just a little prep on Fabio's case the next day, but that would not be a problem. The likelihood of any of these MIP losers hiring me at $1,000 an hour was pretty remote, so for that last seminar I thought, what the hell—tell them the truth. Maybe.

This particular evening there were about twenty participants in the room. Since husbands and wives must attend separate sessions, these folks are all strangers to each other. This supposedly allows for frank questions and uninhibited discussions, during which they can trash their spouse in public. It can be pretty funny. I could see them checking each other out, already thinking about moving on to their next parasitic partner. Hope? Delusion? Necessity? Who cares?

It was a pretty rag-tag group, men fresh from work, some still in suits, women in designer jeans, some in Lululemon workout clothes, like they were going directly from here to boot camp in a local park. Most of the time when I have seen these people in their workout gear, they look like overpackaged human sausages who really do need to work out but for some reason are drawn more to the fashion statement than actual activity.

A few attendees stuck out. An older Black woman, well dressed, sat at the back of the class. Quiet, taking notes, serious. As people were settling into their seats, I had asked her about her situation, just to make conversation. Embarrassed, she fessed up. She was there covering for her daughter, who couldn't make it but needed the stamp on her MIP. Whatever. Beside her sat Ms. Lululemon. In another seat at the front was a young Asian woman with a phone ready to record. I tried to speak to her, but she did not understand English. I needed to stamp her certificate to say she attended, not that she understood a single word of what I said.

A big fat guy in cargo shorts, a Leafs jersey (Darcy Tucker), and work boots sat right up front. About fifty, working out was clearly not his priority. He was taking notes like there would be some kind of bar entrance exam at the end of class. I knew what this doofus was all about the minute he pulled out his phone to record my comments—self-rep. If he recorded me, there could be no truth tonight. I didn't need another letter from the Law Society. But I also knew that he was going to try to do his own divorce. He would be calling me in six months for free advice on how to fix the mess he created after royally screwing up things. Trust me, I would not take that call.

I started my presentation by moving through the usual bullshit, following the script given to me by the organizers about custody, support, and property division. It is a real snooze fest of barely useful information. What I mean is it's technically accurate, but it's missing all the juice, the tactics, the actual techniques of hand-to-hand divorce combat. But I stuck to the script because that extra juice costs money, $1,000-an-hour juice.

As I was working through the material, Mr. Darcy Tucker asked a couple of good questions. Not bad for a beginner but, get this, with the wind in his sails, he turned around and started to give the rest of the class advice. This idiot was suddenly convinced he had a handle on the whole divorce system because he read a couple of cases on the internet and had yellow-highlighted a self-help book so much that the pages were soaked and curling. I had to get him to stop without being too hard on him. Latin may be a dead language, but it is perfect for killing non-lawyers. Okay, I was a little sarcastic and took Tucker into the boards—heavily—so to speak. I even heard one of the business guys say, "Ouch." But it shut him up. In fact, after that little encounter there were very few questions from anyone.

I decided to finish the evening with an overview of the emotional stages of marriage breakdown. Ms. Lululemon, who looked about forty but thought there had been a mixup on her birth certificate and she was really thirty, sat up straight, and I noticed that the only thing she had been doing more than taking notes was making eye contact. Interesting.

I started to explain how going through a divorce is like grieving and that we are in denial (I saw her gently frown), then we become angry (she nodded knowingly), then we get depressed as reality sinks in (she looked down and made a note; I bet she dotted her i with a little heart). I continued to explain that we often go through a phase of false bargaining where we try to find a way out of our divorce dilemma. Her green eyes locked on mine as I continued to explain how the lucky few move on to acceptance, conclude their divorce, and build a new life. (She flashed a weak but pretty smile as if to say, "I wish . . . ") Warming to my subject and her, I concluded by saying, somewhat wisely I thought, that each person must move at their own pace through the stages of denial, anger, depression, and false bargaining to finally achieve the relief of acceptance. To which Mr. Darcy Tucker announced, "I go through those stages every time I take a dump!" and then laughed louder than anyone else at his own vulgar joke. The only people not laughing were the Asian girl, who had no idea what was going on, me, and Ms. Lululemon. Our eyes met through the mayhem, and I realized that perhaps she would need some additional instruction after class. One on one. I would put the "men" in mentoring. Perhaps preceded by drinks down the street at the Shangri La.

After class, we walked down University Avenue, and she filled me in on her situation, basically a routine divorce. No money. No kids. Boring. We paused outside the Shangri La, in front of that mess of a chrome sculpture called *Rising*, and established consent to what was to happen next. Rising indeed.

Now, it's true that lawyers are not supposed to sleep with their clients, but technically she was not a client. Plus she was an adult. What could possibly go wrong?

9

The Uri Nation

TRAFFIC IN DOWNTOWN TORONTO is pretty much non-existent at 4:00 a.m. There are a few cars and delivery trucks, but otherwise it's peaceful. I know that because I am a worrier. All good lawyers are worriers. We wake up in the middle of the night wondering if we filed the expert's report for a trial that's months away, or that we might have missed a limitation period, or did the Supreme Court finally rule on that mobility case out of Alberta? It's an endless stream of worries, and 99.9 percent of the time it is about nothing, absolutely nothing. Yet I drag myself out of bed, drive to the office through the quiet streets, park, take the elevator—no stairs anymore for good reason—and let myself into a dark office.

Bonnie's workstation and record-keeping are meticulous, and in seconds I can pull up a document and determine that I did indeed file the expert's report, that I didn't miss the limitation period, and that not only has the Supreme Court ruled on the mobility case, but it's already in my Factum ready to go. I was worrying for nothing. But 0.01 percent of the time I'm glad I came. Because there it is, the mistake I almost made. So night after night, I still worry, and sometimes in the wee hours I drag myself downtown. Once at my desk there is no point heading back home, so I work until I see the lights come on at the Starbucks across the street. More than once I've been their first customer, waiting at the door for

Daphne the barista to let me in. She knows about my problem and laughs when she sees me, mouthing, "Not again?" She unlocks the door and greets me with a friendly, "You need help. Seriously."

"Yes, I do."

"Tall non-fat latte?"

"With a double shot today." There's no point diving into my kind of work unless my caffeine levels are sky-high. At times my face burns bright red from it.

"No problem, Counsel." She always shakes her head and laughs at me.

One morning, as the espresso machine roared at the touch of her tattooed hands and arms, I watched Daphne and imagined her tucked in bed at 2:00 a.m. Suddenly she sits bolt upright. She is drenched in sweat, worried about the espresso machine or whether there will be enough Venti-sized cups or yogurt parfaits or, God forbid, there's not enough lactose-free milk. No, I bet that doesn't happen. I bet she sleeps like a goddamn baby.

This particular morning, after being out a little too late with Ms. Lululemon, I grabbed the double-shot latte and headed back across the street, steering clear of the stairs that come up from the parking garage. After parking, I used to be able to skip the elevator, run up the garbage-strewn stairs, and come out the street exit conveniently right by Starbucks. But not anymore.

A while ago, I was only halfway up the stairs when I encountered a bum. (Or what I refer to as a citizen of the Uri Nation because they always seem to have pissed their pants.) This particular guy had been sleeping in exactly the same spot for three consecutive days, sprawled across the stairs, lost in the sauce, and lying in a rapidly drying pool of his own urine. The previous few days I had been simply taking a deep breath, grabbing the railing and climbing over him, thinking why the hell am I paying all this money to park, with cleaning staff and useless security guards all over the place, when they can't even deal with this bullshit. It's not safe for me.

Later, on the third day that this had happened, I was on my way to court and Bonnie was out in the street, I assumed having a smoke. There were two police cars, three cops on bikes, a fire truck, and a paramedic ambulance.

I asked her, "What the fuck is going on? Did a plane crash?"

She turned to me with tears in her eyes and said, "You know I don't like it when you talk like that."

Oh brother, here we go. "Sorry, what happened?" I said dryly.

She could barely get the words out. "They found a homeless man in the stairwell, dead. It's so sad. The fireman told me they think he'd been there for days. No one did a thing. This city is getting crazy . . . " She sputtered and then repeated emphatically, "He'd been there for days and no one did a thing."

I watched the scene unfolding outside the stairwell as they carried him out. "Poor guy. What is it with people? Don't they inspect those stairwells?"

Bonnie sucked in an angry breath and pointed at the building across the street. "They're getting the security camera footage from the TD Bank. Its cameras should catch everybody coming and going from that exit." She said this as if this information would somehow explain what happened to this dead citizen of the Uri Nation and deliver accountability.

Shit.

I didn't have time to get into with Bonnie. It was a busy day. I had to get over to Old City Hall again to meet Paul, get him out, and then meet my client Fabio at Jarvis Street court, a.k.a. Poverty Court.

I took a quick look at my phone and saw three texts from my brother: *Call me.* Then I saw a 680 News alert: *Two dead at Don Jail: Two inmates at Don Jail were killed last night while the jail was under lockdown. A spokesperson reported that missing scissors involved in the death of the men had been recovered. No names have been released pending notification of next of kin.* My skin crawled. I ran the four blocks to Old City Hall.

When I arrived at the courtroom on the lower level, it was already half full with anxious family members, lawyers, and God knows who else follows this crap. The door opened at the side of the court, and prisoners filed into a glass box, separated from the rest of the courtroom. It was a rogue's gallery of society's misfits: a tattooed skinhead Neo-Nazi wannabe, a big-haired Rasta drug dealer, some late-night brawlers from clubland, and a bleary-eyed insurance executive in an $800 camel-hair sports jacket, wrinkled shirt, and black slacks who had clearly been through the ringer. At least Paul was alive. He saw me across the courtroom and gave me a weak smile. Within thirty minutes I had him released with instructions to stay away from Chloe and the home.

His handshake was very firm, and he was clearly relieved to see me. I could tell that he was shook up. "Let's get out of here," he said hoarsely.

"Paul, am I glad to see you. I saw the news this morning—the stabbing. Man, your eyes are really bloodshot."

Once we were out on the steps, in the sun Paul shielded his eyes and took a deep breath. "I wear contacts, and I had to keep them in for three straight days. I can't see without them, and I couldn't take any chances." He sounded exhausted. "I need a coffee."

We headed across Queen Street to the Tim Hortons and ordered three large double-doubles and a half dozen donuts, all for Paul. "What happened with these guys being killed? Were you in with some hardcore guys?"

"A few. The prisoners were okay for the most part."

"Really? I saw the guys you came over with in the van. I assume they left the worst ones back at the Don."

"No, those guys were cool. It was the fucking guards. What a bunch of assholes. Messing with people, starting trouble. I'm not kidding, the guards were worse than the guys in there. Mean pricks, every one of them. But I paid attention. I have names and numbers." He tapped his head. "Have a pen?"

I handed him a pen and paper, and he began to write out names and numbers. He looked intense as he wrote and inhaled coffee and donuts. "I wasn't the only guy being fucked with in there." He folded the paper and tucked it into his shirt pocket. "I need to get home, make some calls, but I can be back at your office in two hours."

"Whoa. Take it easy. You need to get some rest, some Visine for your eyes, get your feet back on the ground."

"I'm fine. All I need is a shower and some clean clothes. We need to meet and start working on a plan." He sounded cold, calculating.

"Plan? What plan?"

No answer. His gaze drifted off for a second but then came back with a white-hot focus when I asked about the guy who got stabbed. "What was that about? What happened?"

He looked at me. "I met that guy, Carlos. He was in there for the same bullshit as me. That could have been me. Fucking guards, they let that happen because he was mouthing off."

"What do you mean?"

"He was asking to speak with his lawyer because he was picked up, arrested at his kid's hockey game. His wife had made some allegation that he had beat her up, and the cops came and put the cuffs on him in front of all the other parents, wouldn't even let him make arrangements for his kids to get home. His kids were on the ice. He was furious, even crying, he was so angry. He had words with a guard who was asshole #1." Paul pulled out the sheet of paper and looked at the names again. "The next thing, Carlos was moved to another cell with some psycho, and he had half a pair of scissors in his kidney. Dead. For nothing. I'm not sure what happened to the other guy who died." He finished his coffee and stood to go.

"Paul, let's take some time to cool down and think about this. You've been through hell."

"Bierce, I'm fine. I had time to think in there. You know I came to you for this divorce for a reason. They said you know what needs to be done and how to do it. So now we will do it. Total war." He looked out the window at the people streaming by on Queen Street. "Chloe made a big fucking mistake."

"Go home and get some sleep. I have to get to court. We can talk later." I looked at my watch. Fabio was probably waiting for me at 311 Poverty Court.

But then he turned to me, looked directly into my eyes, and said words we would all regret: "We will fucking annihilate her."

10

Eegs for Sale

I ONLY TAKE ON TWENTY TO THIRTY CASES at a time. Any more than that and Bonnie can't keep up. Mistakes get made. They cost time and money. I learned the hard way when I was trying to carry eighty or ninety cases. It was volume versus quality until I made mistakes and had to live with insurance lawyers and Law Society audits for a few years. Brutal. Now it is quality, nothing but premium.

Fabio fits the premium bill, although you would never know it if you met him on the street. He inherited several very large tracts of land west of Hamilton. His father, fresh off the boat from Italy, had a real eye for future land development. "Go where the people will go before they know they will go there." Not exactly worthy of an inspirational poster, but he was right and grabbed a lot of land on spec. And became quite the property baron.

Unfortunately, the baron had a taste for doing everything himself, including chainsawing a patch of woods alone on some vacant land one day. They don't call chainsaws widowmakers for nothing. He accidentally cut off his own leg while alone deep in the woods. Apparently some coyotes got to him before he bled out and tore him up pretty badly. Fabio found him late that night while searching with a flashlight. Not a pretty scene or way to go. Fabio inherited all the land, but, as is often the case, none of his father's brains or acumen.

Fabio was a decent enough fellow, not a handsome man, about 5'6", 150 pounds, just an average guy, living day-to-day. Was as happy as could be. I gave him credit for one smart move when he set up residence on one of the nicer inherited properties and started a couple of small business-es out of a metal hangar-style garage. You cannot miss his estate as you drive south on 109 near 8th Line. He has a huge—handmade—sign at the edge of the highway announcing to the world in big red letters, *SMALL ENGINE REPRAIRS and EEGS FOR SALE*. I haven't had the heart to correct him, he was so proud of that sign. Why he reprairs engines and sells eegs, I'll never understand. His father's estate trustee immediately sold four hundred acres to a developer, and Fabio now has millions in the bank. He can afford anything he wants or needs—including me.

He made one mistake, however, and I assume he did so because he was either drunk or self-medicated by his home-grown pot. He married a local Welland gal named Christi. She had about as much going for her as the Welland Canal. That is, no traffic in years. After Fabio's father's death, a real estate lawyer advised him to put the property he had inherit-ed into his name jointly with Christi as estate planning. The idiot lawyer recommended this even though the couple was struggling and on the verge of calling it quits. Fabio had found out that Christi was selling more than eegs on Kijiji—you don't want to know. Anyway, this terrible estate planning advice could cost Fabio over $2 million now that they were sep-arated. The lawyer's advice was outright negligence, and I told Fabio that the minute we were done with the divorce, we were immediately going after his ass for whatever he had to give Christi.

But here is where it got interesting. Welland Canal Christi had no idea what the estate was worth and had not even hired a lawyer. To save money, she filed her own paperwork in Jarvis Provincial Court and was looking for custody of their offspring, twins, a boy and a girl. Frankly, it was hard to tell which was which with both of them always dressed in identical Gap sweatsuits. They were both MiniMes of their mom, which was a shame. She of course wanted child support based on Fabio's income from eggs and engines.

Christi considered herself a day trader, and she had been skilfully playing the burgeoning markets—flea markets, that is. She apparently spent most of her time buying and selling crap on Facebook, eBay, Kijiji, and Craigslist. She was so adept, she had acquired a double garage full of junk, which she intended to parlay into a profit from "e-commerce." In her view of commerce, profit was calculated based on your own time being worth about two cents an hour. Abolishing the penny may have been a death blow to her business modelling.

I saw some photographs Fabio secretly took of her home office, and I'm telling you it could have been a scene out of that TV show *Hoarders* shot in the hills of West Virginia, an absolute nightmare of garbage. After the split, she moved in with her parents in picturesque Scarberia for a while but then rented her own place across the street. She said she needed help with the rent, especially for the four storage units that held her resale garbage. Watch for her stuff on display when they snip the locks off in a future episode of *Storage Wars*.

On top of the custody and support issues, we needed to figure out how the twins were supposed to move back and forth between Hamilton and Scarborough every few days. But my main worry was how long would it be before she figured out the juicy property claim.

I had agreed to meet Fabio at Provincial Court at 9:45 a.m. This is the court of welfare moms, deadbeat dads, the Children's Aid Society, child protection, no money, and nothing but Legal Aid, or, worse, self-reps. Lawyers there shuffle around in shabby suits, praying for, I mean preying for, clients. I saw a lawyer there once who had his client's file in a shopping bag, one of those cloth sacks from Sobeys, for Christsakes. I mean, come on, what must the client think? My lawyer can't afford a fucking briefcase? They must have a shelf full of used ones at Value Village.

When I arrived at court, there were about a dozen children, all under the age of six, representing most of the United Nations, running around like it was a goddamn daycare. There was a row of chattering mothers who looked way too comfortable while waiting to speak to the free duty counsel. Those lawyers are usually young lawyers looking for a bit of experience or old lawyers too tired or too cheap to actually go out and market to paying clients. I could see Lester Donald limping around, briefcase screwed up under his arm. Well, at least he had a briefcase.

It felt like the waiting room to lawyer hell. Plus it smelled. Like poverty.

As I gazed around, I recognized a middle-aged woman sitting in the corner. She was at my MIP seminar, doing her daughter's attendance for her. I'd stamped her attendance, even though I knew what was going on. I wasn't sure why she was here, though. This court didn't grant divorces. Then it occurred to me that perhaps she was a grandparent looking for custody of her grandkids. Interesting. Now I remembered talking to her about her daughter's case. She got married to some loser out on a pass from Mapleview Correctional near Milton and had a baby. That meant she could get a better apartment through welfare. She then dumped the baby with Grandma, who was supposed to be enjoying retirement from the TTC. The daughter's girlfriends all had apartments in the same social housing tower near Dupont and Lansdowne. I represented a paramedic who'd been in and out of the building a few dozen times, and he said that the police don't even bother going in there anymore. On one entire floor the tenants took all the doors off so they could wander from unit to unit and party 24/7. You don't believe me? Take a drive by. Poor choice of words. It can be dangerous at night, so go in the early afternoon. I dare you. You won't even go through the front doors of that building.

As the young women waited for court, I noted that husbands and boyfriends are never in court. On the odd occasion, you might see a couple of them slink by with their pants around their knees, hats on sideways, or bandanas. Maybe a judge had threatened to issue a warrant for their arrest for nonpayment of support. They didn't look worried. It's like a bad music video. I smiled at the thought that this would be a much more realistic setting for them, better than a club, a yacht, or sports car. Take over the courtroom instead. Hmm. It occurred to me that my client, Patrick McGovern, who is in the music business (yes, that Patrick McGovern), might be interested in the idea. His divorce trial was coming up. I'd have to remember to mention it to him. Maybe I could get a video credit.

Fabio had arrived on time, and I apologized for being late. He was as usual the happy idiot and seemed without a care in the world. Relaxed, he knew the drill for the day because I had met with him a few days before for a detailed walkthrough of what should be a routine hearing to transfer his case from the hell of poverty court to Superior Court, where I could wage the inevitable war over the property in a civilized way at $1,000 an hour. Every client gets prepped like this, no matter what is supposed to happen in court. We review everything from what to wear to where to park. Clients don't like surprises, and neither do I. So they get prepped. It's expensive but important.

I had yet to meet his ex bride of just a few years, so he pointed out Christi. I don't know why, but the first time I see divorcing clients to-gether—which is usually in a hallway at the courthouse—I try to imagine them fornicating, producing their demon seed. It rarely works in my imagination, although it has clearly worked in reality. It is an abiding mystery to me.

Welland Canal Christi is a big woman, and she could barely squeeze into one of the chairs in the waiting area outside of duty counsel's office. Her velour tracksuit made it a little easier. Shopping Bag lawyer was on duty, so this should be priceless. Wait till he found out the case was worth a few million. If he took it, I would make sure he had to endure WWIII with me, and years from now he would pine for the days of dragging his shopping bag around poverty court.

I heard a familiar ragged voice from behind me. "Hey, Bierce, slum-ming today?" It was Lester Donald, Tim Hortons cup in hand, circulating, I assume, in search of new clients.

"Good morning, Mr. Donald. What brings you here today?" I couldn't care less about his reasons.

"Duty counsel. Third time this week. You?"

I smiled. It was none of his business why I was there. Slumming? He dreamed of a practice like mine—well, at least about the billings. As he rambled on, I could see that Shopping Bag lawyer had nestled in beside Welland Canal Christi, reeling in his catch. If he were retained, I would expect him to celebrate by buying a briefcase and better shoes. From my angle I could see that he was wearing running shoes. To court. A lawyer. In running shoes. What fresh hell was this?

As we were waiting, Fabio giddily told me that his new girlfriend was meeting him at court this morning to provide the dreaded moral support. I really try to discourage this, but clients are hopeless suckers for this approach by the next parasite in their life. Moral support? Sure, while they slide their hand into his pockets. I arranged for us to sit facing the metal security detectors near the front entrance so we could see her enter. The security officers search everyone's bags and purses. This is why they became police officers instead of working at airport baggage checks. Better pension and benefits.

Occasionally they come in handy, though, like that time here at Jarvis court when a client's husband freaked out when I got an order sending him to jail for nonpayment of support. He had a trucking company with a team of long haulers doing runs into the US and was doing well. He refused to pay support. Period. There was no excuse not to pay support to his very lovely family. His wife was a saint. Kids were fantastic. He was the one who set fire to his marriage when it was discovered he had another whole family down south in Texas. First, I garnished his bank accounts, then I took his driver's license, then his passport, and then when his arrears crossed the $100,000 mark, I got an order appointing a receiver manager to run his business and pay the support to my client. I basically turned him into an employee. When he tried to land a haymaker on me, the cops jumped him and beat the shit out of him. Each of them got a bottle of Johnnie Walker Blue later that week.

Fabio suddenly jumped out of his seat and waved to someone in line. "There she is!" I watched the line to see if someone waved back. Nothing. "Charlene, Charlene. Sweetie . . . " Then I saw a woman wave.

Sweet Jesus. She was easily six foot four and weighed at least three hundred pounds. She was wearing a muumuu-style dress that could have been a queen-size bedsheet. From a distance I thought I recognized the pattern from a line of bedding sheets I have on my own bed. She had bare legs and wore those curious gladiator-style sandals laced to her knees. Let me just say they did not flatter her. She looked like she should have a sword in one hand and a shield in the other. I assumed she wore these because there were no size fourteen shoes on sale at Winners. Her hair had been bleached blonde and had otherworldly highlights and frosting on the tips. It was shoulder-length, but only on one side. On the other side was a blunt cut, and a large feather appeared to have been woven into the side of her head. Other long strands of hair were braided as if she had just returned from an all-inclusive in Jamaica. And speaking of fun in the sun, she had apparently been trapped on a tanning bed, since her skin was as brown as a vintage leather football.

I watched as she struggled to get out of a tiny knapsack stretched across her back. It could hold no more than a wallet and maybe a set of keys, which probably had a tiny Smurf attached. The cop, who was dwarfed by her, refused to help, so the next person in line, realizing that no one was getting through security anytime soon unless this knapsack came off, stepped up to help her wiggle out of it. She handed it to the cop for examination and stepped through the metal detector. The alarm went off. She stepped back, shrugged, giggled through teeth bleached so white they appeared almost blue, and removed her watch. "Silly me, I forgot to remove this watch that is the size of an alarm clock." Fabio laughed, enthralled by this female Shrek. She stepped through the security frame again. The alarm went off again. She stepped back, puzzled, but then pulled a thick chain from around her neck. Into the basket with her watch it went. She stepped into the frame again. The alarm went off again. I thought *perhaps she is retarded*. By this point everyone in the waiting area, including Welland Canal Christi, had turned to find out what was going on, because there were now at least thirty people in line and the security alarm was still going off.

A huge smile crossed Charlene's bronzed face, and she announced to Fabio, the cops, and all those present in a relieved, child-like voice, "It must be my nipple ring."

I saw Lester Donald and Shopping Bag lawyer turn to each other and then to me in shock as I'm sure we all imagined a piece of gold as big as a shower curtain ring.

Footnote: Six months later I persuaded Fabio to get back together with Christi. What, you say? Why? Once Shopping Bag lawyer figured out the value of the property in dispute, he wisely brought on

an experienced co-counsel and launched a full-scale attack that was likely to be successful. If Fabio and Christi got back together, the date of
separation that triggered the property valuations would be erased. Live
together, don't share the property, move it around until we could live to
fight another day.

Sometimes in a marriage you need to take the long view.

11

Burdettes

IT HAD BEEN A LONG DAY. Springing Paul and getting Fabio's matter transferred had been exhausting for some reason, and I still had to get to Keg's celebration of life. After wrapping up at the office, I found a parking spot on a side street off Queen Street and dragged myself to the front door of Burdettes, the Temple of Doom, no doubt still harbouring ghoulish body-humpers. Keg's picture was posted in the front window. Not a flattering one, accurate, but surely they could have done better. He looked as if he was furious that he was dead or that perhaps you were there, uninvited.

A half smile crept onto my face at the thought of some guy trying to bugger the Keg. Even dead, he would probably jump up off the table, grab the son of a bitch by the throat, and just pile-drive him into the floor. Man, that would be something to see.

"What're you grinning about, Bierce?" I heard Lester Donald's ragged 10,000-cigarette voice behind me. My God, is he everywhere? With a half-spent cigarette hanging from his mouth, he looked as torn-down as his voice sounded. In a horrible tweed jacket, dark purple shirt, and a crazy yellow tie, he looked like a clown.

"Nothing. Nothing. Poor Keg." I pushed through the front door into a very crowded hallway. A young man in a dark suit was desperately trying to direct people to hang up coats, locate washrooms, and find loved ones, but it was mayhem. And the din. You couldn't hear yourself think.

"Place is packed. I got here about half hour ago." I could barely hear Lester's voice. "Keg's in the Algonquin Room. Open casket." He raised his juniper bush eyebrows and said "open casket" as if this was a terrible idea.

I turned to him, puzzled.

"I heard people were leaning in to see if he had ink stains on his face. They found him at his desk, face down in the Rules of—"

"Rules of Practice. Very funny." I had heard the same lame joke while milling around at court. "Died in the harness, I guess."

"Still. Shitty way to go."

I'm not sure why, but standing there in all the noise, I suddenly recalled how Keg had helped me get my Q.C. after just ten years of practicing law. That's nuts. What I mean is the designation of Queen's Counsel was supposed to be a recognition of distinction, an acknowledgement of demonstrated skilled advocacy before the courts. There was a time when that honour was bestowed upon just a few really good lawyers each year, lawyers who had practiced for 20 years or more. An annual list would be published in *The Globe and Mail*. A few lawyers sat on their porches in bathrobes, scarves, and slippers waiting for the newspaper to hit the stoop reporting their appointment. Those days are long gone now that the Q.C. has been abolished. But those of us who had already received the designation can still put it on our letterhead and business cards, though. Getting mine was an early lesson in how things really work.

Rewind. Keg had called me early one morning, "Bierce, how the fuck are you? It's Keg." He spoke as if we were drinking buddies, even though I only encountered him occasionally in the Barrister's Lounge at Osgoode Hall. Even then I tried to steer well clear of him.

"I'm fine. How are you? What's up?" I prayed that he had not been retained on the other side of some file. If that were the case, I would have to immediately ask my client to double the retainer and batten down the hatches for an insane drawn-out fight. I liked a dustup as much as the next guy, but that kind of money would not be worth having to deal with the Keg.

"What're you up to this weekend?" Oh no, was he going to ask me to socialize with him? I imagined some drunken gathering in an old hunting cabin involving cards, guns, fishing, and becoming part of a story in which someone had their toes shot off.

"I have a trial in a couple of weeks, so I'm up to my ears getting ready . . . ," I lied of course.

"Fuck off. Want to go to L'Orignal?"

I didn't know what to say. What was he talking about? Lorne Nell? Who was that?

"L'Orignal. It's a little piss-ass town up near Ottawa. Was the county seat for a long time. Beautiful old courthouse, though. Have you been up there?"

"No, I haven't." I thought to myself, *What the hell is he talking about? How can I get out of whatever he has in mind?* "What's in L'Orignal?"

"Your Q.C., Biercy boy. Your Q.C."

"My what?"

"Your Q.C. Don't you want a Q.C.?"

"I never really thought about it. I've only been practicing for ten years."

"Fuck off. You've thought about it, you little pussy. Admit it."

"Sorry, Keg. To be honest, I have never thought about it."

"Do you want your fucking Q.C. or not?"

"What is there, some sort of yard sale on Q.C.s?" Keg thought this comment was absolutely hilarious, and he laughed and hacked and coughed into the phone so long that I thought he was going to choke to death. When he had regained his composure after a noisy drag on a cigarette, he said, "No, listen, you know the Sol Gen, Keaton, right?"

"The provincial solicitor general? Yeah, I have met him once or twice at Bar Association meetings," I lied.

"Close enough. He's running for the leadership of the party."

I was aware that a leadership race was on but had absolutely no interest in who won it. There was no money in politics. "Keg, I don't get into politics too much."

"Yeah, no one does. No money, but here's the deal. I'm working on his campaign, and we're going around the province meeting with local folks, you know, kids clubs . . . " (I assumed he meant university and college groups), " . . . local hairpins . . . " (this must have meant local women's associations), " . . . and lawyer groups. We're trying to raise his profile and money. I think he's got a shot at winning. He could be the fucking premier, who knows."

"It's a little far to go, Keg. Is he doing anything in Toronto? Keep me on the list for a ticket to a Toronto event."

"No, no. He's done fundraising in Toronto. We need lawyers. We need bodies in Ottawa and L'Orignal to show the local hayseeds that there's Toronto money behind his leadership bid. There's no fucking money in Ottawa, so we need to put on a good show. Keaton asked me to put together a dozen lawyers to drive up to this event. The fundraiser is five hundred bucks. You just gotta get yourself there—with a cheque." He paused and then said, "Do you know Warren Barry? Why don't you drive up with me and Warren?"

"Yeah, I know Warren." Warren Barry, a.k.a. Dirty Warren. I knew him from law school, where he earned that nickname while simultaneously cheating on his exams and his wife. She was busy working full-time and raising their kids while he went to law school. He dumped her a month after his call to the bar. A real Profile in Courage.

"Great. We can grab a case of beer, drive up tomorrow night. We'll find a place to crash up there. It'll be fun."

Fun? A weekend with Keg and Dirty Warren. Fun? No. Nightmare.

"Keg, it sounds good, but I'm going to have to take a rain—"

"Fuck off, Bierce. Listen up. You buy a $500 ticket. You show up. You kick in another $500 for his leadership bid, and later this year you get your fucking Q.C. That's how it works. Capiche? Are you in?"

"What time do we leave?"

"Atta boy. Meet Warren and me in front of 361 University tomorrow night at six thirty. You grab twenty-four beer. I'm driving a Lincoln Town Car. White. See you there."

I went. Hell of a ride there and back, cracking beers in a cloud of cigar smoke. A few months after the event, as promised, I got my Q.C., along with the others who made the trip, and the next day I ordered new letterhead and some quality business cards.

It was an education of sorts.

With those fond memories front and centre, I moved through the crowd that had gathered for Keg's memorial, following Lester for no particular reason. He turned to me and yelled hoarsely over the noise, "I thought he would OD on anger, you know, his head would just explode." He puffed out his cheeks and made a gesture of a slow-motion explosion with his hands. I could see that Lester had not shaved in days, properly at least. "The guys are saying he must've had a stroke."

Guys is right. There was not a single woman in the place. It was packed with men, a lot of old men. Keg could be hard on the ladies, as he called them. He made more than a few lose their cool, some even in open court. He thought it was hilarious and would tell stories about it in the Barrister's Lounge for hours.

Inside Burdettes was worse than I had ever imagined. It had a dank, musty old carnation smell, as if someone had spilled formaldehyde and tried to cover it up with Febreze. That's what masking death smells like. I felt a little woozy from the heat and onslaught of odours. The air was stifling from thick cigar smoke. I thought of Keg driving to L'Orignal, cigar in one hand, beer in the other. He would love this. I watched as Lester, greeting everyone and moving slowly through the crowd, fired up one Belmont after another. My head felt light and I realized then that I should have eaten something before I came.

A couple of forty-pounders were being passed around. I filled a Styrofoam cup and passed it to Lester. He filled a cup, and the bottle disappeared down the hall. I took a mouthful of what turned out to be bourbon; it tasted good. Within minutes, a bottle of Johnnie Walker Blue came by. Much better, so I finished what I had and refilled my cup. It would do for sipping for a while. But it, too, soon passed. I could see that the young man at the front door had given up and was resigned to squeezing through the crush, picking up empty cups and asking men not to smoke. A complete waste of time, since no one even acknowledged him.

Suddenly I found myself within ten feet of Keg's casket. It looked so small. There was a wide-open area, a sort of no man's land in front of him. Men trickled up one by one or in twos and threes to take one last look at Keg. I just stood there and watched. I couldn't move, and the booze, hot in my stomach, started hitting me. I really should have eaten something. I waited there a few minutes, staring at the casket from a safe distance. Rick Z , King of the B's (meaning top of my list of B grade lawyers) passed me a fresh cup of something and mouthed over the noise: "Oban, single malt." I nodded and made the mistake of starting to sip it. Across the room I could see that someone had made up a cheesy bulletin board with at most a half dozen photos under Dollar Store letters, *K E G: A Life Well Lived!*, cut out and pasted at the top. I noticed there were no flowers, and suddenly I could hear Keg's voice: "Bierce, flowers? You're such a pussy." I looked down and saw that my cup had been refilled.

Just as I was about to unplug my feet and go up—out of pure curiosity—to look at Keg, someone tapped on a microphone and asked for quiet. It took a full five minutes for the place to come to order, with a lot of drunken laughter and shushing. More than one wit called out, "Order in the court!" to laughter. Word spread down the halls into the crowded adjacent rooms, and the old men fell quiet.

Finally, the guy at the microphone introduced himself as Keg's brother, Billy, and thanked everyone for coming. He introduced a few people, several senior lawyers, including Randall Williams. That was a surprise. I was sure he detested Keg. There were some old judges and even a city councillor long since retired.

Billy started, "Tom—"

But someone interrupted and shouted out, "Not Tom! Keg!" And a small, drunken group started to chant, "Keg, Keg, Keg," until the whole funeral home was shaking with over a hundred grown men chanting his name. After a few minutes and more shushing, it calmed down and Billy tried again, "Keg . . . was a hell of a lawyer. I'm told he busted a few heads over the years—"

"My balls too!" A drunken droll called out, followed by much hooting and hollering. Most of what Billy said next was drowned out by laughing and catcalls, but I caught the end of a very forgettable story about something he had done as a boy. I drained my cup and put it up on a shelf filled with fake books. I could see the plastic leatherette spines of classics: *Don Quixote. Bleak House. Crime and Punishment.* How fitting.

His brother concluded by saying, "If anyone would like to come up and say a few words about Keg . . . " A middle-aged man stepped up and introduced himself as Keg's eldest son from his first marriage. This triggered a burst of laughter and comments from those who knew of

Keg's multiple failed marriages. I had no idea he had kids. He apologized that his brothers and sister could not be there. No excuse was offered. I thought he looked very uncomfortable. He told a very short story of going on a trip with his father someplace years ago. I noticed that I had a cup of something in my hand again. I sniffed it. Spiced rum? Good God, what happened to the scotch? I could see Lester across the room, watching, listening intently, Belmont hanging from his lips.

Then Keg's sister spoke of his rowdy youth. "Keg was always an Alberta boy . . . " She started another unremarkable story. I never heard him mention Alberta once. Her recollections were followed by old Judge Pankeratz telling a story about some cross examination Keg had conducted during which he made the witness cry. I could see a large wet spot on the front of the judge's trousers. He had pissed himself. Keg's old partner, long retired, recounted in painful detail a story about how they had taken a trip to Italy with their second wives and got so drunk on red wine the first night in Rome that Keg couldn't walk because of gout. So they flew home. *Is unhilarious a word?* I wondered. I downed the spiced rum and accepted a fresh but large red plastic cup of scotch. As I listened to the next round of stupid stories, I thought that they probably could have been told about anyone in this room and wondered if that made them meaningless or more meaningful. My head was spinning a little.

And then for some reason, I unexpectedly found myself at the microphone. I put my hand on Keg's tiny casket for support, leaned over, and saw his face, still angry, wrinkles etched in his pale, waxy skin and the bags under his eyes still blazing red. Even in death he was furious about something. What? I leaned into the mic and it squealed. "I knew Keg for over thirty years . . . got my Q.C. . . . he . . . did . . . for me . . . look . . . " I nodded to the casket. "He looks angry . . . I don't think . . . I ever saw him smile . . . He never mentioned he had kids . . . He did mention his wife . . . the first one . . . Is she here?" Apparently at that point I put my hand over my eyes and scanned the room as if scouting for her. "I hope not, because he would be really pissed . . . "

Someone shouted out, "You're pissed, Bierce!"

Undeterred, I carried on struggling to get my words in the right order. "He was called Keg for a reason . . . you know . . . " There were a few nervous laughs as some of the old men tried unsuccessfully to get the chant going again "Keg . . . Powder . . . He was angry, an angry guy, always angry . . . I was afraid of him . . . " More nervous laughs from people expecting me to recount some horrific incident. "You never knew what Keg would do . . . you know . . . " I stood there for a few moments, watching the room through blurry double vision. "Does anyone have a happy story . . . I wanna hear a happy story about Keg . . . " I looked at the furious dead man again and shook my head.

Someone shouted, "Get that asshole outta here."

The next thing I knew, I was outside Burdettes in the rain with Lester helping me to sit down on the stone front step of the ancient upholstery shop next door. It was cold and wet.

"Bierce, what did you do that for?" An unlit Belmont dangled from his lips.

"It's the truth. The truth . . . Is true . . . It's true . . . He's angry . . . Still . . . " I slurred my words at the graffiti-covered wall beside me and turned to stare at the wet sidewalk between my shoes, struggling to focus.

"When did you suddenly get interested in the truth?" Lester's voice sounded like God when he is very tired. I think he must have been drunk too, because he started to say something that sounded like it was about sailing, and I think he said something about cargo boats. Unfortunately, his weird insights were interrupted by my violent puke that reeked of spiced rum and scotch. I should have had something to eat before I came to fucking Burdettes.

I could feel the water on the step soaking through the seat of my expensive suit pants, but it felt good to be outside in the cool air with the light rain on my face. I looked up and saw Williams about to get into a huge black Escalade. I could barely make out the face of a pretty young woman who waited inside for him. He looked at me and slowly shook his head, disgusted. Another lawyer, one of his associates, was beside him holding the SUV door. He suddenly reached out and pushed my head. "Nice speech, dickwad. Talk about ruining a celebration of life. Q.C.? You're a fucking joke."

I looked up at him with Gutter Bravado and tried to focus on his face. "Fuck you, ditship . . . Dips hit . . . Dipshit . . . ." I paused and tried to look up into the rain. "Lester?"

"Yeah?"

"They can all just fuck off . . . Am I right? Damn right." Then I shared more puke with the sidewalk.

Lester pivoted on his limp leg away from the growing pool of vomit and said, "Wait here. We need to get you home. I gotta grab my briefcase . . ." He went back inside for his priceless battered leatherette sleeve. I waited until he was gone, staggered to my car, puked again, and drove home.

12

God Help Us All

I HAD TO GO FOR AN EARLY-MORNING RUN to burn off the booze from Keg's celebration of life. Brutal. I could smell the alcohol as it wicked through my shirt and sweats. By the time I got to the office, Bonnie was dug in at her desk getting a matter confirmed for Brampton Court the following week.

"You all right?" She didn't look up. Surely she hadn't heard about my performance last night. "A Lester Donald called here looking for you this morning. He wanted to know if you were okay."

"I'm right as rain." Whatever that means.

A few minutes later, Bonnie called out to me, "Your brother is on the line—again. I'm putting him through." She sounded totally pissed off.

I let the phone ring a few times before picking up. "Andrew Bierce."

"Cut the shit, you know it's me."

"Hi, Sean, sorry we haven't been able to connect. I've been swamped . . ."

"Don't bullshit me. I know exactly what's going on in your world, buddy boy, including your little so called 'speech' last night at Keg's."

How did he know these things? Big brother or not, I hated when he called me buddy boy. "What do you want, brother?"

"Funny. I'll cut to the chase. I'm calling about your client Paul Campbell."

"Yes, thanks for the referral. Did you get the case of scotch I sent as a thank-you?"

"Yeah. Recovering alcoholics need a case of scotch like a nightie needs pockets. I put it to good use, though."

"I'm sure you did."

"I donated it to a charitable auction for—"

"Sure you did." I assumed he had stashed it for the next time he fell off the wagon. "What can I do for you? I have a busy day ahead."

It had been a while since Sean and I could be civil with one another. It's true he's a recovering alcoholic, and it's true that I am painfully aware of it. It is, after all, why he is known as Toronto's worst priest. Well, one of the reasons. The other reasons are related to not being able to keep his pants on.

Until about seven or eight years ago, he had been a credible math teacher at St. Joseph's High School in west Toronto. The real reason he was at the high school, though, was to coach the senior boys' hockey team. He took them to the city championship, then to provincials, and threatened to take them even further until he flew too close to the sun, just like he has his whole life, over and over.

At one time Sean had been a Maple Leafs prospect. That's right, THE Maple Leafs. He faced a choice of either a blessed life in the priesthood or fighting his way into the blessed NHL. And I do mean fight, because Sean had a reputation for losing his gloves and mixing it up over the slightest insult from an opposing player or fan. He could score goals all right, when he wanted to, but that turned out not to be what his coaches had in mind for him. Scoring goals is one thing, but scaring the shit out of the opposing team every time your top line is on the ice, now that is a rare skill in search of a team.

He actually got an offer from the Leafs, a good one, and I thought I would be getting free tickets to Leaf games for the rest of my life. But at the last minute he picked the priesthood. "The Church is a better choice for me," he announced. Choice? This was no choice in my mind. We were talking about the Leafs. I didn't think his time studying to be a priest was even genuine. I assumed he was using the Basilian order just to pay for his university, and then he'd jump back to real life before he had to actually commit to the cult.

Hockey, drinking, fighting, and screwing—not necessarily in that order—that was Sean. Bad boys like that don't become priests, for Christsakes. I said to him, "Sean, anyone can be a priest, but the Leafs . . . Jesus . . . " Notwithstanding my pleas, he still picked what he thought was the higher calling. I thought the whole thing was bullshit and that something else must have been going on. Now it's too late to give a shit.

In addition to the curse of being a great hockey player on the Lord's team, Sean unfortunately also got the looks in the family. Same as our dad. He was Paul Newman good-looking. Cool, charming, fit, he'd never had any trouble with the ladies throughout his life. As a result it was pretty much impossible for him to settle down. He hopped from bed to bed for years—before and after entering the priesthood. I'm pretty sure he has a few kids sprinkled around the province.

So my brother the enforcer Leafs prospect instead became Father Sean and ended up coaching a Catholic high school hockey team . . . and screwing the drama teacher, and the English teacher, and three rather mature Grade 12 students. They became "mature" after they each spent a weekend at the Basilian priests' resort up near Algonquin Park. A well stocked liquor cabinet and Sean's charms resulted in each of them naked in bed with him. "Let your fountain be blessed, and rejoice . . . let her breasts fill you at all times with delight; be intoxicated always in her love." Proverbs 5:18-19. He took the breasts and intoxication part quite literally.

When the girls found out about each other, all hell broke loose at the school. Sean had told each of them that what they shared was special, only she/she/she could move him so powerfully that he would break his sacred vows. The scandal, known in the local community as "The Thornbird Three," almost pushed the school and the archdiocese into bankruptcy after having to pay out what were supposed to be confidential settlements.

Those payouts were on top of the damages to the school van that Sean totalled after getting shitfaced one night. He crashed it after the hockey team lost their shot at a National Championship. A lot of parents blamed the loss on Father Sean and the fact that the day before the big game, the team's first-line centre and top scorer decided he wasn't interested in playing hockey anymore, at least for this coach. His girlfriend was one of the "Three."*

Anyway, the archdiocese ended up having to move him out of teaching into some administrative work that would keep him out of trouble and away from the students. Rumour had it that he then went on to ruin (their word, not mine) a handful of nuns and novices. We all have special gifts, so says the Lord.

And guess what other gift the Church discovered lay beneath the charming exterior of this sexually corrupt, boozing priest? Politics. It turned out he could work a room like the most seasoned political hack. He would lock his baby blues on some little old lady, make her feel safe with his priestly collar, and then pick her pocket at a political fundraiser for some up-and-comer in the GTA. Liberal or Conservative, it didn't matter. The only party he and the Church didn't have time for was the NDP—which he said stood for Not Dependable People.

When Palmer ran for the Ontario Liberal leadership, the archdiocese thought they had died and gone to heaven. Here was an opportunity to have a genuine devout Catholic as potentially the next premier, so they went all-in putting Sean on the delegate recruitment team full-time. When Palmer won the party leadership, it was because my brother had delivered over a hundred delegates, every single one of them, through five ballots and into the wee hours.

Palmer and the delegates went on to victory parties all across Toronto. Sean, however, went back to an empty hotel room filled with leftover booze. He was a goner for months after that celebratory meltdown, but I'll give the archdiocese credit—alcoholic, gambler, sex addict, hell, even a pedophile—whatever your troubles, they will bring in the lawyers (devout Catholics every one) and stick by you in the face of the most damning evidence.

Sean went for treatment and was back on the political schmooze circuit within a year, telling his story of second chances and redemption. Priceless. Unfortunately, while he could stay away from the booze and

---

* Postscript: That kid went on to play in the NHL and spent three seasons with the Leafs before being traded to the Sabres. That's some sort of justice, I guess.

was forbidden to be alone with students, he could not give up the fairer sex, so they agreed to look the other way. I was told by a very reliable source that the archbishop had said, "At least he's not a homo or a pedophile like the rest of them." God bless.

"So, Sean, the referral of Paul Campbell, what's the connection? And by the way, that nut case Chloe asked me to say hello."

Sean took the next thirty minutes to explain why he had referred Paul to me.

God help us all.

13

Quid Pro Quo

THE FILE THAT BONNIE HAD BEEN PREPARING for me was set for a hearing in Brampton Superior Court, trial of an issue. It was a nasty one. My client that day was a pretty-boy actor (you would recognize him from the cop show he starred in, still running). His soon-to-be ex, one hell of a physical specimen, was a soccer player and Olympic athlete (scored a winning goal for the bronze at the Olympics). If I told you their names, you would know both of them immediately, and they desperately wanted something the justice system does not offer you: privacy. If you want to use the public justice system, then you and everything about your divorce are fodder for news of the world. If you want privacy, then opt out into arbitration. These two had decided to try to quietly use the courts.

To facilitate that wish, I had secured at great expense and against all odds a rare order sealing the file so their names would not be in the news. It would appear on court lists with their initials only, R.M. v. A.T. Confidentiality and privacy were important to both of them, especially given the facts. Behind closed doors, celebrities are just like the rest of us, not very nice, maybe even worse. I had arranged through a friendly trial coordinator to have the trial heard in Courtroom 401 at the end of the hall, away from prying eyes.

I was up early and out for a quick run before deciding what to wear that day. I prefer to look good, even if I am going to end up changing into my black gowns for most of the day once I get to court. I take a lot of pride in my appearance, and first-class suits, beautiful ties, impeccable shirts, and top-notch shoes are all business tools as far as I'm concerned. If a client is paying me $1,000 an hour, I better look like I earn $1,000 an hour. Casual Friday? There's no such thing. There's nothing casual about what I do.

I have my own tailor, Manny. He retired from Harry Rosen years ago, and I was lucky to get on his private client list. He works from his home basement studio in Etobicoke and only added me after I helped his nephew out of a jam. By jam I mean Manny's pimple-faced nephew, Joey, all of sixteen, had "been intimate" with some girl at their high school grad party. These teen get-togethers are supposed to be blowjobs-only affairs, but this particular night the teens were hammered on vodka coolers and Red Bull. Things got a little carried away.

Now, you can't walk through a high school these days without someone offering you mint-flavoured condoms, but for some reason neither of these two children had one that night. I believe the young lady's consent might have been an issue as well, but let's not go there. She got pregnant, of course, and paternity of the baby was raised when her family learned of her news. Manny, knowing my reputation, brought me in to help Joey. By the time I was finished with the girl and that family's numbskull lawyer, her parents weren't sure they wanted to have a week-long trial about how many coolers and sexual encounters the young lady had had that evening and the previous week, never mind the accuracy of DNA tests. So they took a walk. Now they are raising a baby without child support from Joey, and Manny does my tailoring. That is what's known as *quid pro quo*.

Manny knows what I like, which is nothing too contemporary. I prefer the classic cut, eleven-inch drop on the lapels, first-class fabrics. I have over forty suits, twenty fall/winter and twenty spring/summer, dozens of sports jackets, hundreds of ties. I have three tuxedos. For my age, I'm in good shape because a few days a week after a morning workout with free weights, I run a minimum 5k, unless of course I have suffered the dreaded night terrors, in which case a morning run is out of the question. I try to hit the street by 5:00 a.m. sharp. I have my route through the city, down to the lake and back. On Saturdays I might stretch my run to 10k. I run alone. I do everything alone now. Sundays I take a break, do a light work-out at the University Club, and head to the office for four for five hours to get ready for the coming week. That has been my routine for a few years now since my divorce.

I felt pretty good by the time I got to Brampton court, which is one of my favourite courthouses provided I can get a fucking parking spot. It is probably the busiest courthouse in Canada, so the parking lot is like ten football fields. They will soon need a Park'N Fly shuttle service, like the airport. The courthouse itself has been renovated and is relatively new compared with some of the other courthouses falling down around the province. It is nothing like Kitchener's palace or Oshawa's alcazar, but with six floors, lots of courtrooms, meeting rooms, and clean washrooms, it is a comfortable place to do business. And like all other courthouses, it is filled with miserable people accompanied by miserable lawyers.

Most of the first-appearance criminal stuff is dealt with on the main floor near the entrance to the Barristers' Lounge, so it is impossible to come and go from the lounge without having to crawl through crowds of guilty people who have dragged half their families and friends to witness their inglorious attendance before Her Majesty. I took a deep breath as I approached this throng and motored through. As I cut a path, I overheard a man yelling at his lawyer, "No, he's living in a barn in New Jersey." Another laughed and said, "Well, he didn't mean to kill all the dogs . . ." What could this possibly mean? I heard a lawyer say, "None of the clocks in this courthouse work." This is true. It has been the case since the court-house opened, not one clock tells the correct time, yet all appearances in court are scheduled for specific times. Another lawyer laughed and said something about the Bermuda Triangle. It is a madhouse. Wandering through the courthouse, I was bombarded by these bizarre snippets of conversation. Not exactly Joyce's epiphanies while wandering through Dublin.

In order to actually get into the Barristers' Lounge and law library, I needed to pass through locked security doors. Lawyers are issued swipe passes. All these locked doors are required before even getting to the entrance to the lounge. I must pass through three sets of doors, each one with a fluorescent paper sign, first in brilliant green, *This area is for lawyers only*, then in hot pink, *Lawyers Only, No Clients*, and then in glowing orange, *Only Lawyers Past This Point*. And yet somehow, non-lawyer idiots still managed to find their way into the lounge and library. So now lawyers have to use swipe passes, even if we want to go into our lounge area washrooms simply to take a piss.

The librarian nodded to me as I arrived, and I wheeled Black Beauty to my favourite spot, a table in the corner along the windows. As I got closer, I saw that even at this early hour someone had already scooped my spot. I immediately recognized the horrible tweed jacket that deserved to be back on the rack at Value Village, comfortably alongside other long since loved but discarded size 48 tweeds. I suppose there was a time for those hearty jackets, when indoor heating meant a coal-burning fireplace, but those times have long passed. Yet there, a thick tweed jacket sat mouldering on the back of one Lester Donald.

"Lester, what's up?"

"Hey Bierce, how you doing? Get home all right the other night?"

Oh, that ragged voice. I wanted to clear my throat the instant I heard it. As Lester leaned back in his chair, I could see a pack of Belmonts tucked into his shirt pocket, the very same purple shirt he wore to Keg's visitation. It was so tight across his gut that a button had popped off. I assume the thread holding it simply gave up the ghost. Released, the button now likely rests comfortably in one of the pant cuffs of his khaki Dockers. It has likely been there for months, if not years.

I had to look away when I realized that what I saw sticking out of the gap in his purple shirt was his hairy white stomach, so white that I assume he had been eating chalk. A paisley tie was splayed in an upside-down V across his chest, the back portion of it blissfully unaware that there was a convenient loop on the back of its brother specifically designed to keep the two parts in good marching order. On top of the tie sat his thick mobster-style reading glasses, hanging from a gold chain around his neck. As I took him in from head to toe, he swung around and with some effort managed to cross one leg over the other. This was not done, I assumed, to show off what were surely orthopaedic shoes. They were chocolate brown and had weird rounded soles, one so thick that I had a flashback to the first man

I ever saw with a clubfoot. He had worked at the A&P where I stocked shelves on the midnight shift while in high school. He was a small, meticulous man with an enormous black wedge of a foot that he hauled around all day as he bagged groceries, stocked shelves, and mopped the floors. I recalled staring in horror at his foot in the lunch room one day, as I now stared at Lester's. Of course, I said nothing, but his curious gait and limp suddenly made sense.

Lester dropped his well-chewed Bic pen onto a long yellow legal pad that was covered in indecipherable chicken scratch and littered with chewed off Roll up the Rim to Win scraps. "Bierce, I'm glad you're here, because I'm at an absolute loss on this motion I have this morning."

"What's the problem?" I had to admit I was curious about the kind of cases that he attracted. He began to explain the situation. It involved a long-standing common-law couple trying to divide their property, which included a business and some investments made from the sale of a second home. He babbled on with his take on the facts and law. I watched him as he spoke, barely listening to what I quickly realized was his complete and total misunderstanding of this area of law.

As I watched him, I could see that his poorly shaved jaw, although peppered with shaving cuts, missed patches and a tiny piece of toilet paper sopping up a careless nick, seemed to perform perfectly well. As he spoke, it moved up and down, words came out, and he appeared normal, for the most part. Yet that voice was a continuous irritating distraction. I considered the possibility that a piece of wet, menthol-soaked fabric—perhaps tweed—was lodged in his throat, flapping with each ragged breath. It must drive judges crazy. And when he stopped talking, I had to resist the urge to reach over and gently lift his messy jaw up about three inches to close his mouth. The hinge seemed broken as his lower jaw hung slack like a broken kitchen drawer at an abandoned hunting cabin, left open, giving a glimpse of the ancient, stained, and mismatched cutlery inside. I could see that every tooth inside his lower jaw had apparently been repaired with tin salvaged from old Players cigarette containers.

One long white hair grew from the left side of his nose. I couldn't take my eyes off this three-inch twig. How could it be missed while looking in a mirror?

Poor Lester topped all of this off with a mop of hair equal parts grey, red, and brown, which gave him an appearance not unlike what I imagined a seventy-five-year-old hyena would look like—if dressed in a tweed sports jacket, a purple shirt, khaki pants, and those bizarre chocolate shoes. I was in perverse awe.

I felt no real affection for Lester, but I did have the urge to assist this odd man who, like a lost senior citizen suffering from dementia, needed help to get back to the nursing home. I would be performing a public service.

"Lester, Lester, stop." For one thing, I could not listen to that voice anymore. I quickly rhymed off the names of three cases—all reported within the last thirty-six months—critical to the argument his client should be making. I referenced the essential parts of these decisions about joint ventures and common-law couples. I had this information at my fingertips as if I had read them that very morning. I glanced at his appallingly drafted pleadings and, with my special edition gold Rolex pen, noted in the column the citations he would need, the appropriate place for amendments, specific rules, right down to the subsections. Unbeknownst to Lester, the latest case law was clearly on his client's side. All Lester needed to do was stand up and recite these cases and rules to hit an easy triple for his client. Sow's ear tailored into silk purse, just like that.

A home run would be possible, but that would require more juice, so I decided not to get ahead of myself. My comments put him not just back in the game but also positioned him to win, and his client would have no idea of the disaster that had been averted. I could see Lester was a little embarrassed but still grateful I had delivered him from failure and humiliation.

"Thanks, Bierce. I haven't, you know, seen a problem like this before. I guess it's a new area . . ."

"Not a problem, Lester. I am happy to help. Who is on the other side?" I smiled, thinking how pissed they would be now that Lester had the edge. He mentioned Derek Strand. I've known him for about twenty years. Able fellow, nice enough, but he would still be a handful for Lester. Because of my growing concern for my pupil, I couldn't resist sharing with Lester the other things I knew, the things I filed away in tidy drawers, the things that elevated my work, the information that could turn a triple into a home run.

"Lester, I don't know if you are aware of this but . . . Derek used to stutter."

He looked up puzzled, as if to say *so?*

I continued. "He had speech therapy for years to get rid of his stutter, but there's still, you know, a remnant, a little hesitation when he gets up to speak in public." Lester just stared at me. "When Derek gets up to do his opening remarks, he will hesitate a few seconds as he collects his thoughts one last time. It's a little trick he uses to avoid stuttering again."

Lester's jaw hung slack. "Oh." He tucked his glasses on his nose, pinning down for an instant that long lonely hair, and looked down at the detailed notes I had made on his pleadings.

"At that moment when he pauses, jump up and interject, make an objection. "

"Why? About what?" Lester was puzzled.

"Anything. It doesn't matter. Just jump up and claim there has been . . . uh . . . a lack of disclosure or some goddamn thing. Just get in his face about something. It can really mess him up. He'll even stutter a bit." I had to chuckle as I explained it. I mean who knows this stuff? No one.

Lester looked back down at his personal hieroglyphics on the yellow pad and pretended to make a note. "I'd better get those cases you mentioned." He got up and toddled off deeper into the library in his crazy clubfoot shoes. "Thanks, Bierce, I appreciate the help. I hope I can return the favour sometime."

I could tell that Lester just didn't get it. Oh well, my good deed for the year had been done.

Besides, I had other things to worry about. As I changed into my gowns, I couldn't get Sean's call out of my mind. What was I supposed to do with that information? My blood boils whenever I think about his life. So much potential, the jams I have gotten him out of, the times I have written him off, only to get embroiled in some new mess of his own making. Now this.

What had he said? Well Father Sean just happened to have been at St. Gabriel's Church on Sheppard Avenue, a few years ago, dropping off political leaflets to the church's Pro Life Group the very day Chloe and Paul—quite on the spur of the moment—came to the church in search of counselling for their very recent but already failing marriage. My brother, who was on his latest last, last chance with the archdiocese, couldn't resist helping (read exploiting) this vulnerable couple and in particular this beautiful young woman. They were having reservations about bringing a child into the marriage so soon. The good Father suggested some "one-on-one" meetings, starting with Chloe. They continued over the next few weeks. His warm words worked their usual magic, and you can imagine what happened next. Chloe was pregnant, and she thought the Father might be the father. She could not be sure. Father Sean suggested an abortion. I'm not kidding. You heard that right. The very priest dropping off Pro Life leaflets "knew someone," no doubt from past experiences. Chloe lost her mind over that suggestion and went home to her failing marriage, with Paul none the wiser.

And then it came down to this—when Sean heard that the young couple's marriage had failed in such a spectacular fashion, he referred Paul to me. He figured he could convince me to make sure Paul didn't ask for paternity testing in his divorce. If Chloe in her rage took the position that Angie was not Paul's child or Paul in his rage thought that it might save him from child support if the child was not his, then Father Sean and the Church would be front and centre. Shit storm. Sean had told me that Chloe threatened to go to the archbishop about the paternity and a certain priest's abortion suggestion unless Sean arranged some "financial assistance" for her during the separation. When he couldn't reach me about what to do, he paid her—from Church funds. It was, he insisted, my fault because I didn't return his calls.

There's only so much boiling that human blood can withstand before it turns to something dangerous.

This is the kind of crap I had on my mind when I was supposed to be fully committed to a client's case in Brampton that day.

The R.M. v. A.T. matter got underway in Courtroom 401 as planned, but after two hours the court had to take a break. My cross examination of the wife probed a few nerves, and things got a little out of hand. The judge decided we should take a break and let Ms. Olympic Soccer pull herself together.

We were all out in the hall, cooling down, when I looked over and saw a tall young man in his black lawyer's robes bouncing a rubber ball off the floor and wall. He was bouncing the ball like a kid would. He threw it at the floor, and it then bounced off the wall and back into his hand, over and over. This was a lawyer, in the hall of a courthouse, in front of dozens of people. All the while, he was talking on his cellphone and to some other lawyers who looked to be his buddies. They sat there as if this was nothing out of the ordinary. No one said anything or did anything.

Except for me.

I handed my file folder to my pretty-boy client, walked over, and stood directly between Bouncing Ball Boy and the wall.

"What do you think you're doing?" I said as I put my hands on my hips, spreading my robes behind me.

He caught the ball and turned to me. "What?" He was obviously surprised someone had interfered with his playtime.

"What do you think you are doing?" I stepped closer to him.

"Do you have a problem?" he muttered.

That particular question ignites a certain fragment of all male DNA. It is a statement that communicates not a question but a fact. It translates roughly as, "Mind your own fucking business." Men who make such a statement and men who hear it always stiffen a little and spread their feet a little bit into a more stable stance in case the confrontation goes further. No real man walks away from that statement, because he would never have put himself in a position to hear it to begin with.

I sized him up. This fellow was probably late thirties, half my age. We were about the same height. He might have been a tad taller, but I could tell in an instant that I had twenty pounds on him. Physical calculations were being made by the fraction of seconds, adrenaline pumped. I was already so fucking pumped from my cross examination that I could probably fly, but I felt an extra squirt of adrenaline that put me closer to the edge. I moved toward him. By now my client had walked over to see what the hell was going on. He was immediately recognized from the cop show, and a bunch of people gathered, asking for selfies.

I was about two feet from the other lawyer's face. "You heard me. This isn't a playground for children." This translated roughly as "I'm prepared to take this up a notch."

He was doing calculations too, like who is this fucking guy? But I literally smelled what he was about to do next. I knew before he even moved—he threw the ball again, and in a second it was in my hand.

"What the fuck? Give me . . . who do you think you—"

I held the ball to his face. "Do you want this?" I held it to the end of his nose. He looked shocked at the level of my hostility. His buddies sat stunned. I pushed it into his nose. My client moved away from my side, clearly alarmed by the imminent confrontation between two fully robed lawyers in a hallway of the courthouse. Other lawyers gathered as we stared at each other. Calculations continued. My blood was on fire. My other hand balled into a fist.

And then came the sound of too many cigarettes and a blown stereo speaker, the voice of Lester Donald. "Bierce, I think that's enough." He stepped between us.

I heard one of Rubber Ball Boy's friends whisper, "It's Bierce." I could see he recognized my name. I didn't know what it could possibly mean to him, but it changed his demeanour. He stepped back to the comfort of his friends and muttered, "Asshole. Thanks, Lester."

I stared at him over the shoulder of Lester's tweed jacket. "Fucking coward."

He stopped and turned to me. I could see he wanted to say something, but before he could find his words, I smiled and said, "Thanks for the ball."

I heard Lester's voice again. "Bierce, come on. That's enough now. Let it go."

I turned to Lester, my face on fire, my hand still a fist. My client stepped forward. "What the fuck was that all about? Man, you were ready to go! Holy shit." He was laughing, thrilled at the possibility of his lawyer throwing it down over a rubber ball. In the corner stood his wife, the one who needed a break from my cross examination. She had witnessed the entire encounter and looked absolutely terrified.

The case settled that afternoon without us even going back into court, and very well for my client. His wife decided she had seen enough and caved. Unfortunately, the next day the carefully protected privacy of my client was lost when his ugly divorce details and a bunch of fan selfies appeared on the front page of the *Toronto Sun* and all over social media. He wasn't laughing anymore.

14

The Underworld

WHEN I GOT BACK DOWNTOWN from Brampton court, I parked and made my way along the PATH, that byzantine network of tunnels beneath downtown Toronto, in search of something to eat. Now, I say the following with no hint of arrogance. It is simply a fact—I know the entire PATH inside out. I have used it so much over the years, I feel like I have lived down there.

Even though it was close to 6:00 p.m., the mad rush to Union Station was still gushing past me. Men and women marched furiously south, streaming to streetcars, buses, GO trains, and even VIA trains, headed to the hinterlands. Fighting to get out of the city core. I once heard a man say that he commuted from Barrie every day. Oh my God.

Beneath the throng on the street creeps an underworld of people who actually do live on the PATH. Near the lower level doors to my tower sits a man of indeterminate age who has begged there for years. He, Mr. Carpetbeggar, sits on a 4' x 4' piece of carpet that looks like it was torn from the lobby of an old movie theatre. He wears a pair of brutalized Nike running shoes, green wide-wale corduroy pants (soiled), and an exhausted ski jacket, its pink shoulder panels and patterns suggesting that it was once the height of fashion on the slopes. There was an unusual shade of pink a few years ago that signalled contemporary but now says simply Value Village. Funny how colour can tell the time.

Mr. Carpetbeggar always has a large Tim Hortons cup at the front edge of his slice of carpet to solicit change from the hundreds who stream by him twice a day, north in the morning, then south at the end of the day. He's expressionless and makes no effort to garner our generosity. There are no crudely printed cardboard signs, no *Homeless need a little help. God Bless*, no *Have a nice day. God Bless*, no *Hard times. Lost my job. Anything helps. God Bless*, no *Trying to get home to Nova Scotia. God Bless*. It's all I can do to keep from saying, "Come on, Carpetbeggar, give me something, anything, a witty *Saving for my MBA, Help put me over the top, only $74,935.43 to go!*" Nothing.

Don't get me wrong. I never give money to these bums. It just encourages them. I will drop a toonie on a busker from time to time because they are actually performing a public service. I'm sure some depressed soul changed his mind about jumping in front of the Bloor subway during rush hour because a cheerful busker just happened to play "It's A Wonderful World" on a didgeridoo. Everyone got to their Pilates class on time. Everyone's a winner.

One time, I tried to get close to Carpetbeggar's cup to take a measure of his success, but Black Beauty clipped the carpet corner and sent coins and bills in all directions. Instinctively, I turned to apologize, but he just sat there staring while a half dozen otherwise busy people crawled around to pick up the day's receipts and put them back in his cup. He said nothing, not so much as a God Bless.

There is another citizen of this underworld near the entrance to the King subway station. Stuart, older, heavy-set guy, again of no fixed age, sits there every day on a nice piece of foam with a simple, neatly printed sign of *Thanks* leaning against a battered vintage top hat, hoping for our contributions. He never looks up to engage those passing by because he is too enthralled with the latest book he happens to be reading. He always has half a dozen paperbacks in a stack, ready to go. One day when I was passing by he was finishing up a hardcover edition of Stuart McLean's *Christmas at the Vinyl Cafe*, hence my calling him Stuart. I thought about dropping off a copy of Covey's *Seven Habits*, but I have to say Stuart's top hat is always brimming with coins and bills. Thriving in the big city, being paid to read. If McLean were still alive, he could probably write a weepy story about how this life of leisure in the underworld came to be. God Bless you, Stuart.

As I got closer to my office, I cut across the salmon run and saw the Leatherlady tucked into her usual spot on a small bench under the escalator near the shoeshine girls. Leatherlady is bent from the waist at a ninety-degree angle like an old Singer safety pin. She is so hunched over that she cannot see straight ahead, so she cocks her head at an awkward angle to estimate where she is going and to make regular course corrections as she pushes her cart. Her hair is shoulder-length, grey, with those strange lemony-yellow discolourations that come with age. She parts it sharply on the left side, I assume to keep it from falling across her face and eyes, thereby interfering with navigation. I have seen her at least once a week for several years now as she pushes that cart, neatly stuffed with all her worldly belongings, around on the PATH. She has been circulating down there 365 days a year for years. And on every one of those days she has been clad in a full-length shiny black leather coat circa 1968. I have to remind myself that these folks who live down here always look ten years older than they really are. So in underworld years I'm estimating she's in her seventies. That is one hardy leather coat.

As I waited for end of day discount sushi, I watched her sitting beneath the stairs, cart pulled close, head bobbing as she struggled to stay awake, and recalled the first time I had encountered her, years ago. I had been cutting underground on the PATH to the courts at Osgoode Hall, planning to come out on Queen Street at the Sheraton Centre. I arrived at the hotel escalators to find that everything had ground to a halt because she had pushed all the emergency stop buttons. People rushing up to their offices looked at each other in a panic as if to say, "Now what should I do? How will I get up to my office? Is this an up or a down escalator? Where are the elevators? Quick, get to the elevators!" But then, just as suddenly as they had stopped, a building security guard reset the buttons and the flow resumed up, up, up. A wave of relief swept across the waiting crowd.

The usual movement resumed, except for one tourist who had observed the whole scene. I assume he was a tourist because, in his sixties, he wore bright white running shoes, had a blue MEC rain jacket that matched his wife's, and a new Herschel knapsack from which dangled his emergency one-litre Roots water bottle. Oh, and he wore a Tilley hat. Dead giveaway. He stepped forward—against his wife's protestations—and, wagging a finger, spoke sharply to Leatherlady as if she was a naughty child. She twisted her head around at an impossible angle to look up at him and began shrieking obscenities. In that moment, I saw in her weathered face tortured madness. He stumbled back safely beside his wife as Leatherlady scuttled away with a jerky, crablike gait, course-correcting every five or six steps.

At one point I considered introducing her to another citizen of the underworld, the Curious Woman, but I have never actually seen them in the same vicinity. Perhaps they have reached an understanding about schedules and territories.

The Curious Woman is a skinny little thing, neat as a pin in black slacks, tight sweater, and laced-up hiking boots. I would guess she is in her late sixties, underworld years. She has a shock of white hair tucked under a tight black headband. Her worldly possessions are packed into one of those common large Red White Blue bags. I overheard a woman on the elevator one day complain that Curious Woman goes into the public washroom and regularly locks herself into the handicap booth. She does her business—as my mother would say—tucks her big bag and overcoat onto the toilet seat and then crawls under the door, leaving her stuff safe and sound for an hour or so while she wanders the PATH.

Why Curious Woman? Although her hair is bone-white, her eyebrows have been drawn on in huge black arches of perpetual curiosity. I followed her one day as she strolled the food court under First Canadian Place, sans her Red White Blue cargo, sampling free tea at David's (*Thank you, dear, is that Ginger Lemon?*), dark chocolate at Lindt's (*Maybe just one with the orange cream. Oh, delicious.*), and the cheeses at Metro (*A new Herve from Belgium? Wonderful.*). The girls with samples all seem to know her and treat her like their grandma. She maintains a constant appearance of happy curiosity as if today, for the first time, she is enjoying all the underworld has to offer.

I assume she thinks this ruse of window shopping fools everyone for an hour or so (I saw her staring in the window at Victoria's Secret, for heaven's sake) until she must head back to the public washroom and crawl to retrieve her bag and overcoat.

By the time I finally got up to my office, Bonnie was long gone and the sun was setting over the city. I could see the streetlights popping on, car and truck tail lights streaming in and out of the downtown. One by one the office towers lit up, and a peace settled in, high above it all.

After a couple of hours of research and docketing the day's work, I turned to look out across the adjacent towers. Once the sun has set, it's actually prettier than during the day, when you can see too many grimy details on the streets below. In the dark I can see right into BCE Place, First Canadian, and the TD Towers. Hundreds of offices, all with lights ablaze, sit empty, computer screens still glowing, papers spread out, and favourite coffee mugs abandoned until tomorrow, when the salmon run will start all over again. I can see the cleaning staff pushing carts from office to office, a supervisor trailing along to make sure they keep up the pace.

I picked up my binoculars (please, everyone in the towers with a window has a pair) and looked across into the TD Tower on King Street. I scanned a few floors, mostly empty offices, but then found an interesting corner office. A woman sat on the edge of a desk, a man leaned back in his chair, they talked, and she threw her head back, laughing at something he had said. Tempting each other. I could see where this was going. They both should have caught their 6:40 p.m. GO trains to the hinterlands, like they promised their spouses. No matter, they would have a couple of hours on the train to mask the smell of each other and make up excuses for their delay ("It was Jason's birthday . . . I had to go for a drink . . . "). Tempting fate.

I scanned over to the former Trump Tower. The outside balcony bar on the thirtieth was packed with young people. Lights were flashing and selfie overtime had begun as buckets of something arrived at the cocktail tables. Even without the sound of their music, I could sense the beat of a great party just beginning high above the streets below. I could always come back to the party later once it had warmed up, so I moved on to other prospects. I stood up straight in the floor-to-ceiling windows and panned into the CIBC tower to find a guy sitting at his desk, looking out the window through his binoculars. He raised a hand and waved to me. I raised my arm to acknowledge him, and he waved again as if to acknowledge our connection, a weird high-level semaphore.

Suddenly the cleaning lady was at my office door, "Scuze, scuze." She smiled self-consciously, as if this was a huge intrusion. I gestured for her to come in and, as she emptied my trash and recycling into the same large garbage bin, I realized that there are no tall cleaning staff. Everyone is 5'3" and not from around here. They are all from faraway places, and by the hundreds they pour into downtown towers each day. They wait underground in basement lunch rooms or food courts for the end of our workday so they can flow up into the towers to empty waste cans, vacuum carpets, spray and wipe desks, scrub and flush toilets, and pick out the gum men inexplicably spit into urinals. They do their work, quickly, silently until the wee hours and then slip away to who knows where. How do they do it? Why do they do it?

When she was done, I sat back down at my desk, put my feet up on the credenza, and looked out over the glittering city lights. I recalled a podcast I had heard while running early one morning. A man had written a novel that had something to do with Einstein and time. It was about villages in Switzerland. Each village experienced time in a different way. One village had time that was erratic, stopping and starting randomly. Another village experienced time quickly on the edge of town but more slowly as one approached the centre of town, where it slowed to an imperceptible crawl. I know, crazy. But one village experienced time, so the higher one went, the more slowly time passed. Fast on the ground and slow in the clouds. People who didn't want to age quickly moved into the hills above the village, then higher into the mountains and once there, built their homes as high as possible on stilts. Height was good. Height was expensive. Height was healthy. Height preserved youth. And the poor? They lived in the village, ground level or worse. If a rich person had to be in the village, they would race down and do it as quickly as possible, since every minute down there was aging them. They would rush back to their homes on stilts high in the mountains. Eventually, the people below forgot that higher was better and just carried on with their lives.

As I looked down from the towers, I wondered where the cleaning staff, the parking lot attendants, the security staff, Leatherlady, Curious Woman, Carpetbeggar, and Stuart were right now. Were they dining somewhere at a food court, comparing notes about their day's activities? I wondered if they had forgotten that higher is better. I hoped so.

15

Breaking a Cardinal Rule

HAVING AN UNHAPPY CLIENT after getting them an excellent result is not a good thing, and I spent a little too much time drowning my sorrows at the Dakota Tavern the night after the confrontation in the hallway at Brampton court. Word spread fast, and there was already a rumour that the Law Society might get involved. Apparently, Rubber Ball Boy was actually a Crown attorney, and he was filing a complaint. And then there was Sean. He alone was a good reason to drink.

In the morning I was too hungover to go for a run, so I ended up at the office wondering why I had chosen to surround myself with people bent on self-destruction. On days like this the phone does not get answered. Emails are ignored. I'll see the name of a client or opposing lawyer on caller ID or in a text message and just look away, knowing they probably want to take some step that will surely make matters worse for everyone. Sometimes it's the tell-tale number of the court office calling to sort out some bureaucratic mess they've created. All are ignored. Bonnie knows enough to steer clear of me at such times. She might send an email: *Can I come in?* If I don't answer, she carries on, knowing that we will need to put in overtime to catch up. These are dark days. There are too many of them.

In an attempt to cheer me up, Bonnie sent an email to remind me that one of my all-time favourite clients was planning to stop by. Now there was a grateful client. Excellent result. I really helped that family.

Sometimes when I'm in this dark hole, Bonnie says half jokingly, "You should write a book. No one would believe what goes on." She's right, so a long time ago I started to make some notes, jot down ideas, and even make a list of some thoughts to help people avoid a lot of the pain of divorce. Clients are constantly suggesting that I should do their divorce for free in exchange for giving me the rights to a book about their fascinating divorce. This usually ends with them saying, "You could make a movie about my life and this divorce . . . You'll make a fortune." The first few times this stupid idea surfaced, I just smiled politely and docketed an extra hour to their file as punishment. The twentieth time it was suggested by a client, it unfortunately coincided with one of my dark days. When I asked why would anyone want to watch a cliché-ridden movie about their boring divorce, well, I lost the file to another lawyer who had professed that quite the contrary, their divorce was truly unique. Probably for the best.

On the upside, though, I have been keeping, in no particular order, a list of rules or truisms based on my professional experiences. Here are some examples:

1. Don't get married.
2. Don't let your stay-at-home wife have a personal trainer.
3. Don't let your husband take French lessons, or singing lessons . . . any private lessons, for that matter.
4. People get worse, not better while divorcing.
5. While divorcing, a small percentage tell the truth, about 1 percent. (Give or take 1 percent.)
6. If your husband keeps a locked safe in the basement, he may very well be a crossdresser.
7. A woman's worst enemy is another woman.
8. A man's worst enemy is himself.
9. The surefire signal your marriage is over? Contempt.
10. Before marrying get a full list of their meds, criminal record, and a credit report.

It's a rough draft, and I keep refining it, but I have a list of over two hundred.

I scrolled through the messages on my phone and saw a number I didn't recognize. As bizarre as it may sound, this sometimes actually acts as an invitation to listen, to reach out. For a few moments I can forget about all my current cases and dive into a new tale of woe, breaking the surface of the pool of misery of a complete stranger. I plunge in and feel refreshed as it washes everything else away. This new number appeared five times, so I relented and listened. Bring on the salve of fresh heartache.

"Mr. Bierce, this is Alvin Shank's sister, Hailey. I'm calling to ask for your help. Alvin needs you. Can you call him at . . . " She recites his number, twice. I continued to scroll through messages but saw nothing from Alvin himself. It had been a few months since Alvin helped me at Old City Hall. We stayed in touch with a coffee now and then, but I'm not much for that sort of male bonding. It was business. Keep things professional.

Out of pure curiousity I called Hailey back, and she picked up on one ring. "Hailey, it is Andrew Bierce. I'm sorry I couldn't get back to you sooner but . . . (fill in pack of standard lies about being busy or in court or dealing with an emergency)." She began by apologizing for bothering me but said Alvin was in a very bad situation.

"He hasn't called me." In response to this, she pushed her tongue against her front teeth and made that unmistakeable disapproving "Tch" sound for which there is no known name.

"I was worried he might not call . . . he's ashamed. He said that you wouldn't understand."

"Well, that is entirely possible. I do divorce work, and he is a criminal lawyer."

"But that is why he needs you. His fiancée broke off their engagement, and he is really broken up."

"Engaged? When did that happen?"

"A few months ago, but it all blew up last week."

"Does he need a counsellor? I can give you names."

"No. No. He needs your help. Please call him. Please, Mr. Bierce." She was pleading.

Now, let's stop right here. I have a cardinal rule: I never call clients to set up a first interview. Never. Certainly, I will return a call, but the client must call me first. The client must call—not their mother, father, sister, brother, coworker, new partner, or neighbour. The client must call. All those people trying to help say the same thing: "Please, Mr. Bierce, Mr./Ms. (Fill in Blank) needs your help! They're in a terrible way . . . Pleeeease . . . "

"So terrible that they cannot pick up the phone?"

They continue, "He/she can't. They don't even know they need help . . . They need you. Ohhh, Mr. Bierce . . . "

I tell them as gently as possible, "Well, when he/she realizes that he/she needs me, he/she can call me. I answer my phone (well, most of the time). You have my number." Years ago, I used to make that first call. I would dial the number given to me, and I would say, "Mr./Ms., your mother/father/sister/brother/aunt/uncle/niece/nephew/cousin/coworker/neighbour/new partner asked me to call you because . . . " You know what happened? Ninety-nine percent of the time I wouldn't get a chance to finish that sentence because the person who supposedly could not live without my help then treated me like an ambulance-chasing scum lawyer. "You lawyers really cannot wait to jump on a divorce, can you?"

When I tried to explain that their mother/father/sister/brother/coworker/aunt/uncle/niece/nephew/new partner asked me to call, their reaction would be, "Well, it's none of their goddamn business. What did they tell you? What did they say? Have you talked to my wife/husband? I'm calling the Law Society . . . " After a few of those I stopped calling, and the cardinal rule came into force. I never make that first call. Never.

But I was going to make an exception for Alvin.

16

No Good Deed Goes Unpunished

BEFORE I COULD EVEN PICK UP the phone to call Alvin, Bonnie called to me from her workstation. "Guess who needs to meet with you?"

"I'm too tired to guess. Thrill me."

"Conchetta and Marco are splitting up. Carlo wants you to meet with her."

"Okay, set something up." Personally? I had expected their marriage to last a little longer. I mean, after all they were barely in their twenties, knew each other less than a year, were expecting a child accidentally conceived, spent over $100,000 on their rushed wedding . . . , I mean what could go wrong? What about Celine Dion? "The Prayer?" What about "And help us to be wise, in times when we don't know. Let this be our prayer when we lose our way." Maybe Bocelli should add a line about prenups.

"And guess who just arrived to see her favourite lawyer?"

"Please, Bonnie, I cannot deal with guessing anything today." I gave her my standard *I'm suffering* look.

"Teresa Savoie."

"Really?" I smiled for the first time that day. Lovely woman, always appreciative of my work.

"I thought you would be happy." Bonnie handed me the latest volume of the multi-volume Savoie file.

"In the meantime, Bonnie, can you pull that file I had a year or so ago dealing with an engagement that blew up . . . ring was in dispute?"

I had been representing Teresa Savoie for at least five years, off and on. It was sort of a charity case because Bonnie snuck her in for a consult, she could never really pay full whack, and somehow she got in too deep for me to back out. Plus, I was having a lot of fun taking the hickory to her deadbeat husband.

Teresa was in her early forties but looked in her late fifties. Someone had driven the vitality out of her, and that someone was her husband Eric. She was with him all of nine years but probably knew after a couple of months of marriage that she had made a huge mistake. However, God bless her, she motored on, especially when the kids started arriving, three of them back to back to back. Once the babies start coming people put up with a lot of nonsense. They develop this innate skill called "explain away or look way." Every once in a while I would catch a glimpse in her pretty smile of what she used to be like, but then it was gone, like smoke.

She and Eric separated about five years ago. She came to me in an absolute panic after she had met Bonnie at one of her charity groups. I probably should have passed on meeting with her. Whatever. When I learned that Eric had been laid off from his aircraft assembly job at Bombardier, I was interested in possibly scooping his severance package for Teresa in the divorce. Easy pickings. But then I learned that instead of taking the package, putting it in the bank, and simply finding a new job, Eric had a brainwave after seeing so many commercials in which young people raved about how well they were doing managing their own investments: "I'm going to be a day trader and play the stock market. I will parlay this package into a mini fortune so I never have to work again!" Of course, he had all the usual qualifications for sophisticated investing: he watched TV—a lot, in particular *Mad Money*, Bloomberg and BNN; early in the morning he would read the overnight news from Asian markets; and, of course, he relied on tips from folks he chatted with online.

Eric was so good at this new career that within seven months he had nothing left. Instead of telling Teresa the bad news, he turned to a different form of online investing called gambling. That didn't improve the family's financial situation because within a year he had racked up a $250,000 HELOC on their modest—previously mortgage-free—family home in Etobicoke. Guess what? They weren't richer than they thought.

Teresa found out, of course, hit the roof, and they split. Eric then joined that secret league of thousands of men around the Greater Toronto Area who are sleeping in a buddy's basement after separating. Eric did that for a while, then he moved in with his parents for a few months and then in with a girlfriend who carried him through his depression for several months. She caught on that he was not working and booted him out. It was a mess.

He refused to hire a lawyer (Too expensive. Why give all our money to the lawyers?), so I cut Eric a deal that would keep Teresa in the house with the kids and he could see them when he wanted, which over time meant not much. Sure, he might show up to their hockey practice with some new $200 hockey sticks, but there was nothing regular. Within a few months she called to say that the kids were stressed out not seeing their dad, and could I do something to force him to see the kids? Hmm, not really. The court can't issue a restraining order to stop kids from pissing their beds.

Over the last few years, she had worked hard to keep the house, with a little help from her parents. Eric chipped in what he could from time to time on the line of credit and for kids' expenses like soccer, hockey, and tutors. She would call me every once in a while to say that she had to sell the house and move to an apartment, but I always told her to hang on, never leave the market, build your equity. It's the best form of savings you can get. She took the advice. After a few years she had another $100,000 in equity. She was grateful and often dropped off something for the office, baked stuff or wine. Nice lady.

If she makes an appointment to come in to see me, it means Eric has stopped paying child support and she needs me to put the fear of God in him, get him paying again. I'm good at it, but many times I was just chasing air. He has never got back to earning like he did at Bombardier. The last time she was in to see me I dropped a grand piano on Eric, took his driver's licence, and his passport. I really cracked him on the head, and guess what? In a few weeks the money started to flow again. The deadbeat suddenly had a pulse. That was about a year ago.

"Teresa, lovely to see you. How are the boys? How can I help?"

"Eric's dead."

My rear end had not even hit the chair. "What? Oh my God, what happened?"

"Drugs."

"No. Overdose? I never saw that coming. I knew he had issues, but I never thought drugs."

"I guess you could call it an overdose." She shook her head as if to say, *I cannot believe this is happening to me.* "After you crushed Eric in court the last time . . . when you took his licence and his passport . . . he vowed to get a job. You really hurt him . . . so he told me he found something, and the money started to flow. He was regular, every month after you did that . . . "

I didn't like the way she kept saying *you.*

"He even called to say that his licence was reinstated. He started seeing the boys a bit more. They were thrilled, and things were looking up."

"What happened?"

"He had seen an ad in the Metro for participating in drug trials. You know when they ask people to volunteer for drug trials."

"I've seen the ads, 'If you are diabetic and between the ages of 18 and 50,' blah blah blah . . . "

"Yeah, that's it. He was desperate after you put so much pressure on him. Eric thought this testing was free money. No work, just show up at the nice clinic, chat up the Filipino nurses for a few hours, hope they throw in some lunch, pick up your cheque, and away you go. He fell in with some guys who do it for a living."

"Do what for a living? What do you mean?"

"Doing drug trials. It's a scam. These guys go clinic to clinic, but they don't tell the afternoon clinic what they had in the morning. Eric was doing five clinics a week, each one giving him something different to test. He figured half of what they gave him were probably placebos anyway."

"Holy crap."

"Anyway, the paramedics found him in a friend's basement. He had a reaction to some drugs and was dead. They think he might have been dead for a few days. There may be an inquest." She bit her lip and looked down. "I think you drove him to it. Your pressure killed him." She started to cry.

Uh-oh.

But as I sometimes mutter to myself in front of certain clients, *Nihil denim lacrima citius arescit* (Nothing dries sooner than a tear). Teresa's dried up real fast when she asked me about his insurance policy. "I'm here to get the paperwork started for the insurance money. There was something in the separation agreement you did about insurance."

I pulled out a copy of their separation agreement and flipped through to the standard insurance provisions. "Here we go, paragraph 17.5. Eric agreed to maintain a policy of life insurance as security for the child support. It was with Utica Life, $250,000. You are irrevocable beneficiary."

"Good. Where is that money? How do you get that for me?"

"Did Eric keep up the policy?"

She looked at me puzzled. "Eric? You take care of that, don't you?"

"No. It says here in para 17.7 that you, Teresa, have the right to ask every year for proof that Eric was keeping the policy in good standing, you know, paying the premiums."

"But—"

"In paragraph 17.9, you can even take over the policy and pay the premiums if you learned that he's not doing that."

"I thought you did that."

"No, that's what you do. Do you know if Eric kept up his premiums?"

"Paid his premiums?" She was clearly panicking. "Eric couldn't even pay for our son's hockey registration, never mind an insurance policy. I tried to have as little contact with him as possible. So you don't have my insurance money? I need that money. I have $230,000 to go on the line of credit."

"Okay, well, hold on. Let's take this a step at a time. Call Utica Life and see if he paid the premiums."

"Oh God, I thought you were doing that."

I started to feel a little angry about all this *you you you* stuff. "Teresa, why would I do that? The agreement is clear. I covered it in my reporting letter to you. Did you read it? That was your responsibility. Not mine. Remember you were always asking me to keep costs down?"

"Oh, all you ever think about is your fees. What am I supposed to do now?"

"Call the insurance company and see if he paid the premiums. Here, I have written the policy number on my card."

She snatched the card from my hand. "First you drive him to kill himself, and now I find out that you haven't protected me by making sure the insurance is there for me and my boys. I'm very disappointed in you." She stood up and stormed out of the boardroom. As she got to reception, she turned to me and said, "I'm going to go to the Law Society."

Within seconds, Bonnie stuck her head into the boardroom. "Is everything okay?"

"Eric OD'd testing pharmaceuticals. Idiot. Teresa wasn't tracking the life insurance premiums."

"I doubt Eric paid them."

"No fucking kidding."

No good deed goes unpunished.

17

Pussycat

"ALVIN."

"Yeah."

"It's Bierce. What's going on?"

There was a long pause before he answered. "I assume my sister called you. Did she tell you to call me? I can't talk right now . . . I'm at court."

"Alvin. Buddy. If you need some free advice, I'm your man. I owe you."

"You don't owe me."

"So I heard you got engaged and now it's fallen apart. I'm sorry to hear, but can I help? Do you need me to take some hardwood to your lady friend?"

Long pause. "I don't know. I've been trying to figure this out on my own."

"Alvin, it's not easy. I know. But sometimes another set of eyes can help."

"She's really been a handful." His voice actually broke a little bit, and I sensed he was going to cry. Not a good look.

"Listen, why don't we grab a coffee? Meet me at Nathan Phillips Square. I can be there in ten minutes."

"Maybe next week . . ."

"No, ten minutes. I'll bring the coffee."

There was a long pause. "Yeah, okay, I'll see you in ten."

For the Pan Am Games they had swept Nathan Phillips Square and put up a big *TORONTO* sign. Other than that it was the same tired mess of concrete, greasy chip wagons, and ice cream trucks spewing diesel fumes onto the green roof at Old City Hall. Well done, city planners. We grabbed a bench near the "fountain" and listened to a band tune up for a jazz festival.

He was quiet, brooding, so I tried to break the ice. "So, how is our friend the Crown?"

"Ms. Novak?"

"Right, Novak. Still busting balls?"

"Oh, she is still the Queen Bee of Old City Hall."

"God, what a bitch." I took a sip of my coffee. "I hope we cross paths again, because brother, I got a long memory . . . and a mean streak." I laughed.

Alvin didn't. "Careful what you wish for, Bierce."

"What do you mean?"

Long pause. "I'm—or was—engaged to her."

"No shit. You have got to be kidding me."

"Nope, and I have you to thank for it."

"Me? What the fuck did I do?" After Teresa Savoie's *you you you* bullshit I felt I was being asked to take the blame for more than enough.

"After you blew up her list that day, when you sprang your client, she lost it, totally lost it. Harold had to adjourn the rest of the day. She was a bit of a mess. Anyway I went over and spoke to her, just sort of a, you know, "Well, that was quite a day." We got to talking, and she was, I don't know, different. Softer. I know that sounds stupid, but everything felt different talking to her. We went for coffee, then drinks and dinner at Harbour 60, and—"

"Please . . . please . . . ," I cut him off. "Don't say it . . . You didn't . . . "

"Oh, yes we did. We went back to her place. She has a condo over at the Sliver."

I know the Sliver. It is a sleek piece of architecture tucked into an impossible little spot between two old buildings near King and Yonge.

Hotel at the bottom. Condos at the top. A Crown would be pushing it buying in there, so I assume she was renting. "Nice. She can walk to work from there."

"Walk? Not her. You've probably seen her downtown. She rides around on a hot pink Vespa, chromed to the hilt. Bright pink helmet. It's a pretty little ride. I've been on the back of it a few times. It's her absolute pride and joy. Gift from her parents when she graduated. She calls it Pussycat. It has little black paw prints up the side." Alvin opened his phone and showed me a picture of it.

"Cute." I raised my eyebrows. "But I may throw up."

"Tell me about it . . . but it's her baby."

Now that Alvin mentioned it, I thought I had seen that Vespa downtown, scooting up Bay or York, black ponytail flying out from under the pink helmet.

Alvin continued with his story. "We started seeing each other a lot. We were in the same courts week in, week out. If I wasn't at her place, she was at mine. It was pretty wild."

"Wild? You mean . . . "

"Oh yeah, unbelievable. Anyway we kept it pretty quiet, at her insistence. We didn't want any conflicts or someone suggesting that I was getting special treatment. Things were secret, things were great."

"So what happened?"

"I proposed. We were taking the ferry out to Toronto Island. It was a beautiful night, and I had been carrying the ring around for weeks waiting for the right moment." He tapped his phone, and a couple of pictures of the night popped up. Alvin took a long pause, and I could see that he was recalling the moment. "She said yes. I put the ring on her finger. It happened fast."

"Sounds great."

"It was. I had never been in a relationship like this. I was crazy about her, but honestly I felt out of control."

The band practicing behind us suddenly kicked into a version of Moe Koffman's "Swinging Shepherd Blues," so I suggested we walk over to the lawn of Osgoode Hall for a little peace, order, and good government. As we walked, Alvin told me of love's demise.

"We would rendezvous at her place after work. At least 99 percent of the time she was there before me, ready to roll, tub running, wine, dressed to—"

"I get it." Even as I said that I recalled her musky scent and perfume in court that day months ago.

"Anyway, this particular night a few weeks ago, I arrived a little early with some flowers . . . some wine . . . God, it's a fucking blur. Is it two weeks already? The doorman knows me, and I talked him into letting me into her condo. So next thing I knew I was in her apartment."

"I think I see where this is going."

"Oh, you have no idea." He took a long sip of coffee. "On her dining room table some papers were spread out, notes that she was transcribing into black leather books. I took just a glance, assuming it was case work, but it was not. I didn't want to violate her privacy or confidentiality on one of her files. It turns out she was writing her memoirs." He raised his eyebrows and threw some air quotes on *memoirs*.

"What? She is like thirty-five. What does she have to write memoirs about?"

"She's thirty-three. Anyway, she's writing her *memoirs*." Again with the air quotes. "She told me she'd been taking a writing course at Humber College. But she said it was for writing some short stories, just for fun. She has been very private about it, but every few weeks or so she would meet with her mentor, Tom Morris, to help her with her writing—"

"Whoa, whoa, whoa. Tom Morris the author?" I recognized the name of one of Canada's top fiction writers. Giller Prize winner. I'd met him at a Curators' Circle event at the AGO. Pretentious dick. And he reeked. So much for having a bestseller.

"One and the same. The mentoring is pretty high-level stuff, and she pays a good buck for it. She goes away for a couple of weeks every summer to a writing camp. Morris has been working with her to polish her writing. I guess she forgot to put it away . . . "

"So you read it?"

Long pause. More sips of coffee. "Yup."

"And? So what's the big deal? She can't write?"

"She has called her draft memoirs *Pussycat,* like her scooter . . . "

"Hello . . . porn?"

Alvin took a look at his shoes, rubbed his face as only he can, and took a deep breath. "It was brutal. If it's porn it's based on real life . . . She has been keeping track of everything, of everyone . . . she . . . you know . . . has ever . . . "

"What? Spit it out, for Christsakes."

"She's been writing about, you know . . . she basically had . . . has . . . many *relationships.*" Again with the air quotes. "Cops, Crowns, witnesses, jurors . . . judges . . . everyone . . . before—and after our engagement."

"Holy shit. Is it true or just fantasy stuff? Fifty Shades of Bullshit?"

"Oh, it's true . . . and it includes Tom Morris too."

"Holy shit. You know who he's married to? Penny Glover, publisher over at AllPublishing. She would not be amused. She was a witness in that IP case, the one involving writers and newspaper rights, you know . . . I watched her give evidence. Brilliant woman. I would not want to tangle with her."

"Well, you would never know he's married, according to her book."

"Maybe they have an 'understanding' . . . "

"Not according to her book."

"So what happened?"

"When Lorelei came in the door, she took one look at the stuff on her desk, and then at me, and she knew I'd read it. I couldn't cover up how I felt . . . I was going crazy. I read names that I knew, over and over again . . . Names we both know." He glanced at me as if to say *real trouble.*

"Like who?"

"Like you don't want to know. We had a hell of a fight. You know what she said? She said that we never agreed that our relationship would be monogamous. She said that I should have understood that she would continue to see other men and women—"

"Hello, . . . women too?"

"Yup. I mean, this is so screwed up. I screamed at her that the engage-ment was off."

"Well, no fucking kidding."

"She said fine, and I said give me the engagement ring back. She said screw you, that she was keeping it as compensation."

"Compensation for what?"

"For reading her memoirs. She went full Crown attorney on me. I felt like a goddamn criminal."

"What's the ring worth? I mean is it worth a fight?"

Alvin looked at me and then gave his face a rub that any experienced massage therapist would have been proud of. "A hundred K."

"What! Where did you get that kind of money?"

"I didn't buy it. It was my grandmother's and my mother's—white gold, huge stones, beautiful, heritage piece. It has a history that goes back into some European royal family. But the value is not the important thing."

"Really? Not important?"

"Her wearing my mother's ring is burning me up. I can't work. I see her in court wearing it like a piece of ordinary jewellery. I see red . . . "

I could see that he was distraught. "Jesus. What a mess."

"I want it back. I want the ring back."

"Getting rings back is tricky business when a wedding gets called off. Never a slam dunk."

"Bierce . . . "

"Let me think about it."

"Bierce, if it is about the retainer, I can get the money. I have RRSPs, a bit saved . . . I know your rep . . . "

I took a step back from him. "Well, what the fuck does that mean?"

"I mean I know you're expensive, and I know you don't work for free and that . . . "

"What?"

"That you can be . . . "

"What? What have you heard?"

"Ruthless. Smart . . . but ruthless."

"You're goddamn right I am." I liked hearing that. Ruthless. "Okay, let me think on this a bit. Don't do anything until we speak again, so let's stay in touch. Tomorrow?"

"Yeah, tomorrow's good. Look, I gotta get back to court. But thanks, Bierce, it feels better talking about it."

I grabbed him by the sleeve. "Alvin, hang tough . . . and . . . you know, get yourself tested. You never know these days. I'll get Bonnie to pull some of my files dealing with cancelled engagements."

"Thanks. I'm actually waiting on some results. Fingers crossed."

Heading back to the office I recalled that day in court with Lorelei and actually got a little spring in my step thinking about finding a way to pull that ring off her finger.

That is until I remembered that I had a trial starting in the morning for my client, Patrick McGovern, the fading rock star.

But ruthless? Yeah, I liked that.

18

Stealing Arrows

PATRICK MCGOVERN. THAT'S RIGHT, the musician who became a pop star. There's a difference, of course. The musician wrote all those hit songs that when played at weddings trigger people gathering into drunken circles and singing their hearts out. The pop star, however, had fallen on hard times, and by hard times I mean he was caught in a time warp and partying like it was still 1999. Tequila and cocaine were consuming his royalties and his career, not to mention him. He was forty-five, looked like he was fifty-five, and dressed like he was twenty-five. Not a good progression. And of course his marriage was toast. Honestly, if it were not for the royalties pouring in, he and his family would be living in postal code BuM FcK, Ontario.

Patrick's wife, Laurie, lovely woman and good mom, and her very competent lawyer, Leslie Kaplan, had been trying for the last couple of years to boot Patrick out of one of their two heavily financed Forest Hill homes. One of them had to be sold and it was not going to be the one that housed Laurie and their five kids. Patrick had paid me handsomely to make sure he stayed put a few blocks from Laurie and the kids. So far, so good. But even his well-known musician neighbours were beyond getting a little tired of this aging rock-star routine and his party shack. (Geddy apparently sat him down one night and said, "Pat, you aren't Keith . . . and the doctors aren't going to let you get your blood changed." Drake refused to speak to him.)

A couple of problems surfaced as the trial approached. For one, we were out of excuses to delay it any longer. I had run his poor wife and her lawyer ragged with motions, disclosure, questioning under oath, appeals, motions to strike pleadings, more questioning, and more disclosure. If a client's case isn't good—and Patrick's was not good by any stretch of the imagination—certain black arts must be called upon. Client's case stinks? Delay. If the facts are bad? Wait, maybe they'll change. Substantive law is not on your side? That's why the Family Law Rules were invented. Spin a sticky web of procedural problems. Can't beat 'em in the courtroom? Keep them fighting in the alley. Burn their litigation budget so they cannot afford to get into a courtroom. But it's not easy. You need to work at it.

When a judge once described lack of disclosure in family law cases as a cancer, he had no idea that its malignant variant is too much disclosure. Death by a thousand paper cuts. With my disclosure requests, I made sure Kaplan hated the case by the time it was called for trial. But to her credit, she hung in.

A while back, as I was thinking about poor Patrick's case, I took a dirty weekend in NYC with my Muskoka client. I know, I shouldn't have. It had already gone a little too far. It was affecting my ability to get her case settled. She had also made comments about how "maybe we shouldn't be doing what we were doing." I didn't like the sound of that, but my hands were tied. *Relationshit*, as they say, was raining down on me. Anyway, I needed to get away from her complaining about her case. I needed a break, so I wandered over to the Guggenheim for some peace and quiet. (I get privileges there as a member of the AGO Curators' Circle.) Drifting around inside it is like touring the inside of a giant psychedelic ice cream cone. No sooner had I started the tour when I came upon a huge wooden boat suspended from the ceiling. The artist, Cai Guo-Qiang, had peppered it with hundreds of arrows.* It just hung there with everyone crowded around, scratching their heads and thinking like me, *Jesus Christ, what is that supposed to be?* So much contemporary art is borderline garbage, but a boat riddled with arrows, that is over the line, right?

---

* *Borrowing Your Enemy's Arrows*, www.moma.org

I plugged in my earbuds and flicked on the audio guide to see what this thing could possibly have to do with reality. It turned out that the artist was illustrating an ancient Chinese story about a lowly member of an army whose general had ordered him to make a thousand arrows— overnight—for the next day's battle. Impossible, right? Well, instead this soldier made a barge with two dummy soldiers on it, tied a rope to it, and floated it toward the enemy lines. When the enemy saw the soldiers, they thought a battle was beginning so they peppered the barge with arrows. The soldier pulled the barge back to his shore and plucked out 1,000 arrows. He had stolen his enemy's arrows. Well, when I heard that, I stopped in my tracks. I turned to the woman beside me and said, too loudly (according to the security guard), "This guy is a fucking genius."

That's what I do. I steal arrows from my enemies.

Now, a year later, after stealing as many arrows as I could from Laurie and Kaplan, Patrick's day of reckoning approached. We had been ordered to trial. Peremptory, meaning no more adjournments. The jig was up.

A couple of days before the trial, I had sat Patrick down to face some realities about the situation. I told him we were really just rolling the dice with a trial, hoping we get a judge who maybe wouldn't have a complete grasp of the situation. Judicial assignments can be a crapshoot. I have had judges assigned for a trial who don't know an equalization payment from an insolvency application—that is, ass from elbow. It's pure desperation when hoping for that kind of judge is your best option for success.

I also knew that Leslie Kaplan was not going to fool around. She had trial experience, was respected by the judges, and would have a field day cross examining the fading pop star. I assumed she had enough of a retainer to go forward with a trial. She had made a reasonable Offer to Settle months ago, but I let it lapse. Maybe she would put it back on the table. Maybe. If she did, we might grab it. But her client's costs had soared getting ready for trial, so why would she do that? I wouldn't.

"Patrick, we are getting ready for trial, and as a part of the prep—an important part of the prep—we need to discuss The Smell Test." I could tell from the puzzled look on his face that he thought I was talking about his Axe cologne. "When you walk into that courtroom and the judge looks at you, he is going to make a snap decision. He will either like you or not.

The judge will ask himself, 'Is this Patrick McGovern the infamous bad boy rock 'n' roll star or just a talented local boy musician who simply fell in with the wrong crowd?' He will 'smell' you."

Patrick's response? "Rock 'n' roll, baby . . . better to burn out than fade away . . . Right?" Honestly. You can understand why I needed to keep this potential train wreck sequel to *Wayne's World* steered away from a courtroom.

"No, Patrick. At the trial you will appear as a father figure, a talented young musician who found success but then lost his way because of the bad people in the music industry. You're working day and night to get back on your feet, reclaim your career, and provide for your family. You are Canadian music's comeback kid."

He looked at me blankly. "I guess. Have I been doing that? Am I really a comeback kid? Cool . . . I guess . . . "

"Not really, but starting now you're just a hardworking dad . . . which means we have something to discuss."

"What?"

"Your appearance needs to align with your actual age." Pretty diplomatic, I thought.

"What do you mean?" He looked at his tattooed arms, bracelets, rings, black jeans torn at the knees and thighs, his snakeskin belt, and tattered Ramones t-shirt. "I guess I could wear a jacket . . . or something else."

Bonnie handed him a typed list of clothing to wear and instructions for personal care. "Can I come and watch this trial?" Notwithstanding his debauchery, Bonnie was a fan and found Patrick quite charming. She's a puzzle, what can I say. I gave her a look that said "some other time."

"Patrick, when you said 'or something else,' it looks like this." I pointed at the list. "Every day of trial you wear the same clothes. This is how I need you to look."

He read it out loud. "Brown sports jacket, grey flannel slacks, blue poly shirt, red tartan tie, broken in dress shoes . . . Where am I supposed to get this stuff?"

He kept reading. "Haircut. I don't think so. Shave every day of trial, no cologne, no scents at all, I thought you said it was a smell test . . . and—whoa, whoa, whoa—Shave off my soul patch? I don't think so . . . Absolutely not."

Now, maybe there's a rock star somewhere who at one time looked good with a soul patch, that little tuft of hair that some guys grow just under their lower lip. I could probably find a picture of one such musician in a dusty old *Rolling Stone* magazine. But men getting divorced because they blew up their marriage, because they were drunk all afternoon (I'm not even going to get into his nanny escapades, although I'm sure Kaplan will), staying up all night in clubs stoned, unemployed while their wife and kids stand by watching in horror, those men, they don't get to wear a soul patch to their trial. "Oh, it's coming off. You can grow it back."

I thought I had been pretty clear that these were not requests or suggestions. And yet, as I stood fully gowned, ready for the McGovern v. McGovern trial to begin and, as specific as I had been, what did I see stepping off the elevator at 393 University, ninth floor? One Patrick McGovern in a two-piece, cream-coloured, linen Hugo Boss suit, toffee-coloured belt, matching Chelsea boots, crisp pink shirt, sharp paisley tie, hair long but gelled to appear shorter, and one very obvious black soul patch. I watched as he made his way through the line at the metal detectors and could not help but stare as he put his iPhone, car keys, money clip thick with cash, pocket full of loonies, and Cole Hahn messenger-style bag into a plastic tray. A pretty and very young woman was at his elbow every step of the way. His niece, perhaps? Right.

I excused myself from a chat with the waddle of penguin lawyers who were awaiting trials in adjacent courtrooms and waited for Patrick to catch my eye. When he finally did, he grabbed his "niece" by the hand and marched over to me.

"Ready to rock and roll, Counsel?" When he smiled, his soul patch turned up and stuck out about two inches.

"I'm sorry. Who are you?"

"Very funny, Andy. Are we ready to roll? This is . . . " He gestured to the young lady.

I put my hand up. "I don't want to know." I turned to his friend and pointed at a bench at the end of the hall. "You see that bench way down there? Go sit there."

"Andy . . . she's a friend . . . she's here for . . . " Oh God, he was going to say it, " . . . moral support."

"First, stop calling me Andy. I'm still trying to figure out who you are, because the client I'm waiting for isn't on his way to a fucking cocktail party on the rooftop patio of the Thompson Hotel during TIFF. My client is supposed to be a straight-shooting father, beaten down by the evil music biz, struggling to make a comeback in his career and family . . . Comeback kid, remember? Look at you. What happened to the list Bonnie gave you? Do you remember? The Smell Test?" I was incredulous.

He looked at his shoes sheepishly, like a schoolboy. "I didn't wear any Axe . . . I couldn't do the other stuff . . . My girlfriend . . . " He looked sideways down the hall, " . . . she's an image consultant . . . and she said I'd just look like a dork. It'd be better if, you know, I looked like a successful businessman . . . like I had already come back." He looked over at the young woman who was desperately trying to channel either Selena Gomez or Ariana Grande. I always get them mixed up. Regardless, it was still the wrong channel.

"You are *supposed* to look like a dork. Not someone who looks like he might screw the nanny."

"She was only doing work as a nanny until she could get her image consulting business up and running." He actually sounded defensive.

"What the f . . . that's the nanny?" I hissed.

He looked at his shoes again, lifted them one by one, and polished them on the back of his linen pant legs. "Well, I guess it's too late."

"No, no, no, it's not. Go to the pharmacy downstairs and buy a razor."

"Andy, there's no time—"

"Then you'd better hurry, and don't come back with that." I nodded at the patch. "Lose the jacket and the tie, put this on." I handed him my crumpled emergency tie from Black Beauty. "Wash that goddamn gel out of your hair. Get rid of the iPhone, the bag, the money clip . . . and don't call me Andy."

"But . . . " He looked over at Selena Grande and polished his shoes again on the back of each pant leg. As the young woman chewed her gum, her face had an expression not unlike that of a mother whose child was about to begin the first round of a spelling bee.

"Take her with you, and don't bring her back. I will try to hold the matter down."

As he made his way to the elevator with Ariana Gomez, I could see Leslie Kaplan watching us, smiling like a shark circling, circling. She grinned as if to say, "The idiot couldn't resist putting on a show with his girlfriend, the nanny, beautiful." She would be all over him.

I ducked into the men's room as soon as I heard the clerk over the PA call the McGovern matter. "All parties and counsel having anything to do with McGovern v. McGovern please enter Courtroom 901." I waited as long as I could in a cubicle, letting her call the matter three times. Finally, I relented and rolled Black Beauty into the courtroom to see Madam Justice Bracken on the bench. *Shiiiit.* It was supposed to be Mr. Justice Horn. They must have juggled the lists. Unfortunately for us, Bracken is a very good judge. No-nonsense. And she was not looking very happy. "We've been waiting, Mr. Bierce. Are you ready to proceed?"

"Good morning, Your Honour. Yes, I'm sorry I was just in the men's room." I smiled and tried to look embarrassed.

"Where's your client? Is he present?"

"He is just on his way, Your Honour. Perhaps we could stand the matter down for fifteen minutes."

Kaplan was on her feet in a split second. "Your Honour, I am certain I saw my friend's client here in the hallway, and then I saw him leaving the courthouse." Her client, the long-suffering Ms. Laurie McGovern, nodded vigorously in agreement with every word uttered by her lawyer.

"Your Honour, my client is here. I assure you. I believe he may have gone to feed the meter. I'll step out in the hall and find him. Perhaps we should stand the matter down for fifteen minutes . . . " I was grasping at straws now.

"Mr. Bierce, we were set to proceed at 10:00 a.m. Sharp. It's now 10:20 a.m." She looked up at the clock on the wall, which, remarkably, showed the correct time. "I won't stand for any games today."

That was an interesting comment at the opening of a trial. Games? She must have read some of the history of the case. The court record was easily an embarrassing seven volumes, and volumes two to seven were games indeed. But no sooner had the words come out of her mouth than the door at the back of the courtroom opened and in stepped Patrick.

He stood there looking lost. No jacket, a wrinkled and uneven necktie wrapped around his neck, no hair gel, no messenger bag, no iPhone or money clip, and in place of his precious soul patch sat a wad of toilet paper soaking up blood from what must have been a massive shaving cut. As everyone turned to look at him, the schoolboy just stood at the door, paused, looked around sheepishly, and then polished one shoe and then the other on the back of his pants. He looked over at me. "Hey, Andy, sorry I'm late. I was in the bathroom . . . " Every inch a dork.

I turned to Justice Bracken. "We are ready to proceed, Your Honour."

I swear Judge Bracken actually smiled at Patrick as she inhaled his seemingly harmless scent. Mission accomplished.

19

Jenga

AFTER WE HAD FINISHED DAY ONE of McGovern's trial, I headed back to the office to dig into some research on couples who fought over engagement rings and the expense of a cancelled wedding. Surely, you didn't think Alvin is the first guy to go through this? More people pull the plug on weddings than you'd think. It's cheaper than a divorce—trust me. But frankly I'm glad more don't pull that plug. I'm trying to run a business, after all.

Getting engagement rings back is not easy. It depends on a lot of things. Who broke it off? Was it a conditional gift? Was there misconduct? A misunderstanding? Turns out your mothers shared the same sperm donor, and you are engaged to your sister? It happens. And then, of course, just like Patrick McGovern, does the judge think my client smells like a fresh batch of cookies or vinegar?

Understand this, in most cases it's basically a crapshoot. Nothing in family law is predictable anymore. Any judge can do anything on any given day. They can head off on some wild rides without a compass and make decisions that no one can afford to appeal. It's not like the old days when you could tell a client in advance whether their case was a winner or a loser. Now, as lawyers, we just go for it. We tart up the clients, scour the reported cases for a little law on which we might hang our client's hat, and then just throw a dart at the board. Of course, there is other stuff too, the martial arts of law, the hand-to-hand combat. Sun Tzu's *Art of War*? Not quite. Sure, in some cases there's nothing wrong with a little strategic planning, but in many cases a simple surprise broadsword to the head can work just as well.

However, there would be no blunt broadswords on this one, not for Alvin. Not for Lorelei. For them I'm going to bake a cake. It took well into the night, but I felt I had developed a plan worthy of Pizarro's conquest of the Incan Empire. Okay, that might be an overstatement, but I was exhausted and I'd had a few drinks.

It was 3:00 a.m., but I sent Alvin a message. "I have found a way, give me a call. Come by early tomorrow morning. Bonnie will be here."

The next morning, he was sitting in my boardroom with Bonnie and a cup of coffee.

"Alvin, look, I'm sorry to be in such a rush, but I have a trial starting its second day, and I need to get to court, but I have some stuff for you to sign. I don't have time to explain, just sign. Trust me."

He only had one question. "What do you need?"

"Your signature on this retainer, $500 for disbursements and your signature on these affidavits and documents."

"Five hundred bucks? I don't want charity, Andrew. I can get the money. I moved some stuff around. I have $15,000 now and I can get more."

"Not necessary, I'm going to do it on contingency." I threw some air quotes on *contingency* with a smile.

Bonnie could not believe that I had just uttered those words. Her eyebrows shot up with good reason as she muttered, "I need a cigarette." First, for years I had always asked for a minimum of $10,000 up front, and second, contingency fees are actually against the rules in family law cases. Specifically banned by statute.

"Alvin, I have worded your retainer so it says this is not a family law matter—instead, I have described it is a 'property recovery' matter—and it says I reserve the right to charge a 'results achieved fee.'" It was splitting hairs but basically it was a contingency fee. Close enough.

"Are you sure? I can't sell the ring to pay you. I can't do that . . . I have some money . . . "

"Don't worry. Bonnie has some stuff for you to sign and I need to get ready for court. What you'll be signing is an Application to court, some affidavits and other stuff. I'm bringing a motion without notice to Ms. Novak . . . *ex parte*. Bonnie can walk you through it. I gotta get into my gowns. Oh . . . is Ms. Novak at court today and tomorrow?"

"Yup, today at Old City Hall in the afternoon and tomorrow in the morning. I'm pretty sure. I can check."

"Bonnie, once you get this signed, I am going to take it with me to 393 this morning and get it issued before the McGovern trial opens."

"Isn't that pushing it a little?" Bonnie gave me one of those looks as if to say haste makes waste.

"I can swing it. Just get me the docs and a cheque for issuance before I go. And call Nick. I want him to serve this stuff." Nick Alafrate is my go-to guy when there is a tricky service involved. He's like a heat-seeking missile and simply will not be denied. One time he dressed up like a nurse and served a guy who was in a bed at Mount Sinai, getting chemo. Another time he served an entire family at a funeral. The best part is listening to him recount the story of how he did it and their reactions. Hilarious.

I took the application to the Family Law counter at 393 University and had it issued. I asked the clerk, who has known me for years, "It's a little early, I know, but any chance Madam Justice Grandmaitre is in her office this morning? I would like her to hear my *ex parte* motion." She's an older woman, has been sitting for about twenty years, widowed, had a bit of a stroke a few years ago, so the local senior judge lets her work in her office most of the time. I would say she is a little on the old-fashioned side. Her office is lined with pictures of her fifteen grandchildren. Perfect judge.

I sat quietly in her office while she read Alvin's affidavit about the ring's history and his grandmother. *Ex parte* motions are not easy. The reasons for not giving notice to the person involved need to be compelling. I was primed to answer any questions. I could see Grandmaitre's jaw clench and unclench as she read. After she turned over the last page of Alvin's affidavit, she looked up and glanced around the room at all the pictures. There were no questions; she simply signed my order as drafted and handed it to me with a frown. "Good luck."

Once back in the hall, I called Bonnie to get Nick to meet me on the ninth floor to pick up the documents for service on Ms. Novak. I called Kaplan to let her know I was in the building appearing before Justice Grandmaitre on an emergency (admittedly of my own making) and that I might be a few minutes late for McGovern's trial, day two. I called Patrick to let him know I was in the building and was on the way. I looked at my watch: 9:57 a.m. I was running on about four hours sleep and now faced a full day of trial. I headed for the elevator to the ninth floor and stepped in to find Patrick alone and dressed exactly as asked. Well done. He was learning. The only thing different about him was a small round Band-Aid now replaced the toilet paper wad beneath his bottom lip. Things were looking up.

Kaplan spent the morning examining Laurie in chief, taking her through some of the financial documents, the problems she was having with the family's finances, and the kids. It was boring stuff about the money problems, which Laurie was trying to manage all by herself, but I could see that Kaplan was building her evidence toward the "big moment" when Laurie caught Patrick with the nanny. I knew what was coming, but Bracken had no idea. Kaplan wanted to deliver a real shocker of a blow, that kind of moment when a judge makes up his or her mind about a person. Done properly, it is a moment from which the client cannot recover. Alchemy of cookie into vinegar.

I had reason to be nervous. You see, there was a particular morning in the McGovern household that brought the marriage down like a teetering Jenga tower. Laurie was working away at the dining room table, kids were running all over the place, looking for breakfast and fighting, just as she opened some unpaid bills and discovered that once again there was no money in the account to pay them. She stormed all over the house looking for Patrick, only to find him cuddled up with Selena Grande in the nanny's bed, sound asleep in the afterglow. There was quite a scene that followed, and Kaplan wanted to lay it out in all its dirty glory.

I waited patiently but as she approached the "climax," so to speak, I stood up to break her momentum and asked politely, "I'm sorry to interrupt my friend, Your Honour, but would this be a good time to take the lunch break?" Bracken, with a grateful smile, quickly agreed and adjourned the court. I mean, even judges have to take a pee. As we shuffled out into the hallway and the clerk locked the courtroom doors, Kaplan threw darts at me with her eyes as if to say, "You fucker." I just shrugged and smiled. *Jenga.*

When I dialled the office, Bonnie picked up on the first ring. "How is it going? I'm pretty clear here, so I thought maybe I could pop over and watch a bit of the trial in the afternoon."

"Bonnie, not today. I need you there to deal with Alvin's matter. Any word from Nick?"

I could feel her usual disappointment. "I'll let him tell you what happened. He is waiting for your call."

After parking Patrick in a safe spot, I called Nick. "Well?"

"Oh, man. You gotta minute?"

"Just a few, but I'm all ears. We're on the lunch break at a trial."

"OK. So, I dressed up like an air-conditioning repairman, you know, overalls, yellow vest, tool belt, and waited in the stairwell at Old City Hall until she came out of the courtroom to speak to a witness. I pretended to be inspecting something but walked over and just stood near her. I got close enough to see she was wearing the ring. I asked, 'Hey, are you that famous Crown attorney Lorelei Novak?' She actually looked proud when she turned to me with a big smile and said, 'Yes, but hardly famous.' So I handed her the paperwork and said, 'Well you're gonna be famous after this.'"

"Beautiful." This is why I use him. He has that extra touch.

"I mean, she was shocked. No smile now. Then she flips through the paperwork quickly and snarls at me, 'Tell him he will never see that fucking ring again.' So I said, 'Maybe you should read that order from Justice Grandmaitre, especially the part about the trustee.' I had your trustee guy waiting with me, and he stepped forward with his copy of the order and his ID. I thought she was going to blow a head gasket . . . I mean, she just stared at us in a blind rage."

The order I got from Grandmaitre provided that Lorelei had to turn the ring over to an appointed trustee forthwith for safekeeping until further order of the court. That was my brainwave late last night. I was worried that if she got notice of the Application, she would "lose" the ring. Alvin's affidavit had a photo of the ring and an old appraisal attached so the trustee could ID the ring.

"The trustee looked at her finger and said, 'Could I have that?' She slipped it off and dropped it into his hand and mouthed, 'Fuck you.' It was priceless, Bierce. Ring is safe and sound with the trustee."

I wished I could have been there to see it, but I needed to avoid the whole scene out of concern that I might accidentally turn myself into a witness, and then I wouldn't be able to act for Alvin.

Satisfied but exhausted, I sat in the hallway and dealt with a bunch of details on other matters. Before I knew it we were due back in court. Kaplan and Laurie tried to pick up the narrative from where they left off, but she never got traction again. Over just a lunch break, Bracken had lost the plot and reminded Kaplan that we have no-fault divorce and she wasn't interested in hearing about finger-pointing and allegations about affairs. And then she uttered the words I needed to hear: "Let's move on." I could see the disappointment in Laurie's eyes. She so wanted to tell her story and have some sense of catharsis, even vindication. But not today. Not on my watch.

By 4:30 p.m., we had finished all of Laurie's evidence in chief. She had told her story, but clearly Kaplan was disappointed. My cross examination would begin the next morning, and I was sure Laurie would be forewarned about how savage that could be. But I didn't feel very savage as I asked Judge Bracken if we could leave our materials in the locked courtroom overnight to save us dragging everything back to the office. Satisfied with a solid day's work, I slid a few papers into Black Beauty and sent Patrick on his way.

I stood in the hallway and for a few minutes watched Lester Donald struggle with the photocopy machine. *My God, does anything come easy to him?* Another wave of exhaustion suddenly washed over me. Adrenaline only goes so far.

My phone buzzed. It was Paul Campbell. "What's up?"

"Just a quick update. I was thinking about things, and I have decided to go for the DNA testing on Angie. You know, just as a backup . . . Can't hurt to know, right? Although I'm a little afraid . . . "

"Well, let's talk about it, let's hold off on the testing. Do you really need the expense?" I couldn't believe I was saying it. Any other case, I would have had the test results in my file long ago.

"Too late. I snipped some of Angie's hair on her last visit and sent it to a lab. They say they can turn it around in a few days."

Shit. Sean. Shit.

20

Pussycat, Pussycat

WHEN I GOT BACK TO THE OFFICE, Bonnie was gone. Her desk, as usual, was neat as a pin. She had left some notes on my desk, so I poured myself a drink and sat back to catch up on the day, scrolling through emails and flipping through letters. When I'm in a trial, everything else seems less important, less interesting. I think it must be the adrenaline highs and lows. When it's high, the day-to-day world of a law practice seems mundane. When it's low, well, the day-to-day world is mundane. Riding this rollercoaster can be a challenge; it's exhausting.

But as I opened some mail on my desk and read a letter from my favourite a-hole lawyer, Fernstein, the least of my problems was a rollercoaster. I was suddenly on a fucking rocket, and my face began to burn with rage. Teresa Savoie was suing me because of her husband's expired life insurance policy on which her OD'd ex never paid his premiums. The letter ended with the usual bullshit: *Please notify your insurer and have your lawyer contact me as soon as possible*. Fucking Teresa Savoie.

My rage was interrupted when the phone rang at 8:00 p.m. I didn't recognize the number and picked up anyway. "Andrew Bierce."

"Bierce, Randall Williams. I've been retained by Ms. Novak. I tried you earlier but couldn't get you. Do you have a minute to chat now?"

Be cool. Put your rage aside. "Sure. I've been in a trial in front of Bracken, start the third day tomorrow. Set for a couple of weeks (gross exaggeration). But I can chat for a few minutes." The last time I had seen Williams, he was sliding into a Cadillac Escalade after Keg's visitation. I still hadn't forgotten his junior lawyer's insults as I sat on the stoop next to Burdettes. Calling me a joke. I just wished I could remember who it was, except the whole night was still a drunken blur.

But this was interesting. Randall T. Williams. Senior family law lawyer with a big-shot firm over in First Canadian Place. Respected. Knows his stuff, has been to war many a time and chopped off a few heads over his thirty-plus-year career. He and I had never had the pleasure of a genuine donnybrook, so Alvin's case suddenly looked even more tantalizing. Novak must have plunked down some cash to retain him.

"I've reviewed the situation with her, and it seems clear that the ring in question was a gift. Your fellow called off the engagement, so she gets to keep it. Seems pretty straightforward. Am I missing something?"

I let him go on for a bit so he would feel like he was doing a good job for Novak. I like to be underestimated. After a few more minutes of him saying the same thing five different ways, I jumped in. "Randall, sorry to interrupt. Did you get all my materials?"

"Yes, I think so. Trustee has the ring. I'm not sure that *ex parte* order will withstand a challenge. I'm confident I can get that reversed, get the ring back and with costs. So again, am I missing something?"

Oh, clearly he was missing something, but I took a sip of bourbon and played it out a bit. "So you have my client's Affidavit of Documents?"

"Yes."

"Did you read it?"

"I scanned it. I have a junior working through it now." He hadn't read it. That's the problem with using a junior to do the grunt work. You have to wait for them to do the work and then brief you. I do it all myself so I own it, front to back.

"When can I expect your Defense and Affidavit of Documents?"

"You will get them in accordance with the Rules. She has time to defend but really . . . are we going to go down this path? What does he want? An apology? I can recommend that—"

An apology? I don't start cases in the Superior Court of Ontario to get a fucking apology. His arrogant suggestion teased my rage back to the surface, so I dropped the hammer. "I want Pussycat."

"What?"

"Pussycat. Her memoirs. I want production of her memoirs." There was a pause, and I could hear him snapping his fingers at junior lawyers and whispering as he covered the phone with his hand.

"I will need to review the manuscript with my client, but I can tell you now that I don't think it's relevant. I hear you and my client have a bit of history."

Interesting that Novak passed that tidbit on, but I was not going to take the bait and change the subject. "The memoirs are very relevant to how and why this loving engagement came apart, and frankly I'm looking forward to some interesting reading about her very active, shall we say, social life."

"Bierce. Off the record. She's a Crown. One of us, so to speak. Can we have a little professional courtesy? Cut her some slack?"

With those words, he blinked. Courtesy? Like the courtesy she showed me in court that day? *I don't think so.* "I'm going to send over an Offer to Settle in a minute. It is open for acceptance until 10:00 a.m. tomorrow."

"Ten a.m.? That's a bit much. How am I supposed to get instructions by ten? She will be in court, for Christsakes. How about a little professional courtesy?"

Again with the courtesy. "It's open until ten. I'll wait to hear from you, but I will be in trial at 10:00 a.m. tomorrow, so don't leave it till the last minute." I could hear more finger-snapping, whispering, and I'm pretty sure I heard the word "asshole."

I sent the Offer I had prepared as a part of the original package of materials. What was my Offer? Simple—Alvin gets his ring back and $25,000 for my costs. I know what you're thinking, that's a lot of money, but I didn't expect them to accept the Offer. You see, I didn't want them to accept it.

I sent Alvin a quick text. *LN has retained a lawyer, Randall Williams. Expenive. I will keep you posted.*

In less than a minute, Alvin hit back to me. *Interesting. But doesn't he have a conflict?*

You mean AllPublishing?

No. I mean the fact that he makes an energetic cameo in Chapter 4 of Pussycat.

Hello. LN and RW?!

Yup. Isn't that a conflict?

It's going to be a bumpy night.

That scoundrel Williams. What did he think he was doing? Had he read the memoirs? Had she told him he was in it? If so, he had a clear conflict in trying to keep the memoirs from being disclosed.

It was 9:00 p.m. I'd had four hours sleep in the last twenty-four, and I was still seething from Savoie's letter. I decided to work a little bit and then try to close my eyes for a few minutes before really digging in to polish my cross examination of Laurie McGovern the next day. I was going to need adrenaline, lots of adrenaline.

When I finally put my head down on my desk, I remembered my call from Paul. DNA testing. *Shit.* I had to let Sean know. I sent him a quick text.

There could be trouble. Paul decided—on his own—to get testing done.

As late as it was, it didn't take long for him to answer.

One word. *Shit.*

21

Paper Cuts

DAY THREE OF MCGOVERN'S TRIAL went better than I expected, or at least better than I deserved. I had fallen asleep at my desk and didn't wake up until nearly 3:00 a.m., so I threw myself at the prep of McGovern's cross examination until Starbucks opened. There was no time for chit-chat with Daphne; I just grabbed two tall lattes each with double shots, ignored her head shaking, and got back to my desk.

When I arrived at the courthouse, even Patrick thought I didn't look so good. "You okay, man? I'm not used to seeing you with the scruff look." He was right; I had forgotten to shave. The best I could do was splash some water on my face and crack a fresh court shirt before beating it over to the courthouse like a mad penguin.

"I'm good."

And you know what? I *was* good. The adrenaline kicked in. Sometimes, when I'm tired or hurting from a late night out, something happens, an extra gear shows up. I get focused. I can really bear down. And that's exactly what I did with poor Ms. McGovern. I drew on some of the residual rage over Teresa Savoie, and she didn't know what hit her.

There is an old Turkish proverb: *Measure a thousand times and cut once*. I have given it my own personal twist: Cut a thousand times and you don't need to worry about measurements. Disclosure of documents.

I call it death by a thousand paper cuts. Master the paperwork. If you have control of the documents, it doesn't matter what cock-and-bull story someone tries to spin or actually believes; the documents don't lie. After two hours of my cross examination, Laurie McGovern didn't know a music royalty statement from a mortgage payment. Based on what she had in front of her in the witness box, she'd spent more time highlighting documents than actually understanding them. She got so confused at one point that she started to cry and we had to take a thirty-minute break.

As soon as we were in the hall, I checked my phone. The offer on Alvin's case had expired hours ago and, as expected, I'd heard nothing from Williams. Suddenly Kaplan was at my elbow and suggested we adjourn for the day and think about settling. Right. Suddenly settling is a great idea because your client melted on cross. I wasn't falling for that B.S. . . . adjourn and ruin the momentum of my cross examination? I don't think so. It's a manoeuvre experienced trial lawyers play on younger counsel. Right in the middle of a trial the senior lawyer suggests a settlement offer may be coming in the morning, The junior lawyer stops working, thinking why spend the night preparing if the case is going to settle anyway? Of course, no settlement offer was intended and none arrives. The next morning the young lawyer is unprepared, off his game. I've done it a dozen times over the years and even to one lawyer twice in the same trial. Some people are just slow learners. But as I thought about it, Kaplan wasn't like that. She was a straight shooter, not slippery enough to try to sandbag me with phony settlement discussions. Maybe there was something there. Maybe. I hid any interest and instead told her to grab a box of tissues for her client as I intended to press on after the break. "And Leslie, you can tell her the hard part is about to begin."

She looked at me with a mixture of disgust and disdain. "Nice, Bierce, real nice. You're something else."

Truth be told, a settlement would be very much in Patrick's interest. As much time as we had spent rehearsing his testimony (of course we rehearse testimony), I was not confident he would be a much better witness than his poor wife. Playing guitar well and writing catchy tunes is not a strong indicator of emotional intelligence. Witness Nickelback.

I parked Black Beauty outside the courtroom, threw my phone on top of it, and wandered over to catch up with the ever present, not really present Lester Donald. He was limping around the ninth floor in his gowns, which were so wrinkled they must have been carried to court in his wallet. But I noticed that there was a kind of spring in his wonky step, so I asked him about the outcome of his common-law case in Brampton. Mistake. He started to ramble on about the facts and couldn't recall who the judge was or any of the cases I had mentioned to him. I was afraid he was about to tell me that he had botched the whole thing when my burbling phone saved me. "Hold that thought, Lester . . . " I darted over to my phone. Maybe Alvin's engagement ring was going to take a turn for the better.

I looked at the phone. Five missed calls, all from Bonnie. I called her back. "Seriously, five calls? What's up?"

"Oh my God . . . " It sounded like she was crying.

"Bonnie, what happened?"

"Paul Campbell . . . " More blubbering.

"What? What about him?"

"His daughter . . . Angie . . . " I think she dropped the phone.

"Jesus Christ, Bonnie, what the f . . . Calm down. Tell me what happened."

Bonnie could barely get the words out through her sobbing. "She's dead."

22

Put Salt in Their Wounds

"DEAD? WHAT DO YOU MEAN DEAD?" It sounded so stupid as I said it.

"She's dead!" Bonnie was practically screaming at me. "Paul's at SickKids right now. He's been calling the office nonstop. I've been trying to reach you. He needs you at the hospital."

"Where is he?" I felt exhausted, as if a huge weight was pressing me into the floor.

"I told you he's at SickKids. What's wrong with you?!"

"Bonnie, stop shouting at me. Do you know what happened?"

"No, they are trying to figure it out now. You need to get to the hospital."

Leslie Kaplan walked over and told me they wanted us back in court in five minutes. I looked at Patrick, who for some reason was chatting and laughing with Laurie. God, I hoped they weren't thinking about getting back together. How was I supposed to carry on with a brutal cross when they looked like that? And when I needed to get to the hospital. "Leslie, were you serious about a settlement offer? No sandbagging?"

"Bierce, you know me better than that. Laurie's had enough of this shitshow. Both of them look like they've had enough. Look at them, a couple of happy idiots."

"Okay. I can recommend a short adjournment to Patrick on the understanding you'll have something to me by 5:00 p.m. today. No B.S. If there's no realistic offer we will be back here tomorrow. Will that work?"

"I'll make it work."

"Okay. Do you mind advising Bracken? She may not be happy having an adjournment on short notice."

"I'll look after it. We can tell her that—"

"No, I have to go."

"What?" She gave me a weird look. "Go where?"

"I just have to go." I looked over at Lester, who appeared to be checking to see if there was a bit of change left in the copier coin return. I called to him. "Lester, can you speak to something for me?" He toddled over. I asked if he could sit in with Kaplan and advise the court that I supported the adjournment and that I had a client emergency.

Lester looked like I'd asked him to co-counsel an appeal to the Supreme Court of Canada. "Absolutely, Bierce. I'm on it. What's the emergency?"

"Just tell Bracken I agree and look after my stuff in the courtroom." Without another word he marched—somewhat—into the courtroom.

I explained the possible settlement situation to Patrick, who seemed content, and called Bonnie as I went to the elevator. "Tell Paul I'm on the way. Text me his number."

I ran three blocks up University Avenue to SickKids and called Paul as I came through the front door. "Paul, Bierce. I'm here at the hospital. What the hell is going on? I heard about Angie. What happened? Where are you?"

He sounded in shock. "I can't talk right now. We're not allowed to use cellphones where I am—we are just off the Emergency."

"We? Who else is there?"

"Chloe's here with her lawyer. The police too. She says I killed Angie . . ."

"Okay, wait for me. And don't say a word to the police."

I hung up, dialled Alvin and left a message for him to meet me in Emerg at SickKids to deal with a client who might have a serious criminal problem or at least to call me back.

The scene in Emergency was insane. And speaking of crazy, Chloe was huddled in a corner with her mental case mother wrapped around her and the equally mental Fernstein storming around, shouting commands like he was the hospital's CEO. Three cops were standing in a circle, making notes. Doctors and nurses were running in five different directions. No sooner did I walk in and Chloe leapt out of her seat, sobbing and screaming. She darted across the waiting area and tried to throw herself at Paul and me but was blocked by two paramedics who were wheeling in a little girl who had been shot at a local playground. Her mother collapsed at my feet as I grabbed Paul and pulled him around a corner to find out what had happened.

He was so pale, I thought he might collapse himself. His words were barely a whisper, "Chloe dropped off Angie at about ten this morning. She was late, as usual. We had words. We've been following the new court order you got from Judge Newsome, you know where you got me more time with Angie."

At the last court appearance I had creamed Chloe—and Fernstein for good measure. After Judge Newsome heard about the movie theatre arrest and Paul's time in the Don Jail, he expanded his access hours with Angie. I could tell that Newsome recalled the case from our first appearance.

When Paul said he wanted to "fucking annihilate her," I took serious steps, so to speak. I really spelled it out in brutal terms for Newsome; admittedly, I did embellish what happened at criminal court and in the Don. Paul wanted results, and he got them. Chloe didn't know what hit her and to pour salt in her wounds, I sought maximum punitive costs. Losing that motion cost her a cool $50,000. It practically covered my bill to Paul.

As we left the court that victorious day, I had said sarcastically to Fernstein but just loud enough for Chloe to hear, "On the upside, now she'll have more time for cleaning the house." More salt, I know, but again, Paul and I were on a bit of a high. Chloe went ballistic and threatened to report me to the Law Society. Paul, on the other hand, was thrilled with the increased time because the current visits had not been very enjoyable. Angie would just nap through the afternoon visit, and he was basically babysitting. So this was going to be a big improvement in having some quality time.

Paul carried on in a daze. "The first full day Chloe dropped her off, it was the same thing. She slept all day. I texted her and asked if Angie had slept the night before. I wouldn't put it past her to keep her up all night just to have her sleep through my time."

"What did she say?"

He showed me a text. *If you can't look after MY daughter, then bring her back to me ASAP!!!*

"It was the same thing each day; Angie would just sleep. I had her tucked in on the couch beside me this morning while I watched TV, waiting for her to wake up. Then I noticed she wasn't moving. I felt her, she was limp, not breathing. I called 911 and they came but . . . she was gone . . . " He broke down in my arms crying. I could hear Chloe screaming at the doctors around the corner.

As I held him I was afraid to ask, but I whispered, "Paul, did you happen to get the DNA test results?"

He stiffened and looked at me with disgust. Without saying a word, he reached into his pocket and handed me a crushed but unopened envelope. "I haven't looked at the results. I just picked it up at the lab. I haven't the heart to look. It never ends for you, does it? She was my daughter, Bierce . . . I just know it."

"I know. I know." I folded the envelope and slid it into the pocket of my waistcoat.

In the midst of all the chaos, Alvin came around the corner. "Alvin, what are you doing here?"

"You called me."

"Oh God, sorry, I forgot, I'm exhausted. It's crazy here. This is Paul Campbell, the guy you helped me get out of the Don Jail." I filled in Alvin as Paul sat in a daze. More cops and detectives arrived, and I edged closer to their huddle with the doctors. I introduced myself to a tiny woman cop. She stepped back, looked me up and down as I stood there in my court pants, waistcoat, and still wearing my court shirt and white tabs and said, "Oh, so you're the divorce lawyer . . . a little overdressed aren't we Counsel?" I could see that Chloe had told this cop her side of the story, and Ms. MiniCop had already decided who was guilty.

"I came here directly from court." Why was I explaining myself to her?

"Your client has a problem . . . two domestic violence arrests."

"He was not convicted. Those charges are B.S."

"Right, the charges are always B.S. You guys are unbelievable."

As we stared each other down, two more doctors came out from one of the medical bays and called us over to a conference in a curtained-off area. Paul, me, Alvin, Chloe (now being physically supported by Ms. MiniCop), Chloe's mom, Fernstein, and the cops were all crammed into this little area. We could hardly hear a word anyone was saying as the woman whose little girl had been shot screamed in the next medical bay. Honestly, it was like a bad episode of *Law and Order*. The doctor in the middle, a little guy, looked through a sheaf of papers on his clipboard and said, "The test results show that this little girl overdosed on . . . dextromethorphan."

With his heavy accent and all the screaming next door, it was hard to make out what he said, so there were a few seconds of silence until Paul said, "What's that?"

The doctor looked up and said, "Cough medicine."

"Cough medicine? Where would she get cough medicine? She didn't have a cough . . . " Paul looked at the floor, puzzled at what the doctor said. He kept repeating it over and over: "Cough medicine? Cough medicine?"

The doctor looked straight at Chloe and Paul. "This little girl was marinated in cough syrup. She had five times the acceptable limit for an adult, never mind an infant."

Paul looked at Chloe. "Cough medicine? Did you give her cough medicine so she would sleep through my visits?"

The group turned and looked at Chloe. She took a step back, looking like a cornered animal. She snarled at me and Paul, "It's your fault . . . You wouldn't leave her with me . . . I'm her mother . . . You can't take care of her like I do . . . You and your . . . your . . . hired gun . . . It's your fault she's dead . . . "

Chloe's mother suddenly turned and with one punch knocked her daughter to the floor. As she went down, her mom landed two more hard punches directly to her face. It took every cop present to pull her mother off and in doing so probably saved Chloe's face, if not her life.

Alvin grabbed Paul before he could jump into the brawl and cautioned him to say nothing. We watched as they cuffed Chloe and her mother on the floor of Emergency. Ms. MiniCop avoided my eyes, but as she frog-marched Chloe out, I couldn't resist, "Good work, Officer. You're a real crime fighter." No response, of course.

Alvin stood with his arm around Paul, who suddenly looked half his normal size. A combination of grief and hate were crushing him, shrinking him before our eyes. I moved toward him and tried to put my arm around his shoulders, but he stiffened suddenly and turned to look at me. His eyes were red and dead. "Bierce, you went too far. Look what you did . . . You went too far . . . " Whatever words followed were swamped by his tears.

That was it. I felt like I had been punched in the stomach. The last ounce of adrenaline was long gone. It was two o'clock in the afternoon. I'd had four hours sleep in the last two days. I had nothing left and sat down amid the crying and chaos of the Emergency. My phone burbled and instinctively I answered. "Andrew Bierce."

"Bierce, it's Randall Williams. We need to talk. I have my instructions. But I'll tell you now she won't produce the memoirs." I was too tired to answer. "Bierce, are you there? We need to talk."

"I'll call you when I get back to the office . . . " I ended the call and in a daze scrolled through my emails and texts. I saw one from Kaplan. *Can't get an offer to you until later tonight. Working on it.* And then another from Lester Donald. My first reaction was one of surprise that he even knew how to use email, but then I read it. *Bierce, call me when you can. I think I overheard Kaplan and her client laughing about sending you an offer tonight. I don't think they're sending one. I think it's a sandbag . . .* I kept scrolling. An email from the Law Society. Savoie had reported me for misconduct, followed by one from Fernstein demanding I get a lawyer to defend her negligence claim, one from Bonnie reminding me that the husband's Answer in the septic tank condom case was due soon, and several texts from Alvin earlier in the day telling me that Lorelei had been texting and emailing him nonstop all night.

Before leaving the hospital, I texted Sean. *I'm at the hospital with Paul and I have the DNA test results. Paul hasn't seen them yet.*

Why are you at the hospital?

Angie is dead.

Remember what I said about an extra gear that kicks in? It kicked in hard, real hard.

23

Circle of Life

IT WAS 5:00 P.M. by the time I got back to the office. I tried to put that awful scene with Paul out of my head, so I poured a drink and sent Williams an email. *I'm back at the office.* My phone rang within minutes.

"Bierce, what's it going to take to wrap this thing up? It's a dog's breakfast."

Suddenly everything is a dog's breakfast when your client is in a jam. "You have my offer."

"I know, but seriously, what does your guy want? She's not giving up the memoirs. Let's not make things harder than they have to be. I have reviewed the . . . "

As he rambled on, I saw another text from Alvin. *Everything OK? LN won't stop texting me.*

I sent a text back. *Leave this with me. Do not answer her. It's under control.*

I interrupted Williams. "If it's not going to settle, let's talk about the memoirs."

"It's simple, she will not produce them. She cannot. It would ruin her career. And off the record . . . she acknowledges that she named names, but she was planning on changing all the names before she published . . . if she ever did publish."

"Here is what is simple: if I serve an appointment to examine Ms. Novak under oath, I will ask her why Alvin terminated the engagement, and she will describe his reading of the memoirs. I will ask what was so offensive and to see the memoirs, she will refuse, and when she refuses to produce them, I will seek an order to have her produce them. I will be successful. I will also seek and get costs. We both know that. Do I really need to draw a map on this? Besides, I have another means of getting the memoirs in draft form . . . "

"Like how?"

"Ask your client about Mr. Morris."

"Who?"

"Tom Morris, her mentor at Humber."

I heard him put his hand over the phone and ask, "Morris?" And then Ms. Novak yelling very distinctly, "Leave him out of this!"

Williams came back on the phone. "You heard that?"

"Yeah. So she's there with you?"

"Yes."

"Tell her I have a motion ready to go to examine Morris as a third-party witness because he has drafts of the memoirs. If he can read them, why can't I? There's no privilege or confidentiality. The ring is tied to the cause of the relationship ending; the memoirs are the cause, they are relevant, they have no protection. I'll get them from Ms. Novak or Mr. Morris, or both, if I'm good. You know who he is married to, right? Isn't AllPublishing one of your clients?"

"Yes . . . "

"Technically, I guess 'anyone' mentioned in the memoirs would be a potential witness. Someone might be asked to confirm or deny whether what is said about them in the memoirs is true or not. There could be defamatory statements in there . . . if they were untrue of course. Once the memoirs are produced, I would then be in a better position to make a list of everyone mentioned in the memoirs and then determine who is a potential witness or not." There was a very long pause. "I hope you don't have a conflict of interest . . . "

"Let me talk to her. I'll call you back."

"Our operators are standing by . . . "

"Fuck off."

I emailed Lester and asked him to give me a call ASAP. I needed to hear more about Ms. Kaplan and her client. To my surprise, the phone rang within minutes. "Lester, how are you, my friend?"

"Great. Thanks for letting me handle that for you today. I think it went pretty well."

Jesus Christ, it was a fucking adjournment. "That's great, Lester. I expect you to invoice me for your time." Not really, but it couldn't hurt to say so. Maybe I can grab him a loaded Tims card sometime. "What's this about Kaplan and her client laughing?" Lester proceeded to explain in way too much detail what I feared most. Kaplan apparently had no intention of making an offer. She was trying to fuck me so I would not be prepared for tomorrow. Big mistake. Who did she think she was dealing with? I had perfected that dodge.

"What're you going to do, Bierce? You could probably get an adjournment and give yourself time to prep. How was your emergency? What happened? Are you okay?"

"Ms. Kaplan needs to learn a lesson . . . " As I was about to explain, I could see Williams calling on the other line. "Sorry, Lester, I gotta take a call. I will call you back."

"Okay, if you need anything . . . "

I picked up the phone. "Andrew Bierce."

"It's me."

"Who is this?"

"Fuck off. She will return the ring." Williams didn't sound very happy, but I'm guessing he had twisted her arm once he realized the prospect of trying to keep the ring was going to cause a big problem with his partners and AllPublishing and an even bigger one for himself. I began to wonder if there was more to Novak's retainer of him than I first thought. I had assumed that she had plunked down an old-fashioned cash retainer, but maybe she had an arrangement. Maybe she told him he had as much of an interest in keeping them out of the public eye as she did. I made a mental note to ask Alvin to give me his best recollection of the names he saw in her memoirs. Who else had an interest in protecting their privacy?

"I'm glad she took your recommendation . . . ," I couldn't resist, "whatever your reasons for making it. It's for the best. Now, let's talk about costs?"

"Don't be an asshole. She's not paying costs. You're getting the ring, count your blessings."

"My offer expired, and it's not open for acceptance anymore unless costs are paid. However, I do want to get the matter wrapped up so I can get back to preparing for my trial tomorrow. I'll accept $10,000 for costs, and I'll do all the paperwork to dismiss the matter."

"Are you nuts? Ten grand? Your client hasn't incurred costs to that extent."

"If your offer to settle does not include costs, then I'll need the memoirs."

"She will give you the ring."

"Yes, you said that, but I need costs. I don't work for free."

"Yes, I've heard about your fees. I will not get instructions to pay your costs. She is a Crown attorney, for Christsakes. She hasn't got that kind of cash. She's already getting a bill from me, and I slashed my fees out of professional courtesy."

"I'm sure you did."

"What's that supposed to mean?"

"We both know what it means. She should have just returned the ring when Alvin asked for it, instead of all this fucking around."

"Where is she supposed to get ten grand?"

I was hoping he would say that. "Wait. I have an alternative. I will email you a solution, but it will be a final offer. She can take it or you can start copying those memoirs."

"You're something else. I'll watch for your offer."

I typed the new terms into an email, marked it without prejudice, and hit *send*. I figured it would take a few minutes for them to digest it, so I called Patrick McGovern. "Hey, sorry about today. Laurie's lawyer said she was sending an offer to settle, but I think it's bullshit. So we're on for tomorrow. Same clothes for another day. Are you good to go?"

"Yes, I guess . . . How long is this going to go on? What was the emergency today? You okay?"

"Nothing. I'm fine. We're just getting started. The accountant and music execs will take a few days to explain how your royalties work. By the way, you and Laurie looked pretty chummy when I was getting ready to leave. You make my job harder when you play nice with her. She needs to sweat, lose some sleep tonight. I was worried you were thinking about getting back together—"

"Well . . . actually—"

"What? Seriously? After all this crap?"

"I don't know. Maybe, my girlfriend would kill me. She thinks we are gonna get married when this is all over."

"Are you?"

"Of course not. You think I'm nuts? Laurie is worried I'm going to do something stupid like propose. She suggests getting back together all the time, especially after we have been you know. . . you know . . . intimate a few times."

"What? When? Recently?"

"Couple of nights ago. Whenever I go over to see the kids, sometimes things get a little carried away."

"Things? You are in the middle of a trial. Why didn't you tell me?"

"We agreed to leave the lawyers out of it. Now that I have cleaned up a bit, dropped the teen rocker look, she told me that she thought we should get back together for the kids. She said Kaplan told her not to do it. She said that she should go through the trial, get a court order to split the assets, get support locked in, and then we could think about getting back together. That way she would have the family back together, but her share of the money would be locked in. I don't know, but that sounds crazy. What's she going to get if we go ahead with the trial?"

"Half your royalties, plus probably $10 million, low end . . . $25 million high end, plus support. That's what I've been saying for months. I've just been stalling the inevitable. What's more important? Royalties or getting back together?"

"I don't know . . . both? I want both . . . I guess. They're getting ready to release the acoustic live version of my hits. You know, sort of like Nirvana did . . . *Unplugged*. There should be a gush of cash from that . . . Canadian Rock and Roll Hall of Fame . . . I might have the ballots this year. Alanis clipped me in 2015, but with a new release . . . could be my year. Jann Arden wants me to guest on her TV show too. It's all coming back . . . "

All I could think was that his child support and spousal support payments were going to skyrocket if he started coming into even more cash. "Does Laurie know about the business plan? The new release? The Hall?"

"No, no way . . . it's hush-hush. We've been sitting on it so there'd be a big splash in the fall."

The phone rang, and I could see Williams's number. "Patrick, I have another call coming in. I have to take it. Let me think on this a bit. I'll call you back. But don't talk to Laurie tonight."

"That'll be tough, cuz I'm over here right now. She's just putting the kids to bed . . . Then it's snuggle time . . . "

"Jesus, okay, just don't tell her what we have been discussing. I will call you back."

"Later . . . "

I picked up the phone. "Andrew Bierce."

"You're one big asshole."

"I think you mentioned that before."

"Where do you get the balls?" I could hear Novak crying in the background. Crying. Now she knew why I told her to pray that she was never in my house.

"Mr. Williams. I'm shocked. Whatever happened to civility in the profession?"

"People like you came along, Bierce, people like you came along."

"Now you're hurting my feelings."

"Feelings? How about she made a mistake and she's prepared to return the ring."

"Please. My last offer was pretty clear, and it was final."

"Okay. She accepts. But it is totally against my recommendation. You know, Bierce, what goes around comes around."

"Yeah, whatever, circle of life. Are we done? I have to get ready for trial tomorrow."

"We're done."

"I'll send you an email to confirm and then pop in to see Judge Grandmaitre tomorrow morning before my trial starts. I'll get an order on consent dismissing the action and allowing the trustee to release the ring. I'll pop by your office later to pick up the paperwork and the costs. Oh, and can you do me one small favour?"

"I'm not inclined to do fuck-all for you, Bierce. What?"

"You know that associate of yours, the one who was at Keg's funeral with you?"

He paused. "Larson? Steve Larson? What's he got to do with this?"

"Larson, yeah that's the guy. Outside Keg's funeral, he told me I was a fucking joke Q.C. Do me a favour, show him the paperwork on this one, will you, and then tell him to go fuck himself."

The line went dead.

A text from Alvin popped up on my phone. *You OK? LN just posted some very unkind things about you.* I called him right away.

"I'm good. We're done for the night. Maybe meet tomorrow for lunch? Steps of Old City Hall? It depends on whether my trial goes ahead tomorrow."

"Sure . . . but . . . what . . . "

"See you then. I gotta go."

It was nearly eight thirty. No offer from Ms. Kaplan. I poured a drink and put my feet up. It took a few minutes and another drink, but I had an idea. I texted Patrick. *Can you slip away for a quick call in 15 minutes?*

Yup. What's up dude?

You remember how you wanted both? I have an idea.

Cool.

I was still dressed in my court clothes and felt something in the pocket of my waistcoat. I pulled Paul's crumpled envelope out and stared at it. I tore it open and spread the two-page DNA test results out on my desk. I'd read a hundred of these over the years and went straight to the bottom line. I read it, sat back, and wondered, "Does he really want to know? Does it even matter now?"

24

Wedding Bell Blues

I POURED A SHORT ONE, waited a half hour, and then sent Kaplan a short, chatty email. *Sorry, I had to leave in a rush today. Looking forward to your offer. Off the record, I'm struggling with trying to dovetail any potential settlement of our matter with a prenup for Patrick. When he marries his girl-friend, I'll be damned if he shares all his royalties again! Some clients can't wait to jump back in with both feet. LOL I'm not sure who'll be providing the ILA on it for the nanny . . . er, I mean fiancée.*

It took a few minutes for her to hit back. *No problem. Didn't realize he'd set a date. Offer should be ready shortly.*

She could save her B.S. for someone younger, so I sent an emoji of a bottle of champagne and wedding bells and let the idea marinate with Kaplan. I called Patrick. "Can you speak?"

"Yeah, I'm out by the pool. Laurie's inside opening a bottle of wine."

"Are you prepared to play a little Texas Hold 'em with Laurie and her lawyer?"

"I guess . . . "

"If Laurie asks about you getting married, about setting a date, say nothing. Don't say yes. Don't say no. Say nothing. Change the subject."

"Okay, not a problem. I'm pretty sure she has other things on her mind for tonight anyway."

"We'll see. That might change in a few minutes."

I sent Kaplan another email. *You've got a pretty good read on Laurie. Do you think there would be a problem if Patrick brought the kids on their honeymoon? His bride-to-be is all over these kids and insists they be at their destination wedding. As their nanny I assume she had a pretty tight relationship with them. Is that going to be a problem? We could deal with it in your Offer and Patrick's holiday time with the kids . . . by the way, I'm still sitting here on hold waiting for it . . . When can I expect something?*

I emailed Bonnie the details of Alvin's settlement and asked her to come in extra early and prepare the paperwork. It was late, but she responded within minutes. "Are you kidding me?"

I sent her the devil emoji and waited for a call.

It took about fifteen minutes, but the phone rang. It was Patrick. "Holy shit! What did you do? I'm outside locked in my car in my underwear, and my shoes and pants are in the pool. She went fuckin' nuts . . . She accused me of everything in the book. Oh my God. I think the police might be on the way. The neighbours had to have heard that—"

"Patrick, Patrick, calm down. Promise me you didn't say anything about remarriage or your new career developments?"

"No. I couldn't get a word in edgewise. I just ran . . . She bounced a bottle of wine off the hood of my car . . . "

"Okay, sit tight. Can you just drive around the block for a minute?"

"Yeah, I gotta get out of here before she comes back or the cops get here."

I hung up the phone and waited. It rang. "Andrew Bierce."

"Leslie Kaplan."

"Hey, I'm sitting here waiting for your offer. What's up?"

"I just called Laurie to ask about something in our offer. I mentioned his remarriage. Did you know that your client is over there right now?"

"What the hell . . . Why's he there? I told him to get a good night's sleep because we might have to go back to court tomorrow if the matter doesn't settle. Is everything okay?"

"Well, off the record?"

"Sure, what's up?"

"My client was hoping they would get back together . . . "

"Seriously? What do you mean? After this trial? Why would they do that? That's crazy. I've been telling him to move on. He wanted to get back together too, but with the trial and the bitterness . . . I told him to forget about Laurie . . . Life with the nanny could work if he has a prenup."

"This wedding stuff has hit her pretty hard . . . honeymoon plans . . . kids . . . She is very unhappy."

"But is she really serious? I mean, their kids would be very confused . . . reconcile in the middle of a trial? Crazy."

"She wants to do it for the kids. She just needs financial security, and she wants him too. She wants both. He seems to have settled down a bit. You've had a positive influence on him." Wow. I can't recall the last time someone said that to me.

It was time to bait the hook. "Well, I have tried to settle him down. Look, I'm just thinking out loud here, but what if I could persuade him to call this wedding off? Maybe give Laurie some financial security? What if he rolled over a couple of million into her RRSP? Would she . . . you know . . . stop the trial and get back together? I mean, obviously I have no instructions from my client . . . and he would take it hard if he had to tell his fiancée that there would not be a wedding. I think a lot of stuff has been paid for, it's a destination wedding. I'm the one who has pressured him to move on, albeit with a marriage contract. I would be taking a little heat on that."

"Let me talk to her."

"Okay, I'll sit tight until I hear from you."

I called Patrick. "Where are you?"

"I'm parked at the corner of our street, what's going on?"

"Sit tight. I'll get back to you. And I need to spend up to $5 million of your money. No questions asked."

"What do I get for $5 million?"

"Maybe what you wanted . . . Both."

It was past ten, and I was coming down from an adrenaline high. I put my head down on my desk and fell asleep. Forty-five minutes later, the phone rang. I let it ring a few times. "Andrew Bierce."

"It's Leslie. I have instructions."

"It's very late, Leslie. I've been working nonstop getting ready for tomorrow. I assumed when I hadn't heard from you that—"

"Listen, here is the deal, and I'm not crazy about it. He calls off the wedding immediately. They reconcile. They get back into counselling, the whole family. Two million won't cut it. But if he rolls over $3.5 million into her RRSPs and puts $350,000 into an account for her, we can settle this thing. The cash is hers and hers alone. They both consent to a dismissal of the Application."

"She releases the rest of his property for good? No costs. If she wants this deal, I cannot recommend it without a full release and no costs. We would need to put it in a marriage contract for them."

"Agreed. They would need a contract. Okay. Full release. No costs. She wants him back and she wants financial security. She wants both. Period. I'll send you an email confirming the settlement. And, by the way, I'm having her sign a release saying she's not going to sue me in six months if the wheels come off."

My stomach churned at the thought of Savoie suing me. I really needed to find a lawyer to take on my defence, but everyone I asked was tied up on other matters. "Hang on, hang on. I need to track Patrick down . . . get instructions. I don't know if he'll do that deal, but I'll do my best. I know it is probably best for this family but . . . I can only do so much."

"Do your best, Bierce."

I did my best and we did that deal. What a joke. I was ready to go to $5 million.

Footnote. Patrick actually saved about $15 million and probably another $10 million on what came his way with the release of the acoustic greatest hits album, a new release for a CBC movie soundtrack he scored (titled *Annus Mirabilis*, did you see it? Me neither), and the bump from his entry into the Hall of Fame. (I got an invite.) I premium-billed him on the millions-plus that I had saved him.

So that evening I sat and enjoyed these happy endings. Patrick and Laurie ended up back in the pool with a fresh bottle of wine. I didn't have to go back to court in the morning. Grandma's ring was coming back to

Alvin. I poured one last drink and sat back to savour the day. Happy clients and lots of rice. I had both, too.

Well, at least until Sean texted me at midnight.

Well?

I let him hang. Why spoil the moment?

25

Paint by Numbers

BONNIE WOKE ME UP when she stuck her head into my office at 8:00 a.m. I had slept in a chair, thinking there was no point driving home to just come back in a few hours. "Bierce, are you okay? It's 8:00 a.m. Aren't you off to court this morning?"

"Bonnie, thanks for coming in. Can you get Alvin's consent order drafted? I need it this morning to get the order."

"I've been here since seven. Everything is ready to go. What happened with McGovern? Don't you have to appear on that?"

"Settled late last night. Kaplan sent a confirming email. I'll forward it to you. Lester Donald is going to attend and speak to the adjournment while I go see Madam Justice Grandmaitre about Alvin's ring."

"Lester Donald? Your new best friend?"

"Very funny. It's easy, and he can do it. It's impossible to screw up."

"Are you paying him?"

"I'll throw something his way. He's a happy idiot."

"You're awful."

"I need the order from Grandmaitre, then I can flip it to the trustee, grab the ring, and swing by Williams's office to get the rest of it wrapped up. That visit with Williams may take some extra time. He and I will need to sit and have a coffee and as counsel make amends. Smoken peace pipe. It got a little testy last night. But I want to meet Alvin at noon."

"You really are awful at times. I cannot believe you are going forward with that settlement."

"Bonnie, please. She got everything she deserves."

I swear that Grandmaitre was smiling ear to ear when I told her Grandma's ring was coming home. When she asked why there was nothing about costs in the order, I told her we had worked it out. "Good, well done. It's good to see that experienced counsel can still work these things out. I wish there were more lawyers like that." I wished Williams had been there to hear it.

At 9:30 a.m., I called Lester to make sure he was ready to speak to Justice Bracken at the McGowan trial. He mumbled something to the effect that he had been doing "research" on settlements mid-trial. Well, I was definitely not paying him for that waste of time. As long as he was there and could tell the judge that we would be filing Minutes of Settlement, he would have served his purpose. To be honest, I probably would've had more confidence with Bonnie doing it, but it had to be a lawyer in black robes . . . wrinkled or not. I made a mental note to speak to Lester about his robes. There is no excuse for that lack of professionalism.

I made my way from the court to the trustee's office at Bay and Dundas. With an original version of Her Honour's order for the trustee, I scooped up the ring and took the PATH through the Eaton Centre, directly to Williams's office at First Canadian Place. No sign of the citizens of the underworld except for the exhausted-looking crews of cleaning staff making their way to the subway and GO train.

I ascended the heights of First Canadian Place to the fortieth floor and the offices of one Randall Williams. His firm's reception/art gallery, which looks out over the lake, dwarfed my entire office. Ensuring my jaw was not hanging open like some younger, albeit better dressed, version of Lester, I stood in silent awe of the firm's collection until I recognized a painting on the far wall. Without even speaking to the receptionist, I walked, hypnotized until I stood before a massive 6 by 7 foot canvas, Kim Dorland's painting *Go Back*.* It depicts a bridge defaced with ominous

---

* www.artoronto.ca and www.equinoxgallery.com

graffiti arcing over a frozen canal. The pinks and purples in his sky radiated a strange eerie warmth. I recalled it from his show in Toronto a few years ago, titled "I've Seen the Future, Brother." Indeed.

I pulled my eyes away from the work only because on an adjacent wall hung Dorland's frightening *Night Swimming*.* A woman's pink body floats ominously in swirling black and brown waters, so dangerous, so disturbing. He does not shy away from the brutality of love. Magnificent.

"Can I help you?" the receptionist called to me cheerily.

"I had no idea Mr. Williams had such an eye for art."

"They're beautiful, aren't they? I find them a little bit scary but still mesmerizing. The larger one is acrylic and oil on linen. Gives the paint a different texture, don't you think? *Night Swimming* is on a wood panel. Still, he maintains a thickness in the paint. I'm a huge fan of Dorland's work." Such professionalism, intelligence, and warmth from a mere receptionist. Amazing. Probably had a degree from some art university. I wondered what she earned. "And who will you be meeting with this morning?"

"Mr. Williams himself. Thank you. Is there any chance I can get a coffee?" I was suddenly aware that again I had not shaved but assured myself that maybe my scruffy look was getting close to fashionable, a little artsy perhaps. Perhaps. "I look forward to discussing this collection with him. I'm in the Curators' Circle at the AGO."

"I'm sorry, and you are?" She scanned the screen in front of her, I assumed looking for a boardroom that had been booked for our meeting.

"Oh, I'm sorry. I'm Andrew Bierce." I slid my card across her desk. Maybe she would see the Q.C. "I'm meeting with Mr. Williams. It was booked late last night, so it might not be in your calendar yet."

"Hmm. Nothing. Let me check with his junior associate."

My heart skipped a beat at the thought that Steve Larson himself might have to deliver the settlement package to me. What would I say? Nothing? Just smile knowingly? We'd see.

She dialled someone. "I have a Mr. Bierce here for Mr. Williams, but I don't see a boardroom booked. . . . Oh . . . oh . . . I see. . . . Well, will someone come out?" She looked up at me with a very different gaze.

---

* www.artsy.net and www.angell.gallery

"Someone will be out shortly. Perhaps you'll want to take a seat." With that she went back to her work.

I waited thirty minutes. No coffee. No more cheery chatting, notwithstanding my attempts. A pretty young woman, probably a student, came through the frosted glass inner office doors with a large envelope under her arm and huddled at reception. She glanced at me and then slipped back through the door.

"Mr. Bierce. This package is for you," Ms. Art Major called out.

"And Mr. Williams?"

"I'm sorry. Apparently he is tied up. He said you were only here to pick up this envelope." She pushed it across her work station.

"Really? No meeting? So, it's like that, is it?"

"I'm sorry. I'm just the receptionist."

"Can you pass a message to Mr. Williams for me? It's about his art collection."

She perked up. "Certainly. Would you like to write it down?" She set a small yellow pad in front of me.

"No, you can tell him for me. Since you're familiar with the artist I think he should consider acquiring one of Dorland's earlier works, from around 2008, it's oil, acrylic, and spray paint, birch trees and graffiti on a huge canvas."

She looked at me, stone-faced. "I think I know it. Not canvas. Wood, actually."

"I'm trying to remember what Dorland called it . . . do you?"

"I'm sure you recall it, Mr. Bierce, Curators's Circle and all. You can write it here." She tapped the notepad with the nail of a finger that looked like it had been dipped in blood.

"That's right. I do recall it. The name of the painting had been carved on the trunk of one of the birch trees . . . " I took out my gold Rolex pen, wrote the two-word name of the painting on the pad, and pushed it across to her.

*Fuck Love.**

"I'll give him your message. Good day, Mr. Bierce."

---

* www.artoronto.ca and www.arsenalcontemporary.com

26

The Ring of Truth

I CALLED ALVIN. "You still good to go for a quick lunch?"

"Yes, sir. How is Paul doing?"

"He's a mess. And angry."

"What a shit show. I'm going to call him later today. Just to check in. Well, do you have it?"

"Yes, and so much more."

"What does that mean?"

"You'll see. Later."

At noon, Alvin was sitting on the steps of Old City Hall. As I approached, he stood and threw the remains of a soft ice cream cone into a garbage can. His mouth hung open in disbelief.

"What do you think?" I was sitting astride a hot pink Vespa with little black paw prints all over it. I held the helmet in my lap. "She couldn't pay costs, so I took her Vespa instead. Basically, it was Pussycat the memoirs or Pussycat the scooter. I picked up the registration and keys at her lawyer's office this morning. It's a nice ride. Oh, and here's the ring." I opened the ring box for him.

Alvin was speechless. He sat back down on the steps of Old City Hall, staring at the family heirloom and then at the Vespa. "I don't know how you did it, but I'm eternally grateful, Bierce. Bill me. Please. You are worth every penny. I just don't know how you did it."

"Well, let's just say she—and her lawyer—really didn't want to produce those memoirs. And you don't owe me anything. Pussycat is reward enough. I kind of like scooting around on it." I pulled on the helmet and gave it a kick-start.

"Well, you're going to be a whole chapter in her memoirs after this."

"Somehow I doubt that. I think she's glad to see the end of me." My phone buzzed. It was a text from Bonnie. *You better get back here. There is a police officer who wants to speak with you.*

I texted back. *About Chloe?*

She wouldn't say. She is waiting.

"Sorry Alvin, I have to scoot." With a twist of the throttle, I was off.

27

It Comes with the Territory

BY THE TIME I DID A FEW LOOPS AROUND downtown, parked Pussycat in the underground, and made it up to the office, guess who had been cooling her heels for nearly an hour? Officer MiniCop from the hospital.

"Officer, I'm so sorry I kept you waiting."

She looked at the pink scooter helmet under my arm and said, "I'm sure you are. Can I speak with you privately for a few minutes?"

"Sure, let's sit in the boardroom. I assume this is about Chloe. She's been charged? Enjoying the Don Jail, I hope." As we sat down, she looked very serious, and I thought, *God, I hope she doesn't want to retain me for her divorce.* I felt drained and realized I had not slept in a long time. I wasn't even sure what day it was anymore. Meeting with Justice Grandmaitre seemed days ago.

"Mr. Bierce, I know you have a difficult job . . . people are unhappy when they divorce . . . "

"True, but it comes with the territory. People aren't supposed to like divorce lawyers."

"We have reason to believe that you may be in danger."

"Seriously? Come on. People say a lot of mean things when they divorce, especially about their lawyers."

"We have sources that I obviously cannot disclose to you, but given what we've heard we are recommending you—and your staff—keep your guard up. Pay attention to what is going on around you. People following you, packages, your car. . . . where you park . . . "

"You're serious?"

"Yes, I'm serious. Can you think of anyone who might want to do harm to you or your office?"

I had to pause and think about that one. I ran a quick list in my head and stopped at ten. "Yeah, I guess there are unhappy people out there, but no one crazy enough to do something."

"Well, think about it. Keep your guard up. Can I leave it with you to explain the situation to your staff? If anything happens or seems odd, you'll let me know? Here is my card." She stood, shook my hand, and left.

Whatever.

28

Tangerine Dream

IT'S ONE THING TO FEEL UNWELCOME at a wedding but quite another to be shunned at a funeral. Bonnie, Alvin, and I were not invited to Angie's funeral a week later but we went anyway. How could we not be there? What a scene, though. Even from a respectful distance, it was brutal. Two parents, one in cuffs, separated by police officers, burying their child—a horror show. It had rained hard the night before, and the little grave site was a muddy mess covered in blue and green tarps with sheets of wobbly plywood for the clutch of mourners to stand on. I thought my head would explode. After that nightmare, Bonnie went off to do some volunteer work while Alvin and I got pretty drunk starting at the Lulu Lounge and ended up being asked—by the band no less—to leave the Dakota. I don't even know how I got home. I was still exhausted and hungover when I dragged myself into the office the next day.

I had to be there. Seriously, no excuses. I had an appointment I could not miss. I had become pretty desperate in my search for a lawyer to represent me in the bullshit Savoie lawsuit about her drugged-up dead husband's insurance. There are only a few lawyers in Toronto who will take on a case suing another lawyer. Yes, I'm one of them, and another one is that jerk-off Fernstein. But he is a total prick who will even take on a total loser case if he thinks he can shake some cash out of the lawyer's insurer. He'll do anything for a fee. No common sense. Total asshole, and I wouldn't be surprised if he took Savoie on simply out of spite from the shit-kicking I gave him on Chloe and Paul's matter. I guess I shouldn't have been surprised Savoie ended up in his slippery clutches, but I couldn't figure out how she was paying him. There was no way he took the file on for a contingency fee. No sane lawyer takes a case on contingency unless he knows he'll win it. Otherwise you're just taking a risk that you will end up pounding sand. I didn't get it.

My insurer gave me permission to source my own lawyer, and I didn't want my deductible going up any more than it already had—that's a long story for another day. But I did have to work from a list of approved lawyers, all of whom were good and therefore busy. But I needed someone who was going to do what I would do, and that was chop off Teresa's fucking head and Fernstein's too.

I was so desperate, I actually asked Randall Williams to at least meet with me to discuss representing me. I know. Hard to believe but I was desperate. I needed serious horsepower, and I was running out of options. I tried to get him to go for coffee, lunch, or a drink, but no luck. But then, out of the blue, his office called and said yes to a meeting at 10:00 a.m. Not ideal for me, since that is prime billable time, but he had one opening, so I grabbed it.

Notwithstanding an early hot shower, when I stepped off the elevator into his reception area I could still smell the bourbon and beer wicking through my shirt. I had forgotten how beautiful the reception was and tried to look cool when I checked in with Ms. Art School. At least this time I had shaved. Good suit too. No chit-chat, so I tucked into an unbelievably expensive teal leather couch that looked out over the lake. The leather was so soft, it felt like merino wool. I had an opportunity to really appreciate that couch because Williams kept me waiting again. After twenty minutes I wandered across reception to examine an unusual sculpture, a chrome baseball bat attached to the far wall. Black tape was wound around the grip, and a string of words had been etched into the barrel. I leaned in to read them and the artist's name. Dean Drever.* Never heard of him. I tilted my head and read the script aloud, "The only way it makes sense to you." Interesting.

______

* www.artnet.com

I turned to the receptionist and asked in my friendliest tone, "Are you going to help me out with this one? Dean Drever?"

She looked up from her work and said cooly, "Industrial sculpture is not really my area, but I read that the artist is interested in depicting the difference between sanctioned and unsanctioned violence in society. Frankly, his work leaves me a little cold." And with that she turned back to her work.

"Cold? It is devastating. It is brilliant."

She said nothing.

I watched her. "Why are you here?"

She took off her large artsy tortoise shell reading glasses and looked up, a little annoyed. "I beg your pardon?"

"You have knowledge about art, you are clearly artistically inclined, probably an artist yourself, you have an informed opinion. Why are you here?" I gestured around reception as if this place was somehow beneath her.

She paused, smiled, and gestured elegantly with her hand. "Why are *you* here?" She said it as if this place was somehow above me. Before I could tell her that she knew nothing about me or why I was there, a very pretty young woman in a tangerine-coloured suit with off-white piping on the collars and lapels came to get me. I recognized her from the night at Keg's celebration of life. Hers was the face that had been waiting in the back of Williams's SUV.

"Good morning, Mr. Bierce. My name is Lindsay Braun. I'm Mr. Williams's associate. He is going to be meeting with you in the Algonquin boardroom this morning. Please follow me."

Very sharp, very cute. Go Williams, I thought. "I would really love a coffee this morning. Is that possible? Just a little cream." I hoped she could not smell the hangover clinging to my shirt and breath.

The eponymous Algonquin boardroom to which I was led was filled with Group of Seven artwork, beautiful, original rare sketches upon which the artists had based their final paintings. I had an opportunity to examine each and every one of them closely because it was another forty minutes before Williams arrived with Ms. Tangerine Suit in tow. Nothing was said about the coffee I requested.

"Good morning, Randall." We shook hands. "I was getting a little worried. It's been nearly an hour."

"Yes, I was on a call." No apology, I noted. "I read your memo summarizing this Savoie situation. Let's talk a little."

"Great." I jumped into a detailed explanation of my history with Ms. Savoie. I was pretty sure as we sat there that they had to be blown away by my grasp of the facts and law surrounding enforcement of life insurance provisions in separation agreements. Chapter and verse at my fingertips. I noticed as I walked them through the details that neither one of them took a note. That's how good my memo was. Twenty minutes in, Williams stopped me mid-sentence and looked at his watch. He spread his hands on the table, flat, palms down, as if holding the table in place so it would not suddenly float away.

"Bierce, it's an interesting case."

"Interesting? It's a great fucking case. Excuse my French. I want you to chop off her head and Fernstein's too. Kill them both. This is crazy. Move for summary judgment. Get costs. It's a slam dunk."

"Well, no case is perfect. You know that. Fernstein's a good lawyer, knows his stuff. There is always a chance some judge . . . "

Oh, I get it. That wily bastard Williams was covering his ass in front of the cute associate, so I played along. "Yes, I suppose that's possible." I smiled and winked at her, thinking about the prospect of working closely with her over the next several months. She smiled and shyly looked down at her hands. What a doll. "So what's next, Randall?"

"As you can see, I'm very busy now, and I would need a retainer of course." He paused. "And given your history with the insurance company, your considerable deductible, I would still need a retainer." He paused again. "Of $100,000."

"What? A hundred grand? You've got to be kidding me? This case . . . " He stared at me. I saw the student smile and look down again. Embarrassed.

Oh, I get it now. He was showing her what a fuck-off fee looked like. *Wow.* I did not see that coming. My face was burning as the full weight of my hangover suddenly fell on me. I clenched my teeth and fought back an embarrassing, "Fuck you." Instead, I heard myself saying from somewhere in a deep well, "Thanks for your time. I will need to think it over. I . . . uh . . . I'm meeting with some other potential counsel so . . . I'll get back to you." *Keep it together, Bierce, keep it together.* I bit down so hard, my jaw ached. Acid reflux chewed into my chest as I stood and shook his hand. Ms. Tangerine Suit offered to see me to the reception area and elevator. I turned, looked Williams straight in his eyes, and said, "I guess what goes around comes around."

He held my gaze and without a hint of a smile said, "I think the circle of life is what you called it."

I did indeed. I don't know what felt worse, walking right into it or that he felt he had to do it to me in front of that pretty associate.

The elevator ride to the concourse felt like an hour as my head spun from the humiliation and my hangover. My mouth went dry, and my head was throbbing. I started to make my way along the PATH back to the safety of my office. I needed to regroup.

As I passed the LCBO at First Canadian Place, I realized that I was sweating uncontrollably. It was running down my face and the back of my neck; my hair was soaked. Stumbling at a forty-five-degree angle, I walked into a mirrored wall and put my hand up to steady myself. I waited a few beats, and then out of the corner of my eye I could see half an empty bench in the middle of the teeming food court. On the other end of the bench sat another familiar face, Stuart, casually making his way through yet another paperback. I made a very determined effort to focus on walking over in a straight line to sit down. When I finally made it, my chest was in a vice and I bent over, gasping for air. Without warning, I puked on the floor, my pants, my shoes. People screamed and jumped out of the way as I threw up mouthful after mouthful of coffee and last night's booze. Three little cleaning ladies muttered something in a language I did not understand as they offered me handfuls of napkins. A brave one asked. "You okay?" As I wiped off my face and pants and apologized to no one in particular, another mouthful of vomit sprayed across the floor, to more screams. Stuart, alarmed, got up and moved to another bench. My throat was on fire from the bile. I put my hands on my knees, took a few deep breaths, and sat up straight in time to see the girl in the Tangerine Suit, standing not fifteen feet from me, holding two large Starbucks, watching me. With concern? No, in disgust.

29

The Devil's Rope

I WOUND MY WAY ALONG THE PATH, through a parking garage, and into an elevator that would get me close to my building. Head down, I ignored the stares and walked close to a wall for support. Somehow I managed to slip into my office without Bonnie seeing me so messed up. I peeled off my tie. Armani, now ruined by puke. *Shit.* I threw it in the garbage. My suit pants, beautiful, just beautiful, sprayed with vomit. That might come out. That *had* to come out. This was one of my favourite suits. My shoes from Loding, black leather, monkstrap, not two weeks out of the box speckled with chunks of God knows what. I'd clean and polish them myself if I had to. With my tie off, I could see that my blue shirt, bespoke tailored from Manny, was stained with brown liquid, coffee—that goddamn second large Starbucks latte I had at 6:30 a.m. I unbuttoned it, held it to the light, and tossed it into the garbage. God, what a mess.

My phone buzzed. Bonnie. How did she know I was here? "Yes."

"I didn't see you come in. Can I pop in? There is someone here to see you."

"Give me a few minutes, Bonnie." I was standing in the middle of my office in my underwear.

"Is everything okay?"

"Can I just have two fucking minutes to myself? Please. Thank you. Jesus fucking Christ." I fell into my chair and replayed the meeting. Williams, what a prick. The image of the Tangerine Girl flashed through my mind. I could see her face like a sequence of still frames from an old zoopraxiscope. A horse runs, a man throws a javelin, a woman dances. In each frame there is no perceptible motion, but then suddenly all of the horse's feet are off the ground, the javelin has left his hand, the woman's skirt is twirling, and the Tangerine Girl's face has an embarrassed smile. *Click. Click. Click.* Each frame passed, and I tried to find that split second when her face revealed the first hint of that smile. I didn't see the corners of her mouth moving from controlled interest to embarrassed smile. It was fractions of fractions of a second. *Click. Click. Click.* I didn't see it coming. The frames rolled by again and again, and anguish washed over me. My gut churned at the thought of Williams telling her his plan.

"First, we will make the asshole wait, use up his valuable billable time. He's been trying to get me to go for a drink or lunch, like I want to spend time with that shithead. I'll make him sweat. Our receptionist said he is a pretentious amateur art snob. Curators' Circle? Gimme a break. Now, when he comes into the boardroom, let him talk a little bit. He'll be strutting his stuff, especially with a pretty girl in the room."

"Oh, Mr. Williams," she would have said softly.

"No, seriously, he'll think he's something special, so watch his face closely. There will be a moment when his face will flinch just as I drop the fuck-off fee on his head like a grand piano."

Did they laugh at that prospect? Did she take notes? Did he make her promise not to laugh? *Click. Click. Click.* The frames rolled by again. I didn't see it coming. Her embarrassed smile was just suddenly there.

My throat still burned, and I felt like I would hurl again, but there was nothing left in the tank. I fumbled through a drawer for Aspirin. Jesus, where did all that puke come from? Did I have that much to drink last night? I washed down three Aspirin with a bottle of water and pulled a fresh court shirt from my desk drawer. I slipped into my double pin-striped court pants, a little formal, but at least they didn't stink of vomit. I rolled my suit pants into a ball and stuffed them into a plastic bag. I'd tell the cleaners that a nervous client threw up on me. Thank God I kept another pair of black court shoes for emergencies. I slipped them on, and they felt like well-worn slippers. More water, some gum, and it started to feel like a normal hangover. Then her face scrolled by again. *Click. Click. Click.* Was she horrified? Disgusted? Puzzled? Sorry?

Maybe she had scrambled back into the elevator with her two celebratory lattes and rushed back to Williams's office. As she sat his pumpkin spice latte on his desk: *"Mr. Williams?"*

"Yes, Lindsay?"

"You won't believe what I just saw downstairs."

Williams would lean back in his high-back chair as she told her tale. *"No kidding? I thought Bierce had a thicker skin than that. Well, it just goes to show you with these bullies—"*

"But Mr. Williams, why were you so cruel to him? He has a good case . . . no?"

"Yes, an excellent case. His memo was first-class."

"Why did you do that to him? It wasn't right. It was so unfair."

Not fucking likely. *Click. Click. Click.*

I buzzed Bonnie. "Sorry about that, not a good start to the day."

Silence.

"Look, I'm sorry. I had a mishap. Things didn't go well with Williams. I'm not feeling well."

"I'm not surprised after last night. There are two gentlemen here to see you. Building security."

"Oh, for Christsakes . . . not again, not today, Bonnie."

"This is the third time they have been here looking for you."

"What is it with these guys? They'll have to come back some other time."

"They said they'll wait."

"Then they'll wait."

"They said they'll wait as long as it takes. Deal with it. I'm taking a late lunch."

Wow. She was in a pissy mood. I looked at my watch. Nearly 2:00 p.m. "Put them in the boardroom, and I'll be there in about fifteen minutes."

Silence.

"And no coffee or water for them. They won't be here that long."

Silence.

I opened my office door to see her still hanging over her keyboard. She didn't even bother to look up. "They're in the boardroom."

Instead of going to the boardroom, I slipped down the hall and into the men's room. My hangover was so rough, I felt like I had entered a goddamn spa. I splashed some water on my face and crawled back toward something that felt close to a terrible hangover. The mirror told the real story. I looked like crap. I had a huge yellowish bag under each eye, and a hive the size of a loonie had emerged on my cheek. More water, mouthwash. I brushed my teeth, more mouthwash. I ran a brush through my hair. *Shit.* I had vomit in my hair. I could see that the pits of my fresh shirt were already soaked with sweat, and my skin was crawling with needles and pins. My whole body was in a fucking revolt.

I headed down the hall to the boardroom and entered without knocking. They did not stand, and they did not extend their hands. Odd, but I didn't have time for their bullshit. "Sorry to keep you waiting, gentlemen. It's been a crazy busy day. How can I help?"

The bigger of the two mumbled first. "My name is Mr. Something. Joseph Something. This is Nicholas Something Indistinguishable."

Mr. Whatever was all of twenty-six or twenty-seven. With his massive baby face, I was quite sure no one referred to him as Mister anything. I estimated that he stood over six feet, that is if he could ever get all 230-plus pounds out of that chair. He was, let's say kindly, heavy-set, and for some unknown reason he had chosen to shave his head. What is it with security guards shaving their heads? His scalp was greyish blue, and it showed a long, thin scar across the side near his ear. That must have been a nasty fight. Hockey skate?

If not for his pseudo-police garb and thick holster holding a walkie-talkie, he could easily have been mistaken for a skinhead. I assumed he wanted to be a cop but fucked up somewhere along the line. Sold drugs in high school? A break-in at a neighbour's home? Assault? Convictions for fighting? Whatever it was, it kept him out of the police academy. Probably for the best.

He looked like he was used to throwing his weight around, though. He probably worked as a bouncer late at night for a bar in clubland, accepting twenties from Richmond Hill kids with too much money, trying to cut the line. They drop $20 to get inside, only to learn that the place is empty and a bottle of vodka costs $300. So what, they are usually so drunk from pre-drinking that in a couple of hours they have no idea where they are and drop another $300 on a bottle they never should have finished. Pretty soon they're puking and pissing in an alley off Queen Street at 4:00 a.m. I looked at him again. I bet he also parked cars somewhere for extra cash, maybe still lived in his parents' basement? Maybe. "Nice to meet you, Joseph. I'm sorry I don't really have a lot of time."

"We have all day, Mr. Bierce. It's been very hard getting this meeting with you, so we need to cover some matters."

Hmm. He sounded a little aggressive. Who is this fellow? I decided to let him do the talking.

"We're with Building Security." (No fucking kidding. It said that right there on his uniform under his name.) "We're responsible for the entire building, including the parking garage."

Oh, shit. It was probably about that goddamn Lexus I kissed. "I have a parking space. The garage gets a little dirty from time to time and the lights are too dim in some areas. That's not safe for—"

"Mr. Bierce, we're not here doing a survey."

Hmm. Pushy. I could see him looking at my court shirt and pin-striped pants almost with contempt. His metal clipboard and file folder looked to be holding some grainy photos. Well, well, what did he have there? *Patience, Bierce. Let him fill the silence.* As I waited, I tallied up the number of cars I might have tangled with in the parking garage. I stopped at seven when the other fellow sat up and added, "We've had some complaints about the parking garage."

I squinted at his nametag. Nicholas Glidden. No one called these guys Nicholas or Joseph. They were Nick and Joe. Some kind of pathetic matched set.

Nick didn't want to be a cop; he had never wanted to be anything. He was younger than Joe, maybe twenty-three or twenty-four, clearly Joe's subordinate. He shaved his head to fit in. He was overweight as well, sweating like a hog through his poly security shirt, which barely contained his belly. It hung over his belt, and I imagined him unleashing that gut at the end of the day in his basement apartment in Scarborough. His moans of relief could probably be heard three floors up in the scruffy triplex. He would throw his belt and walkie-talkie on the used couch he got at Goodwill, flip open a large pizza box, pop the tops off the three extra containers of dipping sauce he asked for, and snap a buck a beer while watching *Sports Central* to see if any of his bets worked out. Some would, some wouldn't, and he would need to ask Joe if he could get him some extra work bouncing or parking cars. But first he would eat the entire pizza, drink six beers, and fall asleep in his clothes.

I watched him. *I've never met you before, but I know you. You just wanted a job to be able to rent your own place so you could move out after your parents split up.*

Wait, I think I do know you.

I leaned over and tried to read the other one's name tag.

Nick interrupted my train of thought. "Cars have been damaged . . ."

"Really . . . ?" Something was bubbling up, surfacing, the connection to these boys.

"A man died in the stairwell coming up from P2 to the street." They watched for my reaction, but my mind was racing, searching for something else, a memory.

"Yes, I heard about that death." I gave them nothing.

Suddenly, the memories came fast, and my skin crawled with a wave of sharp pricks. I'd had a bout of shingles during my divorce, but this was different, worse, like thorns being ratcheted into my skin, biting my arms and legs, my back. They say the Devil hands out barbed-wire blankets upon your arrival in hell, and I suddenly felt like I was wrapped in mine.

These boys were Joe and Nick Glidden. I did their parents' divorce.

It had been at least a dozen years ago, maybe more—a brutal conflagration that burned through their family's savings and the equity in their home as they fought over these two boys. Neither parent had a pot to piss in when they were done. One of the uglier turns came when the dad ran out of rice. His lawyer suggested he cash in the boys' RESPs to pay his bills and stay in the game. My client, the mom, ended up getting custody, though, and moved to some shitty little rental in Barrie while the dad just kind of drifted out of their lives after falling behind in child support. Not an uncommon outcome.

These two boys were supposed to go to university. They were gifted according to the very expensive custody assessment (I think we spent thirty grand on it). Now look at their sweet little boys, they were fucking security guards. I stared at them, reverse aging them in my mind. I could see the once-children in those fat faces.

They stared back at me until Joe flipped open his file. "Mr. Bierce, before we meet with your assistant Bonnie, we have some photos and a video we would like you to look at." I could tell now that they knew who I was. They knew it all.

There are 1,500 types of barbed wire, and as I sat there with those boys, I felt them all. They don't call it the Devil's Rope for nothing.

30

It Comes with the Territory, Part 2

I WORKED LATE for a couple of evenings trying to deal with the Savoie matter on my own. I had to do something until I could get good counsel to represent me. It seemed everyone was "busy." Big mistake doing it myself. There I was, forced to act as my own lawyer—with a fool for a client. Classic.

I was also forced to travel around town on the Pussycat scooter. Any novelty or pleasure riding it wore off very quickly, and frankly it was a pain in the ass. Never mind the clever homophobic comments I suffered ("Does that say Poofter or Pussycat?" "Is the Pride Parade today?" "Hey, Queen of the Road" were a few of the kinder ones), but you're taking your life in your hands trying to ride a bike or a scooter in downtown Toronto. Hell, even being a pedestrian is high-risk.

Why was I forced to use the scooter? Two nights after my meeting with the Glidden boys—which incidentally went nowhere—my car was trashed top to bottom in the parking garage. Total write-off. The insurers gave me a hard time, for obvious reasons, and building security knew nothing, of course. Once Tiny Lady cop found out about the "incident," as she called it, she was back in my office for another visit to discuss the threats. She practically ordered me to stay out of the underground parking garage. It's a wonder I could get any real work done. At least Sean had gone silent and stopped sending me texts about the DNA test results.

Chloe was charged under s. 245 CCC with administering a toxic substance to Angie, along with an s. 218 endangering a child, and faced a max of fourteen years in prison. The Crown had a choice to proceed against Chloe by way of indictable offence or as a summary conviction offence, which would have lesser consequences. Indictable was a no-brainer; a child had died after all.

There was talk of a manslaughter charge. Pretty serious stuff. But. Yes, there was a big but. We are talking about the difference between what the words say in the Canadian Criminal Code and what actually happens in the system. Big difference.

Although unwelcome, I insisted on sitting in one morning on Alvin's no-charge meeting (I guess it happens) with Paul, designed to brace him for what would likely be happening with the charges against Chloe and how her lawyers would make sure nothing was dealt with for a few years. Angie's death had been in the news, and there was the usual two or three days of outrage accompanied by lots of teddy bears and flowers (someone is making a fortune on teddy bears) left in front of their home. Then people moved on to the next basement fire tragedy, impaired driving disaster, school stabbing, gang shooting of someone who was the greatest human being in their neighbourhood but also "known to police," or perhaps it was this month's honour killing. The daily cornucopia of tragedy has shortened our attention span. It has become a bowl of chips.

According to Alvin, Chloe's new criminal lawyer, a young man looking to make a name for himself, had a veritable buffet of delay options available to him: disputes about disclosure of evidence, reports on Chloe's mental capacity, her statements at the hospital, cough medicine experts, juror challenges (too many people without jobs or too many people with jobs but cannot afford to take time to be on a jury or too many men, and on and on), and, of course, there would be a motion for a mistrial because the Crown attorney rolled his eyes during a witness's testimony. Dismiss the jury and start over. And that doesn't even include all the Charter challenges. What a system.

Alvin took Paul through the likely path of insanity that he faced for the next year or more, including the possibility that he would likely be dragged into it and blamed for everything except actually putting the cough medicine in Angie's mouth. He should expect her lawyers to try to shift the blame to him. That's what passes for quality criminal defence work these days: blame some innocent person just enough to create doubt in one juror's mind. "Yeah, this is just like that episode of *Law and Order*!" When Alvin finished with Paul, he was white as a ghost. Even I felt awful.

It's not like the old days when someone committed a crime in April, got caught a week later, pleaded not guilty in May, had a trial in September, and was sentenced to prison in October. No, now you can film yourself throwing a chair off a condo balcony to the busy streets below, laugh about it, post it on social media for personal publicity, blame Facebook, and our criminal justice system will then still take three years to deal with it. I thought family law was bad.

At one point Paul said, "Let me get this straight. Bierce has spent hours telling me how awful the divorce system is, that it's a national disgrace, and now you're telling me the criminal system is as bad or worse?"

Alvin and I looked at each other. Alvin ran his hand over his face and over his shiny scalp, ending with a perfect De Niro smile, and said, "Yeah, basically, that's it." I nodded in agreement. What else could I say?

Paul looked at the floor and shook his head. "How did I end up in this nightmare? Angie's gone, Chloe's lawyer is marching her around like she's the victim. You know, I saw her interviewed last week talking about how difficult it is to raise children while suffering from OCD and being in an abusive relationship. I can't believe people buy her bullshit."

Since we were near rock bottom anyway, I thought I might as well take us all the way to bedrock. "There is more we need to deal with."

"What? What else could possibly happen?"

I took a deep breath. "I've been served with a motion by her lawyer for spousal support. She claims she is unable to work, needs money, and I'm guessing probably cannot afford her lawyers."

Alvin piped in. "No, I heard from someone at Old City Hall that she's on legal aid."

"What?" Paul and I said together. "Legal aid? How?"

"Yeah, word is she got her lawyer on a legal aid ticket because they're going to characterize it as a test case for OCD sufferers."

"So she gets her lawyer for free? Jesus Christ. This is insane." He was dumbfounded.

I jumped in. "Anyway, the motion for support is not returnable for a few weeks. I can get it adjourned at least once. Let me worry about that for now."

"Bierce, my income has cratered. I'm still facing charges for the breach. I'm making nothing, so support is impossible. A joke. I'm going to lose the house in a few months. I'll need to sell it. There will be a huge penalty on the mortgage. I cannot pay you guys, never mind her."

I didn't have the heart to tell him that he could not sell it without Chloe's permission. And while I didn't like the sound of not being paid, I let it pass. He owed me over $25,000. Against my better judgment, I had done the last motion without a retainer in my trust account. Even though I had a costs order against Chloe, Paul was still in the hole with me, since she could only pay it out of her share of the proceeds from the sale of their home (well, actually Paul's home that he had bought and paid for before they got married, but Chloe now had an automatic interest in). I actually needed him to sell his home in order to get paid but Chloe was not agreeing. Rice is rice. So it was getting awkward with Paul. Downright chilly. His attitude toward me had really shifted. I could feel it.

"Can I get a legal aid certificate?"

Alvin answered, "Uhhh, no."

Looking back, Paul was different after that meeting. In retrospect, I think that was the day he gave up.

And then things got worse.

31

Septic Shocker

MY PHONE PULSED WITH TEXT MESSAGES early in the morning as I sat outside Starbucks, Black Beauty by my side. The big bag was fully loaded for a 10:00 a.m. motion at 393 University on the Septic Tank case. The lawyer representing my client's firefighter husband (a young female junior lawyer from a midsize firm, not going to be a problem) was moving to strike all my delicious and colourful photographic evidence of the condoms he'd flushed. According to Ms. Junior LLB, the evidence was not only "irrelevant, inflammatory, and prejudicial . . . it was odious." What a great word. It's from the Latin "odium." Hatred. I need to use it more often. Were these photos odious? Yes. Did they have anything to do with spousal support? With property division? Well, actually, no, nothing, but fighting over them was a hell of a good way to burn some of the husband's budget for legal fees, not to mention burn his face with a little embarrassment in court.* But I had my instructions: make the divorce hurt, make it expensive, make him wish he'd been a better husband and, most of all, make him wish he'd settled and just walked away—without spousal support. That's odium.

I ignored the onslaught of texts (many from Bonnie about Sean; I could not deal with him now so I stopped looking) as I sat there trying to

---

* Truth be told? I was bringing the exact same motion in the Laurier case, to strike the home video evidence, and fully expected to be successful.

load up on caffeine and having a moment of what passes for peace during rush hour at the corner of York and Adelaide. But then the phone jangled. It was Alvin, so I answered. "What's up?"

"You won't believe it."

"What?"

"A friend of mine in the Crown's office just called me."

"Not Ms. Novak, I hope."

Dead silence. No sense of humour.

"Funny. Chloe's cut some kind of a deal with the Crown, and she is pleading out."

"What do you mean pleading out? To what? How?"

"I'm not sure, but it may be this afternoon around 2:30 p.m. I'm trying to find out more."

"Does Paul know?"

"I doubt it. And there's more."

"What else?"

"She's dumped her legal aid lawyer and switched to none other than Royce Hughes, Q.C. He must have cut her some unbelievable deal. Bierce, he's good. He wouldn't plead her out unless it was sweet. That's not his style."

"Hughes? Isn't he the guy who defended the cop that put his dead girlfriend in a barrel of acid?"

"One and the same."

I knew his reputation. Hughes was a guy who actually earned his Q.C. He was in the news every second week: murder trials, drug trials, drunken boating accidents, bikers, and especially cops with problems. The tough cases were his bread and butter. And the tougher they were, the more he wanted them. I heard that he had a team of junior lawyers on call 24/7 and they slept in the office on shifts. Midnight arrest? One of them was on it.

About a month before, he'd wrapped up a jury trial in which he defended a cop who'd cut up his girlfriend and put her body in a barrel of acid. His defence? He had found her dead from a suicide by drug overdose. Why would she kill herself? Well, he said that when he had suggested they postpone their wedding, she took it hard, thinking he was bailing on their relationship. (There was evidence, however, that no one in their entire circle of friends had heard anything about an engagement.)

He claimed that he wanted to protect her very religious family from the tragic news of her suicide, so he told them she had left him suddenly to travel the world on a journey of self-awareness. Of course, it was total bullshit, but the jury was out for three days before they came back with, that's right, an acquittal. One juror bought his tale of woe.

Years ago, I overheard a lawyer in the Barrister's Lounge at Osgoode Hall laugh and say, "Hughes has no soul. He would have to be hollow to defend these people." I had laughed too and thought that it was a little melodramatic, until I learned about how he handled the Goodman murder case a few years back.

By all accounts, Leonard Goodman was a good grinder lawyer doing insurance defence work in Kitchener-Waterloo. I didn't know him, so this is grapevine stuff. They say he worked hard, six days a week, good solid practice, wife, five kids, all girls. One day he came home for lunch (which you could do if you practiced law in a small town; beats a food court, I guess) and found his wife sitting at the kitchen table in a daze.

"Where are the girls?" he asked.

"Gone."

"Gone where? To a friend's? School?"

"No, gone to heaven."

She then led Leonard downstairs to the basement, where he found all five girls hanging from a crossbeam. His wife had hanged them all, oldest to youngest. She said she heard a voice, the Emperor of the Universe of Pain. I tried to imagine the horror of the youngest girl as she saw her sisters, hanging there ahead of her, with Lucifer's shaggy wings flapping slowly and his three faces, all laughing.

Hughes acted for the wife, who pleaded not guilty, and he mounted a defence that stretched it out for years. Every bullshit angle that he could find he worked. Crown didn't want to take a chance, so they took an NCR plea—Not Criminally Responsible—and she went to a hospital for about eighteen months. Then she was out, remarried, and moved away. Leonard was pretty much a shell after that, they say. I'm not sure what happened to him.

Chloe's poisoning of Angie would be right up Hughes's alley. He would have psychiatrists lined up to testify about OCD, abuse, the impact of the divorce, her eating disorder, and on and on. However, there was one person who would not be testifying for Chloe: her equally kooky mother. She had turned on her like a scorpion. Rumour had it that she was trying to get a book deal after she got a guest spot on a TV show called *Mothers Who Murder*.

I had a bad feeling about this turn of events. "Okay. Keep me posted. Can you call Paul? He's not returning my calls these days."

"I heard he's into you for some fees. Maybe he's just trying to keep costs down?"

Maybe. But it felt different than that.

I called Bonnie. As usual, she was in early. "Cancel the new client who is scheduled for this afternoon. It looks like something is going down this afternoon with Chloe. A guilty plea. Very sudden."

"Okay. I'm on it. Can I come to watch this?"

"Bonnie, this really isn't the time."

"It's never the time for you. I want to see this. If the afternoon is cancelled, and I'm caught up . . . I'll take an unpaid afternoon off if I have to."

"All right, all right, Jesus. When I find out where and when, I will call you. I'll let you know," I lied.

"Oh, and the archdiocese called. They were looking for Sean. Do you know where he is? Have you been in touch? I forwarded a bunch of messages from him to you."

"They're calling me? To find Sean? That's rich. I haven't got time to worry about Sean. I'll call him later. I have to get to court to deal with the septic situation."

"I'll see if I can track him down. He's left a few numbers when he's called." Bonnie always had a soft spot for Sean. Sometimes I think she does it just to irritate me. "And call me with the courtroom and time."

"I will." Lying comes easy sometimes.

I beat it up to 393 University, ninth floor. And made it to Motions Court just in time to find out that I was #1 on the list. Hello. That's great. My client sat in the corner with a demeanour of absolute, well, odium. She was looking forward to a morning of reckoning, of someone seeing what her sweet deceitful husband had done. As soon as I was through security with Black Beauty, Ms. Junior LLB rushed over to me with a look of absolute terror on her face. God, I hoped she wasn't peeing her pants over a simple motion against me. I can be tough, but surely not that bad.

"Mr. Bierce, I have been trying to text you all morning. I'm sorry, but I will need to adjourn the motion."

Oh boy, here we go. She seemed in a genuine panic, but I wasn't in the mood to pass up an opportunity to squeeze this little mademoiselle, if she was trying to avoid me. "No, no, no, I'm sorry, I'm not adjourning this motion at the last minute just because you realized that it could not possibly succeed." I looked around and noticed that her client was nowhere to be seen. Oh, so that was it, maybe her client had bailed as well. That's why she wanted an adjournment. Not going to happen. The court clerk called the matter, and I strolled away into the courtroom, pulling Black Beauty behind me with my client in tow.

As we sat down, she was at my elbow again. "Mr. Bierce, really, I need to adjourn the matter."

I didn't even look up. "Tell the judge . . . I will expect costs if you are trying to adjourn this at the last minute . . . " I hadn't even taken time to look to see who would be hearing the matter. I turned to my client and said with a knowing smile, "Someone is running scared? No mercy." She nodded.

The clerk called us to order, and in walked Justice Newsome. Oh God, but I guess we could do worse. Let's not forget that this is the man who never met an adjournment he didn't like.

The clerk called #1 and Junior was on her feet. "Your Honour, good morning. I am here on behalf of the respondent."

"Is he present in court?" Concerned, Newsome looked around the courtroom. There were three people in front of him: me, my client, and Junior. Obviously, the man was not present.

"No, Your Honour, he is not present."

"Is there a good reason for him not being here? This is an important point he raises in his motion, objecting to this evidence." Interesting, Newsome had actually read the materials. It was a good start. Maybe he wasn't in the mood to kick it down the line. I waited to pounce on Junior.

"I agree, Your Honour, it is an important motion. If I could address that as a part of my request for an adjournment this morning—"

"Adjournment? At this point? I spent last evening reading all these materials. You show up this morning and request an adjournment? Have you asked your colleague, Mr. Bierce?"

"Yes, and he opposes the adjournment."

"Is that true, Mr. Bierce? You oppose this request?"

I stood and simply nodded. "I'm as surprised as Your Honour. I am here and ready to proceed."

"What are your reasons for an adjournment at the last minute?"

"Your Honour, my client and I have great respect for this court."

I'll give Junior credit, good beginning. Well done, Junior.

"My client, as you know from the materials, is a firefighter with the Richmond Hill Fire Department. Last night, there was a considerable fire at the warehouses on the Port Lands."

"Yes, I saw it on the news this morning. Terrible. Considerable is an understatement." Newsome leaned forward, interested.

"My client was one of over twenty firefighters who responded to that fire to try to knock down that blaze." She said "knock down the blaze" as if she had been there herself holding a hose and then paused ever so slightly before dropping the bomb. "Unfortunately, he was caught in one of the buildings when it collapsed."

My client let out an audible gasp. Newsome fell back in his chair, stunned.

Junior continued in a hushed voice. "He was pulled from the building by his team and taken to St. Michael's Hospital, where he is in the ICU with burns to 80 percent of his body. The doctors say he will survive but . . . clearly he faces some challenges . . . and he cannot be here this morning." She said the last part as a brilliant understatement. This Junior might have a gift.

"You advised Mr. Bierce of this?"

Oh, shit.

"I sent Mr. Bierce over a dozen text messages updating him last night and this morning on all the details of my client's situation. I spoke to him when he arrived at court this morning, and he refuses to adjourn the motion." Slight pause. "Suggesting that I only sought to adjourn the motion because . . . ," her voice dropped a little, " . . . because I had no chance of success . . . "

Newsome turned to me. "Mr. Bierce, did you receive text messages from your colleague?"

"Your Honour ..." How could I say I had not read a dozen messages?

"Mr. Bierce, that was a Yes or No question."

"Yes, I received the messages, but—"

"Mr. Bierce, did you refuse to consent to the adjournment and tell your colleague that you thought she only wanted to adjourn because she would lose the motion?"

"Your Honour, if I could address the—"

"Mr. Bierce, again, that was a Yes or No question. Yes or No?"

"Yes, I did, but ... "

Assuming these were my client's instructions, Newsome looked directly at her as if to say, *So this is the way you want to play it.*

He then turned to Junior. "Do you have the text messages that you sent to Mr. Bierce available for inspection by the court?"

"I do ... but only on my phone ..." Junior seemed surprised by the question.

"I don't need to see them, but you are telling me that you have them if I want to read them?"

"Yes, Your Honour."

"Clearly, I will be granting your request for an adjournment. I wish to be spoken to about the costs of today."

I was on my feet in a flash. "In the circumstances, Your Honour, my client does not seek her costs of today. Given the terrible circumstances, an adjournment is in order." I had to get out of there, and fast.

"Oh, now an adjournment makes sense, Mr. Bierce? What changed in the last fifteen minutes? Your client does not seek her costs? How noble. And what about the respondent's costs? He paid his lawyer to come here this morning while he lies in a hospital bed because you would not agree to an adjournment." He was pissed.

"Your Honour—"

"Mr. Bierce, you are familiar with Rule 24(9)?"

Oh God. Oh shit.

"Yes, Your Honour, I am ... in the circumstances—"

"It's open to me, on my own initiative, to order that you personally pay the costs of the respondent, Mr. Bierce."

"I am aware of the power that Your Honour has . . . and I would ask—"

"I am required to give you an opportunity to be heard and to explain why you should not be ordered to pay the costs personally."

He kept putting stress on the word *personally* and then turned to Junior to ask her views on the matter. Wisely, she said simply, "I'm in Your Honour's hands on the matter of costs, and frankly I am concerned about more serious matters right now."

What was she up to? What hook was she baiting for Newsome?

Newsome bit. "What's that, counsel?"

Again, Junior addressed him with great understatement. "Well, Your Honour, I know that today your time was set aside to deal with the evidence, the photographs, but I know given my client's new difficult situation that he will likely require spousal support on a scale and for a duration far in excess of what I originally anticipated, and I will need to amend my pleadings to address these new circumstances."

You crafty little shit. She is going for gold.

Newsome was reeled in. "I am prepared to address that issue now, if it would assist. Mr. Bierce, do you have any objection to the respondent being given leave to amend the pleadings? We're here, after all, because you insisted on proceeding. We might as well do something productive. Agreed?"

What was I supposed to say with costs hanging over my head? *Personally.* "Of course, Your Honour. I think that would be appropriate in the circumstances." I would let her amend, get out of here, and live to fight another day. I was already planning to take the hardwood to this little shit first chance I got.

But Newsome had other plans. "And perhaps we should make an order today for his support? Do we have the income figures for your client, Mr. Bierce?"

Fuck me. I was being led to slaughter in front of my client. "Yes, I have the income figures. . . ." I took him to the correct figure in my client's financial statement. His eyebrows shot up, and he pursed his lips when he saw how much she earned.

"I'm going to make an interim—without prejudice—order today for spousal support in the amount of . . . $10,000 per month starting . . .

Monday of next week." My client punctuated this announcement with a gasp that was even louder than the one she unleashed upon hearing about his injuries. "And I am adjourning this matter for five months to . . . " My mind reeled, and I made no note of the proposed date or whether I was even available. " . . . I am seized of this matter so it is to be returned before me." I could hear his pen scratching on the court record as he scribbled out his endorsement, " . . . and Mr. Bierce, we will deal with the Rule 24(9) motion for costs at the same time. If you wish to retain counsel to speak to it, you will need time to retain someone, and I will understand."

Once out in the hall, I sat my client down and tried to explain the situation. "Let me explain what just happened. We can appeal . . . by the time the matter comes back on in five months, I will—"

Absolutely aghast, she stood and cut me off. With her briefcase clutched into her fists and in a voice loud enough for anyone within twenty feet to hear, she scolded me like a child. "He's in the hospital with burns? And you insisted on proceeding? I asked for results not . . . not whatever that was. Mr. Bierce, you will not be doing anything in five months, at least not for me. I will be retaining new counsel. And I do not expect to receive a bill for this display of mean-spirited incompetence today." She turned and stormed away to the elevators, shaking her head; but then, in a dramatic flash, she turned and called out, "Frankly, I could have done a better job myself."

I looked around to see a dozen lawyers, including Ms. Junior LLB, and puzzled clients staring at me. Among them mingled none other than Lester Donald.

Although I stood there in my formal black gowns, I felt naked.

My phone saved me. It was Alvin. "Okay, I got it. It's going to be at 361 University, Courtroom 2A, 2:30 p.m. Weird, but it looks like your buddy Justice Harold will be taking the plea. They are bringing in some Crown from Brampton, someone who handles only guilty pleas and sentencing. A real low light I heard. So deal looks done. I have to finish up something here, and then I am heading over there . . . okay?"

I stood there. Speechless.

"Bierce? You there?"

"Yeah, sorry. What time?"

"Two thirty. Did you know that Bonnie is coming?"

"What? How did she find out?"

"She called me. She said that you okayed it."

"She's been bugging my ass for years to come and watch."

"Well, of all things to watch? Seriously, this could be over in fifteen minutes."

"Well, that's her problem. Does Paul know about this yet?"

"No, I haven't been able to call him yet. I have to go to wrap up a matter here. Call him."

I had not spoken to Paul in weeks. What a way to reconnect.

I called Bonnie. No harm in taking a little credit if she already knew. "Okay, as I promised, the matter is in Courtroom 2A at 361 University at 2:30 p.m."

"I know. Alvin already told me. Don't worry about me." She sounded absolutely thrilled. I felt sick. "How was the condom case? Photo evidence struck?"

"Bonnie, I have more important things to deal with right now. I have to call Paul." There was no way I would ever tell her about that horse-whipping.

"I called him. He'll meet you in the lobby at 393. See you at twoish."

I pulled my briefcase around to the elevators and gave the down button five furious pushes. The doors slid open, and I stepped into a packed elevator, only to wedge between Randall Williams and Ms. Tangerine associate.

"Mr. Bierce." Williams didn't even look at me.

"Mr. Williams." I nodded and turned to smile at her.

Thankfully, the elevator doors opened, and I pretended to take a call. "Sorry, I have to take this. I'll catch up with you soon . . . " They disappeared into the coffee shop, with the young woman pulling Williams's briefcase.

I turned to head toward University Avenue and practically ran face-first into Paul. He had been waiting for me, and he did not look happy. He looked agitated. Actually, he looked downright angry. I wondered if Alvin had already told him the situation.

"Paul, I've been trying to reach you. Have you heard?"

"Only that we need to get to the criminal court. She has a new law-yer? But she is pleading guilty. Right?" He said *right* as if I would be certifying the result, as if I needed to guarantee it.

"Yeah, but I'm worried. He's a lawyer the Crowns fear. He specializes in getting great deals for clients. It's not the guilty plea I'm worried about. It's the penalty."

"She'll go to jail, though. Right?" Again, demanding a guarantee I could not provide.

I tried not to look in his eyes and fumbled nervously, knocking over Black Beauty. "I don't know. Let's get up there and see what happens."

"Let me get that." He grabbed the handle of my briefcase. "Lead the way."

As we headed out the door toward 361 University, I looked back to see if Williams could see my client pulling my briefcase, to see how my clients really do appreciate me. Nothing.

We headed a block south on University, looking and feeling grim.

32

A Busted Wheel

FROM WHAT I CAN TELL, on most weekdays the courthouse at 361 University is pretty much deserted by 1:30 p.m. Most of the tough slogging has been done by noon, and the judges seem to have headed off to Osgoode Hall Dining Room for extended lunches. If court resumes at two thirty, they only have to get back to their courtrooms in time for a couple of hours work before they pack it in for the day. Easy life. I considered applying to be a judge a couple of times but, it's complicated. Let's leave it at that.

I was practically running up the steps, two at a time, to the courthouse doors, with my gown flapping behind me. I thought Paul was running behind me pulling Black Beauty, but as I stopped at the security desk I looked back to see him with my briefcase turned on its side, pens and notepads spilled on the sidewalk. What the hell?

The police officer on security stood up lazily and clapped her hands as if to say, well, here at last was something to do. "Afternoon, Counsel, late for court, are we?"

"No . . . ," I smiled weakly. "Actually, I am trying to be early for a change. Sorry, I have my ID here somewhere . . . " I didn't expect her to recognize me, because I'm rarely in this courthouse, which deals primarily with criminal matters.

As I fumbled through my pockets, Paul arrived behind me, gasping and looking totally stressed. "Bierce, I'm sorry. I think I busted your briefcase . . . the wheel, I wrecked the wheel." He turned Black Beauty on its side, and sure enough one of the rubber wheels had jammed and then it had been dragged on the sidewalk to the point where it had ground down to a miniature flat tire. I tried to spin the wheel. Ruined. "I'm sorry, Bierce. We were in such a hurry, it just stopped rolling, and that's why I stopped. I tried to fix it but . . . I'm really sorry."

Before I could swear at anybody about the damage, the cop interrupted Paul with a snarky remark. "Don't worry about it, lawyers can always afford a new one." And then, under her breath, "And it'll probably end up being billed to your file."

It sounded like she had some experience with the legal profession, but we were in a hurry, so I let it pass. "Paul, just get through security and I'll take care of it." As he emptied his pockets and put his keys and phone through security, I glanced at my watch and gave the officer a worried look. "I'm sorry, we are supposed to be at a sentencing . . . "

She examined my lawyer's ID and waved me through the security. Paul's stressed voice called out again, "Bierce, where're we going? We're going to be late." I hadn't heard such an edge to his voice since I'd picked him up that day in court after the Don Jail.

"Easy, we'll make it. Alvin said Courtroom 2A."

The cop cut into our conversation. "Top of the escalator, second floor, on the right. Have a nice afternoon." She handed me back my ID as if it was a ticket to a matinee at the Cineplex, not the sentencing of a woman who had poisoned her own child. We set off, the clunk, clunk of the broken wheel echoing down the empty hall.

As we stepped off the escalator on the second floor, I could see what appeared to be a half dozen lawyers and clients all waiting for courts to resume. I recognized no one.

Except one.

A tall lanky lawyer of about forty, outside Courtroom 2A, with a thin file folder under his arm, paced back and forth.

The only thing missing was his rubber ball.

He recognized me immediately and turned away, pretending to read the list of cases scheduled for the afternoon. It couldn't take him very long, because there was only one thing written on the list for Courtroom 2A: R. v. Chloe Campbell. Sentencing . . . "

"Paul, wait here. Watch my bag." I approached Rubber Ball Boy and stood beside him, looking at the list. "Are you the Crown on the Campbell matter?" Up close, I could see his cheap suit, probably from the "buy three for the price of one" at Tom's in Kensington Market.

"Yes, what's your interest?"

"I'm Andrew Bierce." I didn't bother extending my hand.

"I know who you are." He was still boiling over our last encounter.

"I'm counsel to Paul Campbell, father of Angelina."

Without even looking at me he said, "Angelina?" As if I was clearly in the wrong place.

"Angelina, Angie, the child who was killed by Ms. Campbell." My voice dripped with contempt for him not knowing this simple fact.

He turned to me with a look of resentment. "This is a joint sentencing submission. Neither you nor Mr. Campbell will be given an opportunity to make any comments. In fact, there's no reason for either of you even to be present in the courtroom. When Mr. Hughes arrives, we will make our recommendation and the matter will be dealt with."

"We'll see about that."

"Don't make trouble, Bierce. I won't stand for your bullshit this time. I'll hand you your head in there."

I looked at my watch. It was 2:10 p.m. No Chloe or Hughes. "We'll see . . . dickwad."

I walked back over to Paul, who had heard part of our exchange. "What was that all about?"

"Oh, nothing. The Crown and I have a bit of history."

"Good history?" He sounded hopeful. "It didn't look like good history."

"I'm a divorce lawyer, Paul. People aren't supposed to like me."

No sooner had I said those words than Bonnie's voice called out from the top of the escalator. "Bierce. Paul." She was smiling, as if she had a front row ticket to Cirque du Soleil. "Sorry I'm a little late. I was trying to finish—" She cut herself off before admitting that she had left unfinished work back at the office.

Paul seemed strangely relieved to see her. "Hi, Bonnie. I'm glad you could come. You should see this . . . " I cringed at the sound of that statement. It sounded like he had his hopes too high. Nothing good happens in a courtroom.

Bonnie looked at Rubber Ball Boy as he paced in front of the courtroom. "Who's that?"

Paul whispered hoarsely to her, "That's the Crown . . . Bierce has history with him." He said *history* like we had been battling through the ages.

Bonnie looked at me as if to say, *Do you have to fight with everyone?* but settled for a simple "Oh no."

We paced around. I looked at my watch: 2:20 p.m. "It'll be fine. The problem may be getting us into court. That Crown may oppose us being present." It looked like Hughes had tried to engineer this thing to be quick and quiet. No gowns. Under the radar. No media. No public. No special security. Small courtroom, afternoon sitting. Midweek. Cooperative Crown brought in.

The court clerk unlocked the courtroom door and stepped into the hall. "Anyone present with respect to the Campbell matter at 2:30 p.m., please enter the courtroom." Rubber Ball Boy was steps behind her as he slipped into the courtroom.

And then the man of the hour arrived.

Royce Hughes, Q.C., alone, glided up the escalator toward us. I had never seen him in the flesh. TV and news photos did not do him justice. It didn't capture his . . . what . . . his charisma. . . . his . . . obvious royal jelly. In his late sixties, he stood over six feet, slim, fit, tanned, hair groomed perfectly, an alchemy of silver and black that brought to mind Michael Douglas in *Wall Street* but with less sneer and more class. His suit was beautiful. I recognized it. Canali, two-piece, royal blue, an unusual colour, but he pulled it off with a crisp blue shirt that had a brilliant white collar. It was a little old-school but well done. He topped it off with a burgundy and yellow paisley bowtie. As he stepped off the escalator, I could see that his shoes looked out-of-the-box new. He carried an immaculate, thin, caramel-coloured briefcase. Leather? No. It had to be something far more exotic. Matte Porosus? Crocodile. Of course.

He stopped and looked at his watch. I shuddered to think what he had on his wrist. This was not a man who wore a simple Rolex. No, I imagined a TAGHeuer perhaps? Patek Philippe? Without a word, he walked directly into the courtroom without speaking to or looking at anyone. But where was Chloe?

"That was Hughes," I whispered to Bonnie. I'm not sure why I whispered.

"Wow. He looks like a movie star." Even Miss Black Clothing Repository was taken aback. "Bierce, I thought you dressed well, but that man is pure class."

"Let's not get all sloppy here, Bonnie. We need to get into the courtroom. Wait here." She really knew how to hurt me.

Suddenly, Paul hissed, "There she is." Coming up the escalator were four people, two very sharply dressed young women in the lead, followed by Chloe, wearing dark sunglasses, and then a very short, grey-haired, but balding gentleman, older, maybe fifty-five. Based on his attire, he was clearly not a lawyer. He hustled along behind the group in baggy wrinkled linen pants, an oatmeal mesh shirt over an undershirt and a multicoloured woven fabric messenger-style bag over his shoulder. Chloe's therapist, perhaps? As he stepped off the escalator, I could see his tired Birkenstocks and that his grey hair had been pulled into a thin, neatly braided ponytail, the kind I always want to grab and pull like a lawnmower cord.

I whispered (I have no idea why) to Paul, "Chloe has an entourage." She looked to be thoroughly enjoying the spectacle of arriving for her sentencing, apparently confident in its outcome. Some of her natural beauty had been restored, or at least so it seemed from a distance. Her hair was a soft brown, styled shorter, nothing fancy, but it suited her. She wore a simple black linen dress, sleeves to the elbow. I could see small simple pearl earrings, barely noticeable, but around her neck was a silver chain with a cross dangling from it. In her hands was what appeared to be a string of black beads. Surely not a rosary? If we didn't know better, we would've assumed that a beautiful young nun, having chosen to bear a cross at the second Station of the Cross, was now arriving at court seeking an indulgence.

It was quite a different story as soon as she saw Paul and me. She simply lost it right there in the hallway, grabbing at the young women in front of her, who had no idea what she was suddenly screaming about. She dropped her beads, pointed at us, and began screeching, "What are they doing here? You said it was private!" The two young women each took an arm and practically carried her into the courtroom, followed closely by Mr. Ponytail, with her dropped rosary beads in hand.

I turned to Bonnie. She looked stunned, overwhelmed by what she was watching. "Bonnie, Bonnie. Are you okay?"

She turned to me, a little afraid, and said, "Andrew, what is going on?"

"Paul, stay with Bonnie." I made a beeline for the courtroom door and wedged my foot in as the clerk tried to pull it closed. "One more lawyer," I insisted with a smile as I squeezed through. A lawyer in gowns? Must be in the right place, she assumed.

"The matter of R. v. Campbell. Are you ready to proceed?" No sooner had the clerk uttered those words than in strolled my old friend the Honourable Justice Harold. Well, well, well. Small world. He marched, head down, straight to his chair on the bench and sat down. He looked tired, more tired than when I had last seen him at Old City Hall. When he finally looked up, he nodded to the court reporter, who sat to his left, ready to silently record the proceedings, and then turned to see Chloe, crumpled in a chair beside Hughes, surrounded by the young women and the old man with a ponytail. She was sobbing uncontrollably. Harold turned to look at the Crown, who stood before him and nodded. It was clear he didn't recognize him. He then turned to Hughes, nodded, and finally, without uttering a word, leaned to one side and looked at me standing at the back of the court-room. Hughes turned to the Rubber Ball Boy as if to say, *Have you got this under control?*

After taking us all in through those exhausted eyes, Harold spoke. "Please be seated." He read slowly from some notes in front of him. "This is apparently a plea and joint submission for sentencing in the Campbell matter." He then held up between his thumb and forefinger a thin slip of paper. "Gentlemen, this is all I have been given, so please fill me in." Not only was he tired, but he seemed frustrated. Perhaps this had landed on his desk at the last minute.

One slip of paper? *That's odd*, I thought. I don't do criminal law, but even I knew he should have a file with at least the charges, the history of what happened, a sentencing report, something. He had nothing. What was going on?

Rubber Ball Boy rose. "Good afternoon, Your Honour, Krell, K.R.E.L.L. initial A, for Her Majesty, the Crown. My friend, Mr. Hughes, acts for the accused, Ms. Campbell."

"Thank you, Mr. Krell. Mr. Hughes needs no introduction to the court. Good afternoon, Mr. Hughes."

Hughes rose slowly from his seat, took off his reading glasses, and said in his most rehearsed humble voice, "Thank you, Your Honour, and it is a pleasure to see that this very difficult and sad matter has been put into your experienced hands. As Mr. Krell will tell you, we have a guilty plea from my client and a joint submission for sentencing. Should Your Honour accept the recommendations, we would ask that you impose the sentence today, to take effect immediately."

Krell was on his feet. "The Crown agrees with Mr. Hughes, Your Honour."

Whoa, whoa, whoa. *Who is in charge here? Who is prosecuting whom?*

Harold looked down at the sheet of paper in front of him and scowled. "Thank you both. That just leaves at least one unanswered question."

Hughes rose again and removed his glasses again, this time with a broad smile. "How may we assist Your Honour?"

Harold leaned to the side again and looked at me. "What is Mr. Bierce's role in all of this?"

"I'm sorry, Your Honour?" Hughes was puzzled and looked to Krell for help.

"Mr. Bierce." He nodded toward me as if to say, *That Mr. Bierce, the one standing at the back of the courtroom in black lawyer gowns.*

Krell rose quickly, knocking his chair over in the process with a loud bang. "Your Honour, Mr. Bierce is not involved in this matter and frankly has no interest in these proceedings. As Mr. Hughes and I said, the submission . . . the joint submission—"

Harold cut him off. "Really? No interest?" He seemed intrigued. "Never a dull moment, Mr. Bierce, when you are around. I thought we had an understanding that you would be sticking to divorce court. No?"

"Good afternoon, Your Honour. May I address the court?"

"Please. Come forward. Mr. Krell seems to think you should be excluded from this otherwise public hearing."

"I'm not surprised, Your Honour." I let that hang out there long enough to beg the next question.

Harold took the bait. "And why is that?"

I had him. "Your Honour may recall my appearance in your court about a year ago at Old City Hall."

"How can I forget it, Mr. Bierce? After your little intervention, the rest of the day was a washout. I hope we're not looking at a repeat today." I swear he smiled a little at the thought of Novak's meltdown and suddenly having a free afternoon.

As Harold and I reminisced, I could see Hughes looking at Krell. He was concerned.

I took pains to remind Harold that he had sprung Paul from the Don Jail that day, that he was ultimately released, and that his wife—who would have only been too happy to see him remain in jail—in fact went on to kill their daughter.

Krell could see it slipping away and jumped in to break up our trip down memory lane. "Your Honour, this is all very interesting, and we are all sorry for Mr. Campbell's loss, the loss of . . . " He forgot her name again. "A loss we should remember is shared by the mother."

Whoa, whoa, whoa, who's his client? Chloe? Hughes stiffened at Krell saying anything about his client. That was his job.

"Her name was Angie, and she was just three, Your Honour." As I added these details, Chloe began to bob back and forth in her chair, sobbing. "And I think there is more to this sentencing than meets the eye."

Krell jumped in again. "A full sentencing report has been prepared, and the Crown feels comfortable that there is more than enough information in that report to assist the court. Mr. Bierce has nothing to offer the court—"

"There is a sentencing report?" Harold asked, surprised.

"Yes, Your Honour, there is. I have a copy for you." He handed it to the clerk, who passed it to Harold without a word.

"Mr. Hughes, do you have a copy?" Hughes simply stood and nodded. He sensed that the less said right now, the better. "It would have been helpful for this court if I had seen this earlier." He was annoyed but interested. "Give me a moment to read this, Mr. Krell."

"Yes, Your Honour. However, I would just like to repeat my request that Mr. Bierce—"

"Mr. Krell, I said give me a minute. Sit down." He was getting angry now.

Hughes was now staring at a pad of paper, fuming at how this bumbling Crown had managed to piss off the judge in less than ten minutes. I don't know if it was the heat coming off Hughes or if the thermostat was broken, but the courtroom was getting warmer by the minute. I could feel that my gowns, already overheated from our mad dash to the courthouse, were soaked through.

While Harold flipped through the sentencing report, I kept my eyes on Chloe, who had begun tugging on her hair and twisting it into tight strands on either side of her face. The wheels were coming off her carefully manicured look, even with her handlers stroking her shoulders and pouring glasses of water. One even wiped her face carefully with a small towel as Mr. Ponytail passed tissues to her. But nothing worked. She was melting in the quiet of the hot courtroom.

Finally, Harold looked up. "Mr. Bierce . . . "

"Yes, Your Honour . . . "

"What do you want here?" He was tired. I could see it.

Krell fell back in his chair, exasperated. Harold noticed. Not good. Visions of Novak that day a year ago.

"Only that Mr. Campbell and I be permitted to observe the sentencing of Ms. Campbell. Surely he has no less a right than any other member of the public."

Krell was on his feet again. "Your Honour, let me repeat—"

Harold was not having any more of his interruptions. He held up a palm. "Mr. Krell, sit down. The next time I want to hear from you, I will ask you to make submissions. Don't make me repeat myself. Understood?" Rubber Ball Boy was finished.

Harold turned to Hughes. "Mr. Hughes, your thoughts?"

Hughes rose. *How will he play this?* I wondered. Was a rabbit about to be pulled out of his hat? "Your Honour, I'm in your hands. Our justice system is open for all to see. It is not a weakness but rather one of its greatest protections."

Beautiful. Well played.

"However . . ."

Uh-oh . . .

"However, I wish to add that I came here today with my client at the request of Mr. Krell, who acts on behalf of the Crown. I was assured that this proceeding was in everyone's interest: the Crown's, the administration of justice, and my client, who is here, ready to plead guilty, ready to accept responsibility and ready to accept this court's punishment." He said *punishment* like she was going to the cross itself.

He was basically telling Harold that he was here to help, Krell was the problem, but they should get on with it. A deal's a deal.

"And what of Mr. Bierce and Mr. Campbell?"

"I'm ready to proceed on the terms proposed by the Crown. I'm in Your Honour's hands." Again, he was telling Harold that they had a deal. *It's your courtroom. Let's get it over with.*

Harold turned to me, and I could see that he had heard enough. "Mr. Bierce, I appreciate your interest in this hearing but . . . it appears that quite a few people have spent time putting together this sentencing, and this afternoon I need to move it forward. There is no need for any delay. I will not be hearing any third-party submissions."

"Your Honour, may I ask one question?"

Krell stirred and half rose from his seat, as if he was going to rise and say something, but Harold shot him a look and held up a pointer finger that must have felt like a slap in the face.

"Of course."

"Would it be appropriate for the court record to show the names of everyone present? Mr. Krell has identified himself. The court record reflects Mr. Hughes and myself now. Who are these other individuals assisting Mr. Hughes? Should their names and role also be a part of the record?"

"I think that would be appropriate. Mr. Hughes? Mr. Krell? Is there any reason these people should not be a part of the record?"

Suddenly, Hughes looked uncomfortable. "They are assistants to me, Your Honour . . . " Assistants? That was a curious description. He turned and whispered to one of the young women. She shook her head.

"Mr. Hughes?" Harold was now curious. "Can we start with the young woman to whom you are speaking? Name? I assume these students or associates are assisting you? Speak up clearly for the reporter."

The young woman stood and looked like she was to be sentenced for a crime. "Veronica McSorley." She spelled out her name letter by letter for the reporter. Ohhh, Veronica. Well, that at least explained the wiping of poor Chloe's face with a cloth on the way to the cross. These names and actions tugged at long-buried memories of my Catholic upbringing.

"And are you with Mr. Hughes's firm? An associate?" He almost seemed hopeful as his eyebrows shot up. It was as if he was mentoring a young lawyer who was new to the process.

She looked at Hughes and then back at Harold. "No."

"Well, what is your role here today? Mr. Hughes, is this young woman a member of your staff? A student?"

Hughes stood. "No, Your Honour, she is not—"

"Well, who is she? Am I going to have to pull teeth all afternoon just to find out who everyone is? Young lady, what is your role here today? Don't make me ask a third time."

"I'm Ms. Campbell's literary agent."

His eyebrows shot up. "Really? And you, the young woman beside Ms. McSorley, who are you, and what are you doing here?"

The young woman stood quickly and whispered, "My name is Sarah Handelman, Compass, Public Relations and Media."

"Interesting. And the gentleman behind Ms. Campbell. Sir, what is your name and why are you here?"

In contrast to the two young women, this fellow seemed genuinely proud to be present. "I'm Simon Hopper. Ms. Campbell's new partner . . . "

"What do you mean partner? Her business partner?" Harold screwed up his face in curiosity.

"No. I am her new partner, I . . . we're I guess what you'd call . . . common law? And I'm the father of her . . . our baby."

Well, the last part struck Harold right between the eyes. He actually cupped his ear and leaned forward as if he could not believe what he was hearing. "I'm sorry, the accused, Ms. Campbell, is expecting?"

Krell rose slowly. "Yes, Your Honour, it is in the sentencing report . . . If you look on the last page . . . under the heading . . . Ms. Campbell's plans for the future . . . "

Harold looked aghast. "Everyone sit down. And I don't want to hear a word from anyone until I finish reading this sentencing report front to back. And I mean not a word." He then actually pointed directly at Krell.

As he read, I swear the temperature in that courtroom climbed a degree with every turn of a page. The only sound was paper shuffling by Krell and water being poured into plastic cups. When he was finished, Harold looked up and sensed that Krell was about to jump up and say something. Instead, Harold held his index finger to his lips. He looked at me, "Mr. Bierce. Thoughts?"

"Thank you, Your Honour. It strikes me as odd that these people, even Ms. Campbell's new partner, can witness the sentencing, yet the father of the infant victim cannot." I let that sink in and then turned and pointed at the courtroom door. "Mr. Campbell is on the other side of that door. I think he should be on this side of it."

Harold looked at Hughes and then Krell, chewed his bottom lip, and said, "I agree with you, Mr. Bierce."

All hell broke loose as Chloe burst into tears and Simon tore off his messenger bag and rushed to embrace her.

Harold called for quiet, and when everyone had stopped shouting he said, "Mr. Bierce, bring in Mr. Campbell." He followed his statement in an exhausted voice, almost to himself, "I know what Lord Justice Hewart would have to say . . . He must be spinning in his grave . . . "

Krell and Hughes looked at each other, puzzled by Harold's statement.

I looked at Harold as I bowed on my way out of court and said loud enough for everyone to hear, "He would say, 'Justice must not only be done, it must be seen to be done.'"

Not exactly what Hughes and Krell had in mind.

33

Stations of the Cross

HUGHES AND KRELL SANK INTO THEIR SEATS as I moved out the doors at the back of the courtroom, bowed again to Harold, and said, "Thank you, Your Honour. I will get Mr. Campbell." Mission accomplished, but now I dreaded giving him the awful news about Mr. Ponytail and Chloe expecting a child.

Bonnie and Paul were standing outside the courtroom door, talking to, of all people, Lester Donald. "Hey Bierce, what's up in there?" His voice sounded as if another thousand Belmont Menthols had been sucked over his vocal cords.

"I'm sorry, Lester, I can't talk now. Paul, you're in, but . . . " He started to push by me into the courtroom, but as he did I grabbed his arm. I could see his alarm at how firm my grip was. "There are some things you need to know before you go in there . . . "

"What do you mean 'things'?"

Before I could answer, Bonnie was at my elbow. "Bierce, will I be able to go in?" I had already forgotten that she was even there. "You promised. Alvin said it would be okay." That reminded me, where was Alvin? I was expecting him to be here by now. I could use his advice on all this criminal legalese bullshit.

"Bonnie, this is not the time. I barely got Paul in there." I turned back to him. "Look . . . two things . . . and you need to be cool. All right? Super cool. First . . . ," I took a deep breath. "That guy with the ponytail . . . he's Chloe's new partner . . . common law."

"Partner? What the fuck?" He was stunned. "New partner? He's old enough to be her father."

"I know, and there's more." I decided just to tear the bandage off. "Chloe is expecting a child . . . with him." Bonnie's audible gasp did not help this news land softly.

It literally struck Paul mute. The word mute is from the Latin *mutus*, meaning speechless. But speechless could not capture the hollow silence that hung around the four of us as he digested that horrible fact. However, it lasted just a few seconds before a torrent of swearing gushed out, interspersed with "murderer," "Children's Aid Society," "justice," "joke," "farce," and more. He tugged free of my arm and stared at me. "What're you going to do about it?"

Me? What was I going to do about it? For a split second I was *mutus*.

"Paul, I'm not taking you in there unless you can keep your cool. I don't think you can handle it. There's nothing I can do about it. I'm a divorce lawyer. This is criminal sentencing. They have concocted some deal, and the best I can do is at least get you in there to watch her receive some form of justice . . . " Some form of justice? It sounded so stupid even as I said it. "But you cannot—"

He snarled at me, "No one is keeping me out of that courtroom."

As Bonnie unhelpfully echoed Paul's proclamation, the court clerk stuck her head out the door. "Counsel, Justice Harold is waiting."

"Thank you. Please tell him I'm just going to be a minute." I looked at my watch: 3:00 p.m. Where was Alvin? I could feel Bonnie at my elbow. I had never seen her so forceful. She simply was not going to be denied.

"Bierce, is this a sentencing submission? Who have you got for a judge?" Again, Lester with more questions. "Is it a joint submission?" He craned his neck to see through the crack in the courtroom door. "Is that Krell? That's the guy from Brampton that you nearly got into a fistfight with . . . the day your actor client was at court."

"You almost got into a fight with a Crown?" Now Bonnie was weighing in. "Do you have to fight with everyone?" Suddenly Bonnie was challenging me. Where was this coming from?

"Bierce, I know Krell. He's difficult. I have done a pile of these pleas. Let me help you. I owe you . . . " Lester was pleading.

I pulled Paul away from the door and turned to Lester. I had an idea. "What if I retain you as my lawyer to assist me during these proceedings?"

"Harold would have to let me in."

I looked around one more time. No Alvin. I turned to Lester. "You're hired. Let's go."

But as I pushed Paul toward the courtroom door, he stopped suddenly, pivoted, and ran toward the escalator. What now? Cold feet? "Bierce, your briefcase." In all the drama, I had forgotten about it. Ever the faithful client, he grabbed the handle of Black Beauty and dragged it across the hall to the courtroom door, the broken wheel thumping.

"Okay. Thanks. Let's get in there before Harold changes his mind."

Lester and I and then Paul, pulling my briefcase, began squeezing one by one through the door into the small and stifling hot courtroom. Bonnie would have to wait for another day, especially with all her attitude. I wasn't going to risk blowing this over her desire to witness a court hearing. There would be others.

Within seconds, Krell was on his feet. "Your Honour, Mr. Bierce asked for Mr. Campbell to be present and now he has a . . . a . . . more than . . . that . . . " He sounded so stupid.

"Mr. Bierce, please." I could see that Harold was getting tired of the delays.

"Your Honour, first, if I may, this is Mr. Campbell."

"Good afternoon, Mr. Campbell. I'm glad you are able to join us. But Mr. Bierce, what is Mr. Donald's interest?"

Lester stepped forward. "Good afternoon, Your Honour . . . ." Oh God, that voice had even Hughes clearing his throat and reaching for a glass of water. "It's a pleasure to see you again. I've been retained by Mr. Bierce to assist him in understanding the proceeding. As you know, I am familiar with such plea arrangements . . . "

"Indeed."

"Your Honour, I think having Mr. Donald assist me with understanding the process will allow it to move forward more smoothly." I pushed Paul onto a bench and tried to look helpless.

But no sooner had I spoken those words than everyone turned to look at a bald head that had just poked through the courtroom doors. "Good afternoon, Your Honour. Campbell matter?"

Harold actually seemed amused. "As a matter of fact it is, Mr. Shank. May I ask what your interest is?"

"Thank you, Your Honour. I'm counsel to Mr. Campbell on pending criminal charges that are scheduled to be withdrawn by the Crown. These were charges that arose out of allegations made by Ms. Campbell, the accused." Alvin nodded toward Chloe, who now sat sniffling and sobbing. Her face was red and puffy, mascara streamed down her cheeks, and her carefully coiffed hair was a tangled mess. She looked like she had seen the devil himself. Hughes leaned over to her, brushed Mr. Ponytail aside, put all five manicured fingers on her shoulder, and urged her to calm down. She looked to be coming unglued with every new entry into the courtroom.

Alvin carried on, "I'm here to monitor this sentencing and, if you will, as a friend of the court. If there are any questions about the concurrent charges against Mr. Campbell, I can address them." Even I thought that was a stretch, but Harold just nodded. Krell looked over at Hughes, clearly concerned that their deal was headed into the ditch. There were two experienced criminal lawyers in the room now (well, maybe one and a half). This was far more than any of them had bargained for. I looked at my watch: three thirty. And we had not even started the sentencing yet.

Harold looked around the room and asked no one in particular, "Can we proceed now?"

That was when Bonnie came in.

The court clerk rose to intercept her, assuming that she was in the wrong courtroom. (It happens constantly.) Harold thumbed through the sentencing report again, waiting until Bonnie had been steered out the door. But suddenly Bonnie piped up, "I'm Mr. Bierce's law clerk, and I have an important message for him." She held up a piece of paper. Perhaps a war had broken out and I was being conscripted—no, commissioned to lead a battalion. She stood holding the single slip of paper aloft, waiting for someone to say something.

Harold just stared at her. After a few long seconds he nodded toward me and said, "He's there." As if perhaps she did not recognize me, being the only person in the courtroom—other than Judge Harold—wearing black gowns.

Bonnie turned robotically, handed me the note, and then took a seat on a bench, waiting dutifully behind me and Paul. As I looked at the note, I could see Paul's leg twitching furiously. He was ready to explode and glared at Chloe's new husband. Ponytail, unnerved, wisely slid down his bench to the far side of the courtroom out of his line of vision.

The important note? It said simply, *You promised.*

I pretended to read it, nay, to study it, as if it said far more. I pursed my lips in contemplation, folded it, and tucked it into my vest pocket. I hadn't noticed, but everyone in the courtroom was looking at me, waiting for me to say something. After all I had just been handed "an important message." Surely it called for some action.

Harold broke the ice. "Mr. Bierce, is everything okay? Do you need a minute?"

"Thank you, Your Honour, I will need to give the matter a few minutes consideration. I will take necessary steps as soon as we conclude this matter." I had been pretty clear with Bonnie. Wait in the hall. This was so not like her. There would have to be consequences.

Harold just shook his head. "Very well, let's proceed."

As Krell prepared to finally get on his feet and make submissions, I pulled the note from my pocket and scribbled on it. *When we get back to the office . . . I'm going to kill you . . . and don't write back to me.* I turned and handed it to her with a sinister smile.

For some reason Krell felt he needed to preface his submissions with a request for a warning from the judge. "Your Honour, I would ask you to caution those present to avoid outbursts."

Sensing something might be up and with Chloe reduced now to mere sniffing and moaning, Harold took the cue and announced to the court, "Over the next while I expect to hear only four voices in this courtroom: mine, Mr. Krell, Mr. Hughes, and possibly Ms. Campbell, should she choose to address this court. Any outburst and you will be excluded. Understood?"

There were mumbled responses in agreement, to which Harold simply stated, "Mr. Krell, proceed."

Krell rose and began to read from a prepared statement. "Your Honour, this is a very sad case, and I'm pleased to report that the Crown and defence have worked together to achieve a guilty plea and a sentencing recommendation—"

Harold interrupted him. "Mr. Krell, I know that already. Please get to your submissions."

This seemed to throw Krell off his script, and he paused, searching through his notes and papers for a starting point that would be something Harold actually wanted to hear. Embarrassed, he turned and looked at me out of the corner of his eye. I caught his glance and mouthed, "Problem?"

"Mr. Krell, please." Harold was getting annoyed again.

"This is a very sad case, Your Honour, and—"

"Mr. Krell, what are your submissions?"

"Yes, thank you. Let me begin by recapping the charges . . . "

He seemed to find his feet, and even I felt a little relieved. But as Krell read the background and the ugly facts around Angie's poisoning, I could feel Paul stiffen beside me. He clenched his fists and grabbed handfuls of his suit pants into sweaty wrinkled bunches. I put my hand on his leg, which was jumping as if an electric current was running through it, and whispered to him to take it easy.

Chloe turned to look at Paul every few seconds as if acknowledging that even she could not believe she had done this to their daughter.

Krell reached his conclusion in a stunning understatement, which could barely be heard. "And therefore the Crown is accepting Ms. Campbell's plea of guilty to the charge of reckless endangerment of a child . . . "

Paul hissed, "What did he say?"

Harold looked surprised, and even the court reporter's eyebrows shot up. Reckless endangerment? The child was dead. I assumed it would be a guilty plea to manslaughter. Chloe turned and looked at Paul, her face a mess, her eyes blank. Veronica slipped between them, and I was grateful as every glance seemed to increase the voltage to Paul's electrified leg.

Alvin and Lester leaned into me and said almost in unison, "This is B.S. . . . they have switched it to a summary conviction. Now I know why they put this in front of Justice Harold instead of a Superior Court Judge." Unhelpfully, Lester also handed me one of his Egyptian chicken scratch hieroglyphic notes that for the life of me I could not read. The first word appeared to be "restaurant." I tucked it in my vest pocket and waited to hear what Harold had to say.

He simply turned to Hughes. "Mr. Hughes, your submissions?"

Hughes rose and said, "Thank you. First, Your Honour, let me acknowledge the work of Mr. Krell. He has made what could have been a difficult matter much easier to deal with."

Lester's unmistakable voice could be heard muttering, "No kidding."

Harold's eyes shot to Lester. "Counsel!"

"I'm sorry, Your Honour."

Harold turned back to Hughes. "Counsel, please begin."

The courtroom fell silent for the great man's words.

34

Captivated

HUGHES BEGAN WITH HIS VOICE just above a whisper, making everyone turn an ear to hear his every word. Even Harold leaned forward, straining to grasp his special take on this tragedy. He looked directly at Harold, not a piece of paper in his hand, his thin crocodile-skin folder opened before him on a short, battered wooden podium. He spoke from memory, from his heart about Angie, a child he had never met. He spoke as if she had been his own.

I was captivated.

Hughes then changed direction, subtly shifting from Angie to Chloe. Imperceptibly, his tone changed too, firmer, less personal, no longer the compassionate friend but now a professional, a neutral observer of an accident scene.

"Your Honour, our professional lives do not include divorce. We labour here in the criminal courts, and yes, we hear awful things, we see unspeakable things . . . " He paused as if he was searching spontaneously for the right words. "But in divorce, when the custody of innocent children, babies, flesh and blood, become like a piece of furniture caught in the bitter crossfire between mother and father, we truly see some people at their absolute worst . . . "

Where was this going?

"Your Honour, I had the opportunity to review the divorce proceedings between Paul and Chloe . . . " (ah, no last names now; he had personalized their battle) " . . . and I read firsthand the terrible things they said about each other. Both of them are guilty of that. We must wonder how such people could ever profess to have been in love. It is a mystery how love can be poisoned and turned into what? Bile? We cannot hope to understand it, but their bile poisoned Angie as surely as the cough medicine."

He paused again, and then summoned a new tone, a judgmental one. He turned, raised his arm, and pointed directly at me.

Uh-oh. Shiiit.

"I had not expected Mr. Bierce to be in court today. But I have seen his handiwork." He said the word as if I had mutilated a body. "Chloe, we know from the sentencing report, struggled, struggles still, with a medical condition. Medical professionals call it obsessive-compulsive disorder, and her struggle with that medical disorder was laid out for all the world to see in the divorce proceedings. It was used skillfully, like a sharp knife, to carve her up, to mock her, to make her out to be some kind of monster. And it was ultimately used to try to take her child away."

Before continuing, Hughes let that analysis hang over the courtroom as Saint Chloe rocked in her chair, sobbing. Harold glanced at me and let out a deep sigh. "Does Chloe take pride in her disorder and its curious manifestations? Of course not. Does she want these humiliating compulsive behaviours stalking her movements day in and day out? No, no one would. Is a person who suffers from Tourette's not ashamed of what his brain and mouth can combine to spit out at an unsuspecting world? Should we use that disorder to mock that person? Shame that person? Take their children away? No. But that is surely what Chloe felt: shame, shame, shame." Each time he said "shame," it was a little louder and held a deepening tinge of anger. "Each time Paul and his counsel rubbed her nose in her disorder, that is precisely what she felt: shame."

Chloe's crying had settled into a low moan again, and Paul, horrified, was now strapped to an electric chair, both legs bouncing as Hughes skillfully spun a narrative that turned her from murderer to victim. I looked at Harold. He, too, was riveted by Hughes's words as he climbed to the climax.

"Chloe admits to administering the cough syrup." He said it quickly, getting her admission of guilt out of the way. "She does not deny it. She doesn't ask that you see her medical disorder as excusing her horrible actions. She asks only that you see her actions in the context of that medical disorder and the divorce proceedings. She doesn't deny that it was a misguided attempt to hang on to her daughter, to keep her from being taken away, taken out of her life." Then Hughes paused and looked up at Harold. "Parents do terrible things as they divorce. Look what this divorce drove her to do." He turned and looked at me and Paul as if to say, *Look no further than these two devils.*

Hughes was not finished. He softened again. His voice fell low. "Things went horribly awry, and now we, you, Your Honour, must do the impossible. You must determine a suitable punishment for Chloe, a punishment . . . " and here his voice fell to a hoarse whisper, ". . . a punishment that could certainly be no greater than the cross she must bear for the rest of her life, the loss of her own child at her own hand . . . all the while raising another child . . . " Chloe clutched the cross around her neck with hands still bright red from bleach-induced dermatitis and began to sob again, gasping for air. "If there is such a punishment, I cannot think of it, Your Honour." Hughes sounded exhausted, as if he truly had wracked his brain to think of a suitable punishment but had given up and was leaving the terrible task for Harold to decide.

And then the rabbit was pulled from his hat.

"Mr. Krell and I have conferred and—as this is now proceeding as a summary conviction offence—our joint recommendation for this young woman, as an expectant mother, is one year probation on condition that she participate in counselling and treatment for her condition as recommended in the sentencing report."

Paul's legs suddenly stopped jumping. He simply froze. I expected him to gasp, as both Lester and Alvin did behind me. A fog of injustice settled around us.

Justice Harold, clearly moved by Hughes's words, turned to Krell. "Mr. Krell, does the Crown concur in the recommended sentence?"

Krell barely rose from his seat, bent at the waist and said, "Yes, Your Honour."

Harold turned to the martyr. "Before I impose sentence on you, do you have anything you wish to say?"

She did.

35

An End

BEFORE CHLOE ROSE TO SPEAK, Hughes leaned into her and whispered a few words of encouragement, reminders likely. I assumed he had rehearsed with her an appropriate statement filled with regret and humility. Mr. Ponytail moved closer and helped her from her seat. As she stood before Harold, she began to tremble uncontrollably, and her prepared pink sticky notes spilled from her hands onto the courtroom floor. Instead she clutched with one hand the cross around her neck, leaned heavily on the old wooden counsel table, and gasped for air.

"Take your time, Ms. Campbell," Harold said patiently.

"Your Honour, I . . . I . . . I miss my daughter . . . I miss Angie . . . I'm so sorry . . . " She reached down and placed her hands on her abdomen. "I want to be a good mother . . . again . . . with . . . " She reached for Mr. Ponytail's hand. "With a good man by my side . . . " Before she could say another word, she was convulsed by sobs and collapsed into her chair.

I could see that Harold was unnerved by the scene. He swallowed hard and resigned himself to the role of executioner. He cleared his throat and announced, "This court accepts the recommendation of Mr. Hughes and the Crown. I find you guilty of . . . " His words disappeared as any remaining oxygen left the stifling hot courtroom. "And I impose the recommended sentence with the conditions as set out. This tragedy is over."

I'm not sure either Chloe or Paul heard a word of what Harold actually said. They were still in their personal fog of war. Harold mumbled something to the court clerk, who stood and announced that the court was adjourned. He was out of the courtroom in seconds, probably headed for a stiff drink in his chambers.

Lester leaned over my shoulder again and said too loudly, "Like I said in my note, Bierce . . . " He turned to Alvin. "Am I right?" Alvin was speechless and just shook his head in disbelief. I looked over at Chloe and Hughes. The crying had stopped, and she was on her knees, gathering her pink notes from the floor, apologizing to Hughes for not saying what they had rehearsed.

Hughes took her by the hand, helped her up, and seemed to inject her with his cool calm. "It's okay, Chloe, leave them. It's okay, it's over . . . Let's get out of here." I watched as he reached for his folder and nodded to the two young women to get Chloe moving. "Let's move." He said it with cold authority.

I turned to Paul, Alvin, and Lester. "Wait for them to leave. Hang back, and we can discuss what just happened." As I spoke, Paul calmly reached down beside the bench into the zippered pouch on the outside of Black Beauty. When his hand emerged, it held a small black handgun. He rose from his seat and pointed it across the room at Chloe and Hughes.

He called out. "Chloe!"

He squeezed off shot after shot. Words would not come from my mouth to stop him. I heard Alvin shout, "Don't!" as Paul wheeled around in my direction. I pushed his hand away, but the gun went off like a cannon inches from my face. A bullet ripped into a TV monitor over Chloe's head. I saw Veronica fall underneath the weight of Hughes. Ponytail scrambled over the courtroom benches but tumbled into a heap as Paul fired around the courtroom. I tried to grab him, but someone pushed me hard to the floor as I heard Alvin again, screaming at Paul to stop. Shots rang out again and again as people screamed and fell to the floor.

And then suddenly in the stifling heat there was silence.

With the weight of someone piled on top of me, I could not move, but I could hear Alvin saying over and over, "Paul, Paul put the gun down. It's over." The hot chamber filled with the smell of burnt wool.

Through the benches I could just make out Bonnie lying on the floor near the courtroom door, her legs twisted into an impossible position and her black skirt twisted up around her waist, exposing her panties to the world. (They were, of course, black.) I called out to her, but she didn't move. I could hear crying and moaning all around me, and then suddenly the room was filled with new voices, angry voices, shouting at Paul. I looked across at Bonnie again and recognized the woman cop who just over an hour ago had ushered us so warmly through security. Her face was not warm now. She knelt over Bonnie's back and snarled at Paul to get down, get down, over and over again.

My face felt wet. I could smell stale cigarettes and a pungent spicy body odour as a police officer knelt beside my head. I was being crushed by the weight of people on top of me and cried out, "Get off of me, get off! I'm okay."

The officer called to no one in particular, "This one's hit." I wondered who he meant. "Lie still, help is coming, just lie still." He called out again, "Another one here," as paramedics suddenly scrambled over the scene.

I tried to roll on my side but couldn't move. Paralyzed, I was wedged between two benches, and my black robes were wrapped tight around me like swaddling. I struggled to free a hand and ran it across my sweat-soaked face. My face burned, my ears were ringing and the smell of wet wool filled my nose.

"I'm fine. I need to get up. Bonnie . . . Bonnie." Nothing.

"Lie still." The officer's voice was almost angry with me. I looked at my hand. It was covered in thick red blood. When I turned to Bonnie again, I could see that she was now on her back, and a paramedic hovered over her. She was not moving. In a fury I wiggled my shoulders and tugged at my robes enough to be able to turn my head to the right. There I found myself just a few inches from Lester's face. His eyes were wide open, a brilliant blue. His lips mouthed something to me as bright ruby-red blood pumped with a sickening low gurgling sound from a hole torn in his throat.

Blood pooled on the floor, framing our faces as we looked at each other.

"Lester . . . Lester . . . "

His lips moved again as he tried to speak to me, but his words were lost as a cop pressed handfuls of my black gowns onto his neck to try to stop the bleeding. I watched as Lester's eyes blinked rapidly, his eyelids fluttering. And then his lips trembled one last time, and he exhaled a long, stale menthol breath directly into my face. He was gone. It was over.

36

Defrocked: *Ad Poenam*

THE NEXT FEW DAYS were not good. The media could not get enough of what had happened. After Paul was arrested, new revelations tumbled out almost by the hour. It was soon reported that Paul had made the wrong kind of friends during his brief stay at the Don Jail. The fellow he met, Carlos, it turns out was not a very nice person. He was very guilty of horrific domestic abuse, not to mention some other unsavoury things, and very much deserved to be arrested, kids' hockey game or not. Paul had stayed in touch with Carlos's friends, and they were only too happy to get him a Glock 19 in exchange for getting money to Carlos's family. *Quid pro quo.*

It was humiliating, but I had to admit to the police that Paul had fooled me with all his fumbling with Black Beauty, breaking a wheel so he could slip the gun into the side pocket and have me bring it through security. The *Toronto Sun* had a field day with that tidbit: "Unwitting Lawyer Smuggled Gun Into Court House: Partner Gunned Down." I tried to explain that Lester was not my partner. No one cared.

What really hurt, though, was how quickly some in the legal community lined up to offer criticism of me. Williams in particular seemed to be in the news every day, milking it as a "leading member of the bar." In one interview, he was quoted as saying, "My colleagues and I are not sure why

Mr. Bierce was even there. A divorce lawyer, in his lawyer's gowns no less, doesn't go to the criminal courts . . . and drag their secretaries along to be entertained by the show. That poor woman . . . I'm calling for a Law Society investigation . . . This reflects on the whole legal profession . . . a suspension may be in order, but I don't want to prejudge his actions . . . " What a prick.

And then an ambitious *Globe and Mail* reporter uncovered Sean's relationship with Chloe and his long, soiled history with the archdiocese. Oh my God, you would think it was a journalistic coup worthy of a Pulitzer Prize. When the Church read the story and learned about Sean's attempt to arrange the abortion, there was a terse announcement that Father Sean had used up his last last chance. Of course, for the Catholic Church that was simply a bridge too far. Everything he had done to that point in time, the affairs, the drinking, the lawsuits, the damages he had caused, that could be tolerated, but abortion? Oh, that was simply too much. Laicization was even mentioned. Now there was a word the journalist had to look up. The Church was going to *defrock* my brother, remove his liturgical vestments, take his alb. Effective immediately, there was to be no officiating at Mass, baptisms, weddings, funerals, or communion. There might even be a canonical trial. Father Sean, they said, was entitled to due process but suspended in the meantime. Sean didn't care about due process; he was gone for forty days and forty nights with forty ounces and was no doubt being ministered to by the angels.

Speaking of frocks and albs, in all the chaos at court my gowns had disappeared. I'd had those gowns for over forty years. The last I saw of them, they were wrapped around Lester's head as the paramedics wheeled him to an ambulance for one last fruitless attempt to save his life. My calls to the detective went unanswered, even though I explained repeatedly that those gowns were very valuable and that I needed them for appearances in court. I tried not to think about what state they would be in, but ugly images of their black folds being pushed into Lester's throat and that stale menthol breath flashed through my mind every day. And what had Lester been trying to tell me?

Of course, Chloe's media team used every opportunity to mention that her book release would now be delayed because of what had happened but would be available soon with additional chapters telling the "inside story" of what had happened to her at court that day. Title? *The Cross I Must Bear.* I wanted to throw up.

As all of this unfolded in the days after the shooting, I ended up sleeping in the office a lot. Reporters were hanging around my condo. At least here I could try to get some work done while the dust settled. I also had no car to get back and forth as anything I parked in the underground was immediately trashed, including Pussycat. Something had been poured into the gas tank, and it was going nowhere. I couldn't even rent a car given my track record, so any movement was strictly by Uber. The building security squad was of no help but promised to undertake an investigation ASAP. They seemed to think the whole thing was pretty funny, kind of just desserts. Pricks.

As I scrolled through emails, I saw a letter from the Law Society marked *Personal and Confidential. Urgent.* I opened it to see that, unlike their usual snail's pace on anything important, they were indeed going to launch an immediate investigation into the incident, and it was to be led by none other than Mr. Williams. The letter urged me to seal Paul's file and preserve all potential evidence for the inquiry. And until further notice, I was suspended on an interim basis. They also urged me to retain a lawyer. Pricks.

Loud noises from the reception area doors and whispers snapped me out of the Law Society's *ad poenam.* It sounded like someone was forcing their way into my office. It was a Saturday morning, so I was not expecting any little Portuguese women to clean the office. I could make out a man's voice, too confident, almost belligerent, laughing. "Got it. It was no problem." Then heavy footsteps coming slowly down the hall. I crouched down behind my desk and waited. The footsteps stopped outside my office door. I waited in silence, a fury growing inside me. I looked around for something I could use as a weapon and grabbed my old heavy metal notary seal. It would need to do. I sprang from behind the desk wielding the seal like a hammer and screamed, "Bring it, you motherfucker!"

Bonnie's scream probably would have been heard at street level had it not been drowned out by my screaming. "What the fuck are you doing here? Why are you breaking into the office?"

She was trembling and looked absolutely terrified. "What are you doing here on a Saturday? I haven't got my purse back from the police yet. My office pass is in it. I had a security guard let me in. Why are you hiding behind your desk with . . . your notary seal? You scared me to death." She started to cry.

"I have been sleeping here . . . trying to get a little work done . . . get ahead on a few things . . . "

As she stood there crying, I could see the large brown and yellow bruise all up the left side of her face. She got it from hitting a courtroom bench as she was pushed to the floor by Alvin. She had been knocked out cold. Probably for the best, because she missed the horror. Six shots. Only one person killed. Lester, of all people. Hughes and Alvin were credited with saving lives when they pushed others to the floor. They were heroes. His Royal Highness Royce Hughes, Q.C., was front-page news, with pictures of him and Chloe (clutching her cross) shielded under his arm, his beautiful blue suit flecked with blood and his declaration beneath the photo, "We survived by the grace of God." Jesus Christ.

"Bonnie, come in. Sit down. It's been a lot . . . "

Still crying, she sank into my prized authentic Arne Jacobsen egg chair. I could not recall in all our years together her ever sitting in that chair. It was considered off limits to anyone but me. She usually stood at the door, pen and pad in hand. This day she looked different. She looked drawn, tired, older, and she wore no makeup. Perhaps more extraordinary was the fact that she also was not wearing black from head to toe. She had on some plain jeans, not designer, a nice blue sweater, and, of all things, a pair of worn cowboy boots. I waited a few minutes while we both collected ourselves. "Nice boots." She didn't see me wince or pick up on the sarcasm.

"Thanks. I usually wear them on weekends when I take my riding lessons."

"Whoa partner. You take riding lessons? Seriously?" Maybe she had brain damage from her fall.

"Yeah, over at the CNE, the Horse Palace. I've been going for over a year. I told you."

I looked at her, clueless. I had no recollection of her saying anything about riding or horses.

"You never listen to me. They wouldn't let me ride today, with the head thing . . . I have a concussion. So I came straight here. I always do on Saturdays after . . . " She seemed to lose her train of thought and touched her face gently, as if checking to see if the bruise was still there. "Anyway, I figure Wednesday and Thursday will be tough days with Lester's celebration of life and funeral. Do you want to close for a couple of days? Things can be adjourned. People will understand."

I didn't have the guts to tell her I was suspended and couldn't do anything anyway. I had no gowns. I had been defrocked. "No, no . . . it's better to work through this stuff. There will be new files coming in," I lied.

"It looks like we got a couple of Notices of Change on some files . . . "

Shit. A Notice of Change meant a client was notifying me that they were terminating my services and switching to a new lawyer. "What? Which clients are switching?"

"I'll check and get you a list. It might be a good thing. You need . . . we need a break."

I didn't look up. All I could think was, *Wait till she finds out I'm suspended.*

"Lester's celebration of life. Are you going to be okay with it?"

"Yeah, whatever. Where is it?"

"Same as Keg's. Burdettes."

I stifled what I really wanted to say. Fucking Burdettes. Not again. "Yeah, I'll be fine." I flipped through some papers, which was my cue for Bonnie to leave my office, but then added, "Look, Bonnie, I want to make sure there is a good turnout for this thing, so let's really rally the legal community. Let's give Lester a good sendoff." She looked at me as if she had no idea what I was talking about. "Never mind. Leave it to me. I'll send some emails, make some calls." She shrugged and turned to go. "And Bonnie, have they published anything about the celebration of life? Is there a webpage or something. Facebook thing?"

"Nothing. I saw the story in the *Star*, you know, with the follow-up about Chloe and Hughes. He is becoming quite the hero . . . " I did not take the bait. "But no details about a service. Maybe his family wants it that way. It has been a bit of a circus." Bonnie was right about that. It had become a three-ring circus that now involved the attorney general strik-ing a task force to look at courthouse security.

I sat staring at my phone. I had no idea who to call, who to send an email to, especially on a weekend. I slid from behind my desk and walked over to Bonnie's work station. "I'm going to grab some lunch and a bit of the hair of the dog at the pub downstairs. Do you want to join me?"

"No, thanks. I'd better get started here. I only have an hour or so."

"Do you need a . . . " I made a puffing gesture.

"I quit months ago."

"No way."

"Yes, way. I told you. I've been on the patch." She started to flip through papers on her desk, and I wondered if that was her clue for me to shove off. "I need to get started on some of this stuff if you're going to be out of commission after the celebration of life. I remember what you were like after Keg's . . . "

"Very funny. I'll be fine."

"Well, just in case you aren't 'feeling well' I'll get a few things out of the way."

I picked up a letter out of the pile of mail on her desk. It was another letter from the Law Society. Assuming it was simply the hard copy of the letter about my suspension, I tore it open to discover it was in fact a letter from the Discipline Committee. Ms. Lululemon had reported me for professional misconduct. My stomach churned, and a wave of pins and needles crawled over my shoulders. Pricks.

As I stepped away from Bonnie and headed for the door, she called after me, "Shall we send some flowers to Burdettes for Lester?"

I thought back to Keg's rousing celebration and smiled. "Flowers? That would be such a pussy move."

"Don't use that language!" She was pissed. "Sometimes I don't know you. Why do you talk like that? Honestly."

"I'm sorry. It's not what he needs—flowers—he doesn't need flow-ers." I muttered to myself. He didn't need flowers. He needed a proper sendoff, and I vowed to make it happen.

And why does everyone end up at fucking Burdettes?

37

A Quality Sendoff

I DECIDED TO PRETEND that I had not opened the letter from the Law Society, suspending me. There were things that needed to be done, and I was not about to put down my pen and stop work just because of the shooting and the Law Society inquiry. I slept at the office again for two nights and slipped down to Starbucks to wait outside the doors at my usual spot. When I caught Daphne's eye, she opened up early and told me she had seen the news about the shooting. She seemed genuinely concerned and even asked if Bonnie was okay. I guess they train their people well to look like they give a shit.

When I got back to my desk, I closed my office door, sat, and tried to think of lawyers I should call or email about Lester's celebration of life. I sent a reminder to Alvin and a few emails to guys I thought might have known him, but I didn't feel I really knew enough about him to reach out to his circle of colleagues. Others would need to look after it. Besides, I had other problems.

Fernstein was all over me about the Teresa Savoie matter. I still didn't have a lawyer, and now that I was suspended, I could not even represent myself. He would just love that turn of events. Prick.

There were two messages from the Glidden brothers trying to book yet another meeting with me. Apparently they had finished their "investigation" and wanted to meet before the matter was turned over to police. I resolved as I sat there that the best course of action might be to reach out to the property manager to see if I could get them fired for their incompetence and ongoing harassment of me. I had given him and his daughter some free advice a year ago about her situation with an abusive boyfriend. Might be enough to call in a favour. Frankly, I didn't have the time or the energy to worry about it; the last couple of nights I had done enough worrying for ten men. I was exhausted.

I looked at my watch: 11:00 a.m. Where had the morning gone? When I opened my office door, there sat Bonnie, yellowing bruise and all, working away as if nothing had happened. (And yes, she was dressed in black from head to toe.) She is really unbelievable. "Hey . . . "

"Hey." She did not look up.

"How're you doing?"

"Good. Did you sleep here again?" Still not so much as a glance at me.

"Yeah, I put in a pretty solid morning on a few matters already, so I'm going to pop out and get some air and stop by the LCBO to grab something for tonight."

That got her attention. She stopped and looked up at me. "Something for tonight? Something like what?"

"For tonight, to pass around, the guys like to down a few at these events. I want to make sure there is a good supply of quality scotch . . . " For some reason I said the word as if I was doing a Sean Connery impersonation. "*Shhcotch.*"

"Event? It's a celebration of life at a funeral home." She looked at me, totally dumbfounded.

"And I need to get some cups, some styrofoam . . . no, not styrofoam. I'll get some clear plastic, that's better . . . " I was pretty much talking to myself.

"No visitation that I have ever been to has served booze. You're thinking of a wake. This isn't a wake." She went back to work.

"Yeah, a wake. That's what we should have, a wake."

"It's not a wake. It's a visitation in a funer—"

I wasn't even listening to her. "And I need to grab some cigars . . . "

"You can't smoke in a funeral home. What are you thinking?"

"Bonnie, trust me, these things can get a little hairy." I smiled at the thought of the men chanting at Keg's visitation. "When the boys start getting into it, it can get a little crazy."

"The boys? What are you talking about?"

I grabbed my phone and left for the LCBO. I was back in an hour with four twenty-sixers: two Johnny Walker Blue, an Oban single malt, a nice Glendronach, and a vodka in case some women showed up. I scooped up two dozen cigars at Sleuth and Statesman. As I stood in their humidor, inhaling the rich tobacco scents, I had Edmundo box twelve Cohibas and twelve Romeo y Julietas (which I am partial to when I am in the mood for a celebratory cigar, so they would not go to waste).

On the walk back to the office, I vowed to make Lester's visitation a quality sendoff.

38

Burdettes

I SAT IN THE UBER in front of Burdettes for a few minutes after we'd pulled up. I could see Lester's picture in the window. It was a poorly cropped version of a picture he'd taken with my client at Brampton Court the day I almost fought Rubber Ball Boy. He was smiling, thrilled that he had met the star of one of his favourite cop shows. Little did he know.

"Everything okay? Is this the right address?" The Uber driver looked at me in the rear-view mirror.

"Yeah, can you pull around to the other side of the street and drop me there? And I need to get my briefcase out."

He waited for a streetcar to pass, wheeled around to the opposite side of the street, and popped the trunk. I stepped out and noticed a growing clutch of exhausted people, young and old, men and women, building outside the steps to Burdettes. Some would shake hands, throw their arms around each other, pat each other on the back, and then solemnly turn to go inside. A few grabbed each other, kissed, and hugged like long lost friends. Others, young moms and dads, with shy children wrapped around their legs, seemed to have not seen each other for some time and paused to introduce their little ones and catch up before dragging themselves inside. I could see the grief gathering around them like thick cobwebs weighing them down. It was pulling me down too. I couldn't move and stared as a dozen people, mostly women, now crowded around the entrance. Shit, it suddenly occurred to me that I might not have enough vodka. I could always send Bonnie out for more at the LCBO over on Brock Street if needed.

I wheeled my old backup black briefcase across the streetcar tracks and down the broken, heaving sidewalk to the ugly, painted-brick funeral home. The briefcase was heavy, loaded with the booze, cups, and cigars. The police had seized Black Beauty as evidence and just laughed when I asked how long they might keep it. Whatever. Pricks.

As I got closer, I checked my watch and looked up to see Lester's smiling face in the window. I suddenly said out loud to no one in particular, "Why do they do that?" Is it for people who aren't quite sure they're at the right funeral home? They jump out of their car, check the picture in the window. "Yup, honey, this is it, terrible photo, but that's Lester. Park the car and I will wait here for you." Or is it for the bored passerby who sees the picture in the window and thinks, *Hmm, this dead person looks interesting. I think I'll just pop in and see what this is all about.* It's a mystery.

My briefcase thumped step by step as I carefully dragged it up to the front door. I had a flashback to that day in the library at Brampton Court, Lester's awful clothes and the mess he was making of that case. How did he survive all these years?

A few people streamed by me as I stood in what was supposed to pass for a lobby. I noticed that the bold floral-patterned carpet was the same style used in old movie theatres and thought of Carpetbeggar's magic carpet. A young man in an extraordinarily simple black suit looked at me, tipped his head to his left side, and said in a soft, robotic voice, "And which family are you here to visit with?"

"Uh, Lester Donald, of course . . . " *The same guy whose fucking picture is out front in the window. What a jerk-off,* I thought. It never occurred to me that there could be more than one visitation in this little funeral home. Keg's turnout had filled the place from top to bottom. It had been a good old-fashioned sendoff, and Lester deserved the same, even better.

Robot Boy raised his right arm and tipped his head. "The Donald gathering is here in the Algonquin Room." His left arm rose as the right descended, and he gestured to a small cloakroom behind a black curtain. "You can leave your briefcase in here."

"No, it's okay, thanks . . . "

He smiled at me. "It's a free service we offer."

Like that makes a fucking difference. "No, thanks. I'll just tuck it in the corner of the—"

"The Algonquin Room. Wonderful." With that, he turned to another arrival. "And which family are you here to visit?"

Yeah, the Algonquin Room. How many rooms in this country of ours are called the Algonquin Room? Enough. More than enough.

It was then that it hit me. I felt myself swoon as a wave of Febreze and formaldehyde filled my lungs. I fought the urge to gag and put my hand on the wall just outside the door. Two thoughts swirled: I should have eaten something, and I needed a drink.

When I gathered myself and peered in, I scanned the small room. I saw that its walls were covered with prints of Group of Seven paintings. Prints. I felt a longing for the vibrant art in Williams's reception area, the chrome bat, *the only way it makes sense to you*, and wondered if the artsy receptionist ever thought of me. Did she worry if I was alright after the shooting? The Febreze was affecting my brain.

A quick head count of Lester's mourners came to six. I recounted. Still six, and one of them was Bonnie, appropriately dressed in black from head to toe, with matching bruise still evident. As soon as she saw me, she popped out of her chair and walked over, concerned. "I came a little early to help. It's pretty quiet." Typical Bonnie. I don't think I had heard a word of complaint from her since the shooting. She had always been so, so, I don't know, polite. I bet she would've apologized to the bench she hit if she had not been knocked out cold.

"It's early yet. It won't really get going until seven or eight. I'm going to set up a little . . . " I mouthed the word *bar*, " . . . over here." I wheeled my briefcase into a corner and pulled out a Johnny Walker, cracked it, and stood the bottle with a string of plastic cups. I laid a box of the Cohibas on the bottom shelf of a bookcase, along with my personal cutter and some matches. I poured a large one for myself and downed it. It would hold me until things got going.

When I rejoined Bonnie, I nodded in the direction of an elderly woman dressed in a dark burgundy two-piece wool suit, which I am confident was purchased through an early edition of the Eaton's catalogue, when it was still in its rivalry with Simpsons. "Who's this?"

"That's Lester's secretary, Ida," Bonnie whispered. "She was his secretary for nearly forty years." The tiny woman looked to be over a hundred and could have been Lester's grandmother. I realized then that I didn't know how old Lester was. I guessed late seventies and then tried to do the math for how old Ida would have been when she started working for Lester. I gave up. Exhaustion and JW Blue had clouded my calculations.

"Who's the other one?"

"That's her older sister. She came to keep her company."

"Older sister? I must ask her about the War of 1812 . . . "

Bonnie gave me her standard *don't start with that nonsense* look and asked me what was really on her mind. "Have you been drinking?"

I ignored her question and turned my attention to a tall, impeccably dressed man in his eighties sitting in a corner, trying to look invisible. "Who's the Jimmy Stewart?"

"Very funny. You *have* been drinking." I said nothing and waited. "I'm not sure who he is, but he's been here since six, hasn't said a word, and prays a lot. He also brought a box of condolence cards. He left some on the table over there."

"Is there a board of pictures of Lester or anything?"

"No, not yet. Maybe his family is bringing one. Traffic has been bad."

"Yeah, it's early yet. Flowers?" I smiled.

"None, yet."

Out of the corner of my eye I saw Lester's casket at the front of the room. Open. I knew I needed to see him one last time and pay my respects, but I was not ready. Soon, but just not yet. Instead I slipped over to the lower shelf, pretended to get something from my briefcase, and poured myself another drink. I downed it, looped by a table to grab a condolence card, and slid it into my pocket. Just another concerned mourner; no one was the wiser.

I headed over to speak with Ida. Gently, I said, "Hello, I understand you worked with Lester." I reached to touch her hand. "I'm so sorry ... He was a good man."

She looked up at me, tears in her eyes, obviously heartbroken. "What am I going to do?" She grabbed my hand with a vice-like grip and squeezed so hard, I could hardly feel my fingers.

"I'm sorry. He must have meant a lot to you." I winced as she maintained the grip of a pioneer woman.

"What am I going to do? I needed that job with Lester . . . I don't know what I'll do . . . " She looked across the room at his casket, lost.

Her sister took her other hand and said, "Ida, you can move in with me. We'll be okay." She looked up at me and pulled at my sleeve. "Are you a lawyer?"

"Yes, I'm Andrew Bierce." My God, did these people not have a television or read the papers? My picture and Lester's had been in the news for days now.

"Do you need any secretarial help? Ida has lots of experience."

"No, I'm good right now. But I can ask around when other lawyers start arriving." I tugged my hand from Ida's, and it seemed to uncork something in both of them as they sat, holding each other's hands, crying. I let out a deep sigh and turned to see Bonnie watching me console them. She burst into tears and turned away. What was her problem?

Lester's casket caught my eye again. He was waiting for me, just a few steps away, at the front of the room, but at that moment it might as well have been ten miles, uphill all the way. I decided to head out to the lobby to round up late arrivals.

Robot Boy was still there, greeting people as they entered, head tipping to and fro and arms directing the grieving. Left to the Tom Thomson Room, right to the Algonquin Room. He turned to me. "Yes, sir, can I help you?"

"The Donald family?"

"Yes, the Algonquin Room." His arm floated up to point at the room I had obviously just come out of.

"Yes, I know, but has the family arrived yet?"

"No, I haven't met them, but it's early yet. While you wait, there is coffee just over here in the lounge area." Again with the floating arms. "It's complimentary."

I winced at him. "No, no . . . wait . . . Is there a washroom nearby?"

His arm directed me to a stairwell leading to the lower level. I shuddered to think what went on in the basement of Burdettes and made my way quickly to the men's room. I threw some water on my face and stared at my reflection in a cloudy mirror that had seen better days. And based on the bags under my eyes, that mirror had seen better faces. I checked my watch. Nearly eight. Where was everyone? Where was his family? *Stay calm. It's early. It'll happen. Not to worry.*

As I reached the top of the stairs, a wave of relief washed over me. The lobby was filling up, and there stood Rick Z, King of the B's, and three of his associates. *Thank God, it's gonna happen.* I stepped between him and Robot Boy to grab his hand. "Rick, Mr. Z, great to see you. Lester's over here in the Algonquin Room. We're just getting started . . . "

"Lester?"

"Yeah, Lester Donald's here. It's his celebration of life. It's here. Tonight. Great you could make it."

"Wow, he's here too? We're here for the Bronsons. Their son, a ten-year-old, died in a boating accident up near Haliburton. Our firm is looking after the litigation, so I thought we should stop in and pay our respects." He looked over at the Tom Thomson Room, overflowing with people. I could see a dozen flower arrangements, a memory board chock full of photos, and a flatscreen playing a slideshow of the beloved boy. "Lester's here too, eh? God that was terrible. What a nightmare."

"Yeah, Thanks. I'm okay, I'm hanging in." As I said those words, I realized he had not actually asked how I was doing. "Listen, can you drop in after you're done at . . . that one?"

"Yeah, I guess. I'll try."

"Well, pop in for a drink at least."

"I'll try. A drink? Is that allowed in here?"

"Yeah, you know for the toast, like Keg's . . . "

He looked at me, puzzled. "Okay, I'll try. Not sure about the drink, though. I'm driving, and I have to get back to the office. Got a trial coming up. Usual B.S. You know."

"Yeah, I know, but try to make it. It's Lester, after all."

"Right. Sure. See you later."

By eight thirty, no more than a dozen people had graced the Algonquin Room. The celebration was to end at nine. I had invited a few to help themselves to the Johnny Walker Blue, but it sat untouched except for my refills. I wished that I had eaten before I came and had a horrible flashback to sitting in the rain outside this awful place with puke on my shoes. I promised myself there would be no repeat tonight.

I walked over to chat with two elderly gentlemen, Lester's former law partners, both long retired. I'd never heard of either of them, although they said they had each practiced law for over forty-five years in Toronto. One told me that Lester had nearly gone bankrupt late in his career after a nasty divorce. They couldn't seem to agree about what had happened to him after that, bickering back and forth based on two totally unreliable memories. Bad investments? No, no. Trouble with his kids? Maybe. No, no. He didn't have kids. Yes, he had a son. All they could agree on was that Lester "had" to work, needed the dough, and that it was sad how things had turned out. They excused themselves because the special TTC bus for the disabled had arrived. They left, slowly.

A couple of Lester's former clients came and went. A real estate agent floated around. One fellow arrived to pay his respects, and I was certain it was the lawyer from poverty court who carried his client files around in a shopping bag. Justice Nelson wandered in. He was followed a few minutes later by two cops who were at the shooting. Nice gesture, but I didn't expect any of them to join me in a drink. Nelson simply nodded at me, paid his respects, and left. I thought he probably had a senior's subscription for theater tickets at the Royal Alex and could still make the second act. Alvin finally arrived. I saw him milling around and chatting with Bonnie but he always seemed to be on the other side of the room. Was he avoiding me? I watched as he made his way up to Lester's casket, knelt, and prayed. I would have never figured Alvin to be a religious man. I moved to intercept him as he headed to the door. "Hey what's up my friend? No time to catch up? How are you holding up? It's been a shit storm hasn't it?"

There was none of his usual goofy smiling and facial massaging. He simply looked at the floor and said, "I have to get going."

"I was hoping we could grab a few ales."

"Nah, can't."

"What's up, Alvin? Grab a drink with me. Did you see what I got stashed over there? There's some quality scotch over there."

"Look, Andrew, I have to be straight with you. Given everything that's happened I don't think it's best for us to hang out. I've been told it's not good professionally." He threw air quotes on *professionally*.

"What do you mean? Who? Who would say something like that? Law Society? Who?" For good measure I threw some air quotes on *who*.

"I'd rather not get into it. This day is tough enough as it is."

"Alvin, I think you owe it to me. If you're pulling the plug on this . . . this . . . I don't even know what this is."

"Do you really wanna know?"

"Of course. I'm a big boy."

"OK. As a part of the Law Society investigation Williams took me aside and told me to steer clear of you. He said . . . well it wasn't very nice."

"What? What did he say?"

Alvin's voice fell to an embarrassed whisper. "He said, 'Lay down with dogs and . . . '" He couldn't finish the sentence.

"Lay down with dogs, wake up with fleas?"

"Yeah, something like that."

"And you agree with him?" There was a long pause. "Not a problem. Thanks for coming. I know Bonnie appreciated it."

"Look, Bierce, I'm sorry." And with that he turned and left.

I turned and watched as the tall man who had been keeping to himself rose, walked up solemnly to Lester, reached into the casket, blessed himself, turned on his heel, and left without saying a word. I followed him into the lobby, but he had disappeared into the crowd that was starting to exit the Tom Thomson Room. There I saw Rick Z and his associates heading out the door, popping umbrellas in the rain that had started to fall. Pricks.

I returned to Lester's room and realized that it was just me, Bonnie, and Lester. She was sitting at the back of the room, hunched over in exhaustion, looking at her phone.

It was time. I had been there three hours, and I had still not summoned the courage to face Lester. I took a deep breath, finished my cup of scotch, and walked toward Lester's casket. As I approached, I could see it was a common dark brown veneer, large brass handles, and a white silk lining. So simple.

I stopped a respectful two feet from him and peered in as if looking over the edge of a cliff. There was Lester's face, immaculately clean-shaven, not a missed hair, razor cut, or piece of toilet paper to be seen. Who did that? I wondered. Did one of Burdettes's undertakers lather him up, make idle conversation about the big day that lay ahead, and in his death give him the best shave of his life? With his mop of hair mowed and neatly combed in place, twig of hair plucked from his nose, and his bushy eyebrows trimmed, Lester looked better in death than I had ever seen him in life. How is that possible?

A stiff white collar on a fresh shirt covered the damage to his throat from the bullet that had killed him. The body of his dress shirt was a nice crisp powder blue. It reminded me of his eyes, which I had seen so clearly on the floor of the courtroom that day. He wore a sharp navy blue blazer. I could tell from the brass buttons that it was Brooks Brothers. Simple grey flannel slacks. His tie, blue and white stripes and neatly Windsor knotted, was from Upper Canada College, of all places. I recognized the seal and their motto, *Palmam Qui Merit Ferat*—Let whoever earns the palm, bear it. Indeed. Where were Lester's palms? An antique silver tie clip held his school tie in place, just in case, I guess. I could see that someone had tucked some Belmont Menthols into the breast pocket of his blazer, and his glasses, still on a gold chain around his neck, sat on his chest. This was to be Lester's outfit for eternity. I stared at him, trying to conjure up that ragged voice, thinking of his last few moments beside me on the floor, his lips moving with a purpose but that voice, torn away, finally failing him. I knew that it had been Lester who pushed me to the floor, who fell on top of me. What had he been trying to tell me?

I felt Bonnie at my elbow. "Andrew. It's almost nine thirty. It's just us now." She looked exhausted, and any makeup that she had used to cover her bruised face was failing miserably. "Are you staying?"

"Bonnie, let's have a drink. Have one with me." My mouth was dry and my voice hoarse. I knew my breath must have been awful.

"You've had too much already. And you know I'm not much of a drinker."

"Well, just have a taster then, just a sip, enough for a toast to Lester. Come on."

She frowned. "Okay, just a sip. For a toast."

I poured two full cups and handed her one. She held it to the light and frowned. "Why do you never listen to me?"

We raised our cups to Lester, and I said, "May you roll up the rim to win, Lester."

"That's awful! That's not a toast. What is that supposed to mean? You're terrible."

"What? What should I say?"

"At least read something meaningful. Goodness, you are something else. There's a prayer in the condolence card. Read it."

I reached in my pocket, pulled out the card, opened it and read,

I laid awake a whole night long
Waiting for the sun to beat down on my head
In this broken bed
I laid awake and dreamt of ships
Passing through the night
Searching for shelter
Stopping at no harbour
I heard the screaming waters
Call sixty sailors' names
Raging words, pounding on the sail
Like an angry whale
I felt the iron rudder skip
The smell of seeping oil
The heat of slipping rope

Failing hands, failing hope
Every sailor asks
Asks the question about the cargo
He is carrying
God's anger broke through the clouds
And He split the cargo for all to see
The fault of the sailor
The fault of he who asks no questions
*About the cargo he is carrying . . . ***

"Andrew . . . Andrew . . . " Bonnie's voice was miles away. "That's a song . . . a poem by Daniel Lanois." Her words made no sense.

I stared at Lester's hands folded neatly on his stomach. They were tracked with huge veins and brown spots. I scanned my own hands. "When does that happen? You know, the spots?"

"Andrew . . . "

I stared at my hands and thought about my brother, Angie, the Glidden boys, Paul, and Alvin, all of them. A deep loneliness sawed through my bones, through my very being.

Bonnie whispered to me, "Andrew . . . Why are we here?"

I looked up from my hands and around the empty Algonquin Room, at the unopened bottles of scotch, the expensive cigars that lay unsmoked in unopened boxes, at the unused cups, and at Bonnie. My eyes returned to Lester and worked their way down his pale clean-shaven face, his sharp new jacket, crisp shirt, his school tie, and then, finally, they settled on his shoes. His crazy chocolate-brown, well-worn, thick-soled orthopaedic shoes were laced tightly in place. They would carry him into the next life.

And then I sat down by Lester and wept.

———

* The lyrics to "Fisherman's Daughter" are reprinted here with the generous permission of the artist, Daniel Lanois. The piece appears on his 1989 album *Acadie.*

ABOUT THE AUTHOR

Michael Cochrane is a Toronto author and lawyer. He has published a number of best-selling books about Canadian family law and is frequently featured on television and radio as an expert. Over his forty-plus years of practice, he has been an advocate for a more humane system for separating and divorcing families. He was the host of BNN television's national legal affairs program, *Strictly Legal*, for three seasons.

He is Counsel to the firm Brauti Thorning LLP in Toronto, Ontario (www.michaelcochrane.ca), and can be reached at mcochranellb@me.com.